Love and Wine
by
Paula Marais

Logogog

Copyright © 2016 Paula Marais
First published in 2016 by Logogog Press
Cover design by Kara Peters
ISBN 978-0-9922155-4-5 (printed book)
ISBN 978-0-9922155-9-0 (e-book)

This is a work of fiction. Names, characters, businesses, places, events and incidents are
either the products of the author's imagination or used in a fictitious manner. Any
resemblance to actual persons, living or dead, actual events or actual places is purely
coincidental.

DEDICATION

To my father, Louis Marais,
who is always so generous with both his love and his wine.

♥

Love and Wine

by

Paula Marais

ACKNOWLEDGMENTS

Love and Wine has taken several years and three computers (and some lost data) to pull together. So if people who helped along the way have not been acknowledged by name, this is not because I am ungrateful but because I didn't yet store everything on dropbox and save myself a great deal of heartache. That said, it began out of a conversation I had with fellow author Ron Irwin: something along the lines of 'sexy love triangle set in South Africa', which I suppose would be the one-liner pitch you would use in a lift but doesn't really cover the realities of character or emotion.

My husband Dave van Wijk has done some of the arduous hard yards with me: staying in Franschhoek, tasting wine and making sure the food in the region is as good as people say (it is). He's also pushed me to finish, when I kept pursuing other books. Dave was tired of people asking him when the next novel was coming. Well here it is!

Thank you to my talented sister, Kara Peters who's designed my beautiful cover and advised me on web marketing, websites and other fun stuff. My editor Nicola Rijswijk, who cut me down to size making my writing tighter and less fluffy. We didn't agree on all aspects of the book, which is appreciated. She gave me honest feedback without totally breaking my heart. To my mother who loves reading as much as I do and always gives me honest feedback on my writing. To Kirsty Savides for her marketing savvy and friendship. To Sabina Mtenda for being my rock. To my friends at Common Ground Café – still the best coffee in Cape Town and my very happiest place to write. Thank you for the welcome.

Other thanks go to: Jenna Blignaut, Jenny Bright, Jude Duk, Liz

Buisman, Liza Caryer, Nerisee Marais, Nicola Marais, Rob Duk, Sally Veary, Robyn Hopkinson and Vicki Erskine for feedback on the cover blurb and to everybody who voted on the cover – you know who you are! To Elaine Walmsley, who left us, but whose last interaction with me was words of encouragement on *Love and Wine*. Thank you to my readers, and for your support and encouragement on my previous books. Hope you enjoy this one.

For *Love and Wine*, I also used many resources in Franschhoek, including visiting the Huguenot Museum. A particular book was of great use to me: *The Genealogy of the De Villiers Family*, compiled by Juna Malherbe and Alet Malan, published in 1997 by The Huguenot Society of South Africa.

Finally there are two special people to acknowledge but their names have been lost in earlier notes and a move from Johannesburg to Cape Town. The wine expert from Franschhoek who spoke to me in 2010 and who gave me so much advice on the process. Thank you! And our tour guide from Mont Rochelle Vineyards, whose surname was Mouton (sheep in French, which is why I remember that part). Please get in touch at paula@paulamarais.com if you read this!

Finally to my children Jed and Cole, who light up my life, keep me busy, and spread joy and chaos in equal measure wherever they go. Love you, my boys.

CHAPTER ONE

elen watched June leave, the little Uno puffing its way back up the hill.

Pull yourself together, she thought.

But when was the last time she'd been truly, undeniably and absolutely alone?

Though she and George had been married for five years and together for two years before that, she'd had a series of boyfriends from the age of fourteen. *A serial dater,* her faithful (and brutally honest) friend Olivia had said, *afraid of your own company.*

Well, this was her chance to prove Olivia wrong.

Standing on the wooden deck, Helen looked out towards the ocean. George had never been a man for the beach. He didn't like the sand; he hated sun cream sticking to him. And the sooner he could wash off the salt water in a decent warm shower, the better. George's idea of a holiday was a cityscape. Prague, Venice, New York. Helen had never complained. She liked to shop, spend hours in museums studying the daubs and strokes of the masters in the great galleries of the world. She liked sitting in cafés watching people pass. She loved eating in chic restaurants and riding on unfamiliar public transport. But the more she considered it, the more she wondered if she'd liked it for George, or for herself.

Helen studied the waves, wondering how she would capture the grey in paint. It wasn't charcoal, or cinereal, or oyster. There was something smoky about the water, the spray coming up like pearls. Or harlequin opals. To the left, a finger of land tipped into the water. Rocky and black. Wavelets combed the edges, cascading foam and onyx-coloured – was it seaweed?

George wouldn't have been caught dead in this isolated, windswept place.

And that's what decided her. Kicking off her shoes and shrugging off her clothes, she dug into her suitcase for a swimsuit. Winter? This wasn't winter!

By the time she got to the beach, Helen could feel a cold breeze beginning to rise and so what? She strode into the water, feeling her toes blueing. Her calves. Her thighs. Then she was up to her chest, the Atlantic waves closer, advancing on her. Helen took a deep, hungry breath and dived.

Welling within her when she emerged – teeth chattering, legs goose-pimpled – was a sense of triumph she hadn't experienced in years. Wrapping herself in one of her Uncle Alec's fluffy towels, she walked back up Scarborough Beach towards the path that led to the house.

She could do with warming up, though, and decided that she rather fancied a cup of coffee: frothy and foamy with chocolate sprinkles on top. She hadn't thought to ask June where to go, but how difficult could it be? She'd have a hot shower, get dressed, then test out the Opel Uncle Alec had lent her, following the coastline so she didn't get lost.

♥

She'd been so nervous on her arrival at the airport. June had tapped her on the shoulder, picking her out immediately.

'Helen? I'm June. Welcome to Cape Town. I'm parked illegally, so let's zip back to the car.'

About five foot three, and gently rounded, June had a soft caramel-coloured skin, and a crop of short black hair that collected in points over her ears. She'd been wearing an unfashionable woolly jersey, but her smile was warm. Helen wasn't used to her accent though – it didn't sound much like the South Africans she'd met at home in London.

As Helen had settled into the passenger seat, June had leant over to help her with her seat belt.

'There's a trick to this,' she'd said. 'A little jiggle to the left ... See?'

Helen had smiled weakly to herself. She wasn't good with strangers. Or was she? It was a long time since she'd managed a stranger without George.

As it turned out, June didn't need her to chat.

'So this is Gugulethu. It goes on for kilometres.' June had waved her left hand, gripping the steering wheel with the right.

Helen studied the endless array of corrugated-iron-and-plastic shacks. Electricity wires hooped down, and every now and then she could see an enormous street lamp, which must have lit up the area like a football field. People passed between the shanties on ramshackle bicycles or on foot. As June's car slowed down in the morning traffic, Helen could see that a man had set up a barber shop in a large shipping container and was shaving hair in the morning sun. Men were smiling, chatting.

It hit her hard in her midriff. *When was the last time she'd smiled like that?*

June's little car whined as she changed gears.

'Everybody's coming into work,' she said. 'In half an hour this won't even be moving. I've learnt a few tricks. My brother's a taxi driver.'

'Right,' Helen managed.

'So Alec tells me you're an artist,' June said.

'Yes. Acrylics and oils mostly. I'm fascinated by light. It's liquid quality, you know, how to capture its ephemeral nature when everything else seems to be so dense. To me, light resembles the states of water, sometimes solid, sometimes diffuse and transparent ...'

June smiled.

'Sorry, I'm waffling on. I also do smaller-scale sketches and paintings for books – that's my bread and butter. Not my passion; I can't express myself as well in such a small space.'

'Well, you won't find a more beautiful city to paint than Cape

Town. We do things big here: big skies, big clouds, big mountains. And Scarborough changes every day. Especially from your bedroom window. You can sit in that one room and see all the seasons.'

'So Alec said. Have you lived there long?'

'Five years. Not really sure how it happened. I was a nurse at one of the private hospitals – oncology. One of my patients left me the house in his will. No family, you know? I was the closest thing to that. Old toppie was in and out that hospital for almost a year. I nursed him on the weekends sometimes. Finally gave in.'

'Poor man.'

June nodded. 'And good,' she said. 'I would have nursed him anyway. He was kind. And so lonely.'

A loud hoot erupted in front of them as June braked and flicked on her hazards. The car shuddered to a stop. Helen gripped on the sides of her seat with both hands. 'What's happening?' Helen asked, wondering if she would die in this odd place.

'Must be an accident. Don't worry. It'll clear. Good time to study our most famous landmark.'

Helen had been so focused on the traffic that she hadn't even noticed it. Rising above the entire city, the landmark was actually impossible to miss. It was like the body of an enormous whale, gliding through an ocean of sky. Above it, an apex of cloud built like a blowhole. The scenery seemed almost staged; an intimate departure point, she hoped, for a new phase in her artistic and physical existence. A setting that could conspire with the weather and her moods to create something life-affirming; something real.

'You can't get lost in Cape Town,' June said, grinning. 'Just follow the mountain.'

♥

All ready to go in pursuit of her coffee, with no apparent grasp of simple mechanics. The difficulty, she soon discovered, was getting the car out the garage. For some reason, she couldn't work out how to get the gears into reverse. What a fool. She wondered if she should phone June, but the thought of needing help so soon made her cringe. Helen pictured Olivia's knowing smile and slid out the car.

She'd walk. She was not to be foiled on her next attempt at freedom ... well, not *that* easily anyway. She picked up her handbag, closed the garage door, and turned the alarm on with the remote control, as per June's instructions.

Fifteen minutes later she came across a small cluster of shops, recognising a little corner store with a sign saying 'Fresh pies'. Considering the puppy fat she'd gained since the fiasco with George, Helen decided against the pies. But next door was a little café-restaurant with wide green-and-white-striped awnings and the smell of brewing coffee, which was enough to draw her in.

A woman in her forties, with a green-chequered apron tied around her waist, came to serve her.

'Good morning, dear. Where've you blown in from?' She had a portrait face, just the right number of lines to make her interesting.

'I walked,' Helen indicated. 'I'm staying in one of the houses near the beach. The one with the glass frontage, and wooden deck. Shaped a bit like a ship.'

'Alec's place,' the woman said. 'You're holidaying at a strange time of year. We're expecting another storm by this afternoon. Good thing you came now – you can't walk two metres in a Cape downpour.'

'Really?' Helen said as she studied the white trail out over the ocean.

'Oh, don't rely on that,' the woman laughed. 'This is the Cape of Storms. Now what can I get you?'

'A latte, please. And maybe a muffin or something like that?'

The woman scuttled inside, and returned a minute later with the coffee, a muffin and a newspaper.

'Sit awhile,' she said. 'If you're on hols you've time to watch the world pass. I'm Madeleine by the way.'

'And I'm Helen,' said Helen.

♥

The storm came, just as Madeleine had predicted, when Helen was safely back at the house. But it wasn't as windy and whipped up as Helen had expected; the grey skies simply sluiced out seemingly endless quantities of water that marred her view of the sea as silver droplets congregated on the windows.

Helen liked the rain. So she pulled a chair to under the shelter of the porch so that she could watch the waves, which seemed fiercer in the half-light. White water crashed on the rocks, then crocheted into foam doilies on the abandoned beach. With only the sound of ratcheting, churning water, Helen felt as though she was the only person in the whole world.

She wondered if this is what Alec had pictured for her. Endless thinking time. Mulling over her shattered hopes.

Being alone, alone, alone.

Her womb scraped out, her doctor's words echoing through her mind: *I'm sorry, Helen, but your egg quality is really poor. And it gets worse in your thirties. We've done what we can about your uterine lining; we'll just have to wait and see what happens next time. Now don't give up, alright? I can't tell you that a baby is impossible. Miracles do happen.*

The empty chair beside her in the consulting room.

Dr Maas hadn't said anything about George's absence, and Helen had simply assumed that his absence was normal; that all men avoided the idea of a baby-in-a-bottle. But sitting outside now, watching the rain, she began to remember the anxious would-be fathers in the waiting room, holding their wives' hands, fetching them cups of tea from the table in the passage. On the two occasions George had come with her, he'd checked his email obsessively on his phone, and paced furiously: *Why, for Christ's sake, can these doctors not run to schedule?* Instead of calming her, he'd made her stomach churn and her heart thunder in her ears, so by the time she'd seen the doctor she'd been shaking with nerves. What a way to make a new life.

Or not, as it turned out.

Helen sipped the wine June had left her. It wasn't really white-wine weather, but it made her feel wanton, drinking on her own. And during the day! Her mother would have tut-tutted the wine back into the fridge: *Now you look after that liver better than Grandad did, dear. The drink's genetic, Helen – you know that.* It always boiled down to her genes, it seemed. Her hair (*We're carbon copies, darling*). Her breasts (*Granny Morris. So you can blame your dad's side of the family*). Her artistic bent (*I wish I could take the credit, Helen. But you do have my imagination*). Her infertility ... (*Victoria battled for years, darling.*)

Was nothing entirely hers?

Helen looked out across the waves. The churning rain had turned the water opaque and dense, cloud and sea merged and would only be perceptible if a boat came over the horizon.

A crimson ship, perhaps, slicing open the horizon like a knife through grapefruit.

♥

Later, when darkness overcame the view completely, and lights began to shimmy from the few occupied houses below, Helen moved inside. She hoped that the sight of her blank canvases, sketchbook and boxes of neatly assorted paints would make her feel herself again.

Her suitcases remained where she'd left them next to the front door, though split open in her search for a bathing costume. Gripping a handle, she still felt the pull on her shoulder from lugging her belongings on the Tube to Heathrow.

No one had come to wave her off, though some had offered. Even George, for goodness sake. But she'd felt humiliated, as if she was running away, and she hadn't wanted a pom-pom brigade.

What a way to leave.

CHAPTER TWO

The rain continued for days and Helen began to wonder why she hadn't just stayed in England. It was summer at least with long days and enough sunshine to keep her cheerful, well, more cheerful than this. But then she remembered. Everywhere she went there, she bumped into sympathy. In bucket-loads. She couldn't bear it. It was just so awfully hard.

Then June popped by, her Labrador on a leash, and showed her how to put the car in reverse.

'Grip and pull,' she said, as the dog pulled against her, ready to leap into the back. 'Sorry. This mutt thinks we're going for a drive. He loves the wind in his face.'

'Well then, why don't we?' Helen said, proud of her spontaneity.

They decided on Muizenberg.

Uncertain of the car, Helen kept well within the speed limit, travelling over the mountains with June directing. The dog, who June had named Desmond 'after Desmond Tutu', salivated excitedly, head half-extended out the window despite the rain. His barking combined with the beat of the downpour made conversation almost impossible, but the sudden release from the house and the realisation that she had fully – albeit temporarily –

escaped from her life gave Helen the urge to laugh, to just let go. And June, picking up on her hilarity, began to laugh too.

They travelled along the coast, through Simon's Town and then Fish Hoek, the main road clogged with construction work, antiques shops and pedestrians taking the gap. Minutes from Muizenberg, Desmond retired to his seat and fell soundly asleep.

Finally able to talk, June closed the windows.

'Muizenberg has had its ups and downs. It's being restored at the moment, but it's quite a historic place. You know Cecil John Rhodes?'

Helen wracked her brain. 'The mining guy?' she guessed.

'Well, a little more than that, seeing as Rhodesia, now Zimbabwe, was named after him. He spent his later years there. And Rudyard Kipling lived in his cottage after he died. Now it's all about surfing. Beautiful waves, great for beginners. Even in weather like this we'll see people out on the water.'

Helen looked behind her at the sleeping dog.

'Have we exhausted him?' she wondered aloud.

'*Nee wat*, he'll spring to life as soon as he hears the waves.'

'You'd think he'd be used to them.'

'Who could get used to water like that?'

'You're right.' Helen nodded, looking beyond the parking lot towards the sea. Certainly the colour of the ocean had nothing on the aquamarine allure of Scarborough, but the beach seemed to stretch for miles.

'How far does it go?' she asked.

'The beach? Oh at least thirty, forty kilometres. Don't ask me in miles. All the way to Gordon's Bay, I do know that.'

'I don't think I've ever seen a beach that long. I know it's raining, but can I get out?'

June laughed. 'I don't think we'll melt.'

Helen slipped out the Opel, feeling sure that the clouds were becoming lighter, patches of blue beginning to show in the distance. If they waited a little, perhaps ...

Hearing the click of Helen's door, Desmond yawned and opened a chocolate eye.

'That's right boy,' June crooned, 'walkies-time.'

Desmond cocked his head, then leapt over the seat and through June's door, squeezing his furry body past Helen. Off he scampered over the white sand, skidding to a halt in the shallows, his coat immediately drenched.

'Shall we?' asked Helen, grabbing an umbrella as she followed the dog onto the beach.

June pulled on a hooded jacket.

'Yes,' she replied. 'I think we should.'

♥

With a steaming cup of hot chocolate in front of her, Helen tucked her stringy damp hair behind her ears. The umbrella had upended and she'd given up on it after a few minutes. She and June were now sitting in a bakery, the smell of yeasty bread wafting towards them as the ovens opened.

Helen's stomach grumbled. She didn't know how far she'd walked, but it had taken the best part of an hour. June had found a piece of driftwood to throw for Desmond and they'd remained fairly close to the parking lot, while Helen had surged on, her eyes on the meandering shoreline ahead.

She looked across the table at June. June was kind. People like June who healed for a living often were. June didn't ask questions. And right at this moment, Helen didn't feel like answering any. By her calculations, George's new baby was due any day over the next two weeks.

♥

'I don't know how to tell you this, but I thought I'd better call. It's a girl. I bumped into George's mother outside Argos, heaving a pink travel cot into her boot.'

Silence.

Helen and Camilla Shaw had been close once, but Olivia, protective as ever, would have bristled anyway.

'*Are you there, Helen? Are you still there? Oh, I'm sorry. I'm hugging you across the line.*'

'*I'm here.*'

'*Oh God, it was awkward, Helen! I didn't entirely know where to look. But then I thought, to hell with it and I walked up to her and said, "The divorce isn't even through, you do know that don't you, Camilla?"*'

'*And?*'

'*She had the grace to blush. And then she said she wasn't proud of what her son had done, but this was her granddaughter, and what was she supposed to do?*'

And that was just the thing. This wasn't George's *daughter's* fault. It was *George's* fault. George and Rose's. Any day now Helen's solicitor would get in touch again, coaxing her through the mechanics. *You're not demanding enough, Helen, don't buckle.* But what did it help to drag her heels? A baby wasn't exactly reversible. Rose had won. All the money in the world wouldn't fix that.

I want the paintings, Helen had said.

The paintings?

She remembered the consternation in her solicitor's voice.

Every last one.

George had never been particularly artistic. Where she was flamboyant (and she *was* flamboyant once) he was sensible. He could do budgets and balance books. She could decoupage almost anything, paint effect the walls. George changed plugs and light bulbs. Helen wrote limericks that made them laugh. He made roast chicken. She made Crêpes Suzette that almost set their curtains alight – twice. He drank wine. She knocked back shooters – the more colourful the better, though never in front of her mother.

Well, she used to drink shooters.

Over the years they'd begun to rub off on each other. George would suggest an exhibition at the Tate Modern; Helen might actually remember to file her credit card slips. But the paintings were hers, and she'd be damned if she let George have them. Helen had always told him they'd be the first thing she'd save if their house burnt down.

'*And what about me?*' George once asked.

'*You'd help me, of course,*' deliberately misunderstanding him.

Now that their home was burning to feathery ash, she would save whatever she could.

♥

Alec phoned three times in the first week to check on her.

'You don't have to worry, Uncle Alec,' Helen told him. 'I'm not about to top myself.'

'Thank God,' he replied. 'Imagine the palaver of getting your body back to England on British Airways.'

'Oh, don't bother about that. Just take me back in a little urn and scatter me somewhere with a spectacular view.'

'Darling, then I may as well leave you in Scarborough.' Alec cleared his throat. 'So has the char come in?'

'Happiness? She doesn't exactly live up to her name, does she? Not that I should talk.'

'Darling Helen, you're actually sounding much better.'

'The house is spectacular. People have been lovely. I like Madeleine. I like June. I *love* Desmond – he appreciates the value of company without conversation.'

'Who on earth is Desmond?'

'June's dog.'

Alec chuckled. 'Good girl, making friends. No more wallowing!'

'Wallowing? You make me sound like a hippo.'

'You're in Africa, aren't you? But listen, darling, I wanted to ask you: have you noticed how empty the wall in the lounge is?'

'Actually, no. I spend most of my time on the porch watching the waves.'

'You're being deliberately obtuse, my dear.'

'You're not commissioning me, are you?'

'You need a project. I can't have you slothing away, wasting all that talent.' Alec's voice took on a business-like tone. 'I've ordered a canvas – it's being delivered tomorrow with an easel, so make sure you're around to receive it. You'd never fit it in the Opel. It's gigantic.'

♥

But even after this short time, Helen was out of practice.

She hadn't realised she could be quite so good at doing absolutely nothing – she'd never attempted it before; she hadn't even opened her paints since she'd arrived. Even as a child, she'd kept busy, and her mother had carried a set of crayons in her handbag for all eventualities: delayed trains, long flights and boring meals in restaurants, which required Helen to sit still. (Never her strong point.)

Unpacking, Helen realised she even loved the sound of her paints. Cadmium Yellow. Pyrrole Orange. Perylene Maroon. Cerulean Blue. It was like stepping into a magical fairyland where all the senses combined so that you could smell a sound or hear a colour. Helen had read something about that – synaethesia, like Kandinsky hearing music as paint splashed to the canvas. What would Crimson Red sound like? Taste like? She'd once bit her lip, two deep grooves from her incisors, bleeding – maybe that was the taste of crimson. Helen had been warned: *If you do fall pregnant, you're going to have to watch those chemicals. Not good for a baby, paint fumes.*

But they were good for *her*. And there was no baby.

Twisting the lids off the tubes, she sniffed luxuriously. How could she have waited so long? She squeezed paint onto her palette, and one by one the colours curled onto the surface like garden snails, glistening.

She didn't know what to paint at first. Something cheerful like the David Kuijers she'd seen in a gallery in Hout Bay. But not as humorous; she couldn't quite manage that yet. Possibly beachy? She plotted a seascape, but as she was sketching giant strokes across the white, it came to her: light filtering through the clouds onto Muizenberg beach, striking the Victorian-style huts in a warm glow. She exaggerated a bit, and dispensed with accuracy; she would capture the light reflected on multi-colours, and perspective didn't matter. Helen picked up her roller, swishing it up and down in giant blocks of colour, laying the foundations. She swept across the canvas till her arms hurt.

Helen loved acrylics. They suited her temperament, didn't require the endless patience of waiting for colours to dry. Even the thicker layers were hardening onto the surface. Watercolours always seemed wishy-washy to her – not that she couldn't use them. Actually, she was quite good. It was a requirement of her profession; pastel baby books or princess tales marked up with neat strokes. And oils, she luxuriated in their texture, the thick globules she could blend on the canvas, with time to change her mind.

Though she didn't easily change her mind. Why else had she pushed herself through IVF after IVF when nothing seemed to be going right?

♥

It was ages before Helen stood up again.

She stretched, opening the porch door only to be assailed by the brackish smell of rotting kelp. The sun was just beginning to dim, impaling itself onto the horizon in a riot of colour, tingeing the clouds cerise. Without thinking, Helen locked the door behind her and headed towards Camelrock Road. There was a shortcut down to the wooden walkways crossing the beach rock, but this time she meandered onto Seagull Road, studying the strange mix of houses, some looking so abandoned while others – clapboard painted in blues and whites, proteas trimmed back, grass neatly cut – seemed remarkably lived in. She walked past 'For sale' signs, pine trees, wattles just beginning to burst into yellow blooms, rows of lavender. Scarborough was eclectic. Remote as an island.

Not for the first time, Helen asked herself what she was doing here, not speaking to a soul for days. Sometimes she watched smoke rising from the chimney of the house behind her, wondering who lived there. Cars passed on the road from Kommetjie heading beyond Scarborough to Misty Cliffs; they never really seemed to stop here. No reason to. Unlike Helen. The only sign of life was the cluster of shops around the coffee shop. Madeleine seemed to pull in the crowds from pure will – and good coffee, of course.

A dog barked. Desmond probably, although she'd seen a few other hounds scampering across the beach, their owners cloaked in Macs or disguised under umbrellas. Nobody passed her as she walked. And no one but Helen ever bathed. People stepped close to the water, warmly wrapped, and on the odd occasion, Helen had looked back to shore and seen them watching her. The madwoman from Hilltop Road.

The thought made her smile. Maybe Helen could reclaim her eccentricity, and de-George herself.

Helen, reborn.

She sighed.

If only it were that simple.

CHAPTER THREE

Helen woke up, and stretched the width and length of the bed. Had she ever been this alone? So untouched?

After all the predicting of timings and ovulation, the measuring of her temperature, she'd once thought she'd never want a physical relationship again. The whole process was so mechanical. Missionary position for a girl. Alkaline for a boy. The Shettles Method. The Whelan Method. Potassium from bananas or apricots for boys. Magnesium from spinach or black beans for girls ...

George had wanted a boy, of course. (Even Rose hadn't got that right.) The stress of trying to fall pregnant had only been made worse by the thought that she could get it wrong, create the wrong type of Shaw. Was that why she hadn't conceived at all?

Helen had almost forgotten what it was actually like to fall into bed in a fit of lust ... and at one point in her life, even a bed had not been compulsory. Before George, and not all that long before either, there had been Peter. Pete. She remembered Guy Fawkes Night. Fumbling behind his Land Rover, her skirt up, back against the spare wheel ... She'd hardly noticed the fireworks above them. Even now her heart quickened at the memory. So many people about. The danger of discovery. She scarcely recognised that girl in the mirror these days. Left to dry naturally, her normally smooth brown bob was lank and thin. Her skin was blotchy, and her lips dry and slightly cracked.

Helen slid her legs out the bed. Though overcast, it wasn't raining today. She thought she might head up to Madeleine's with a book. Pass the time drinking lattes, and heighten her senses with caffeine. She could hear Olivia's voice: *For Christ's sake, Helen, just go out and get laid. You're in a foreign city. Your accent will kill them. Just use protection, that's all.*

Of course Olivia herself hadn't had to follow that sort of advice for at least eight years: sex with some random stranger wasn't part of her agenda. She had Frank.

But Helen was beginning to think she wasn't meant to be alone.

Although she'd shunned conversation when she'd first arrived, especially when it went past the 'how-are-yous', she had to admit that she was now craving company. Getting dressed, she decided to head to the only place she seemed assured of a welcome, albeit as a paying customer.

♥

Seeing Helen padding around the corner, Madeleine waved.

'You're up early,' she said.

'I can't sleep forever,' Helen said. *Much as I'd like to.*

'The usual?' Madeleine bustled off to behind the counter and returned moments later with a muffin and a copy of the *Argus*. She pointed at the front-page image. 'Can't miss that,' she told Helen. 'And on such a beautiful day!'

Helen raised her eyebrows as she followed Madeleine's finger.

'The West Coast flowers!' Madeleine exclaimed. 'You're an artist, so you'll really appreciate the spectacle. Listen, Helen. I know I'm a busybody – my husband tells me that all the time. But you can't stay here every day confusing the locals with your crazy swims and warming up on bran muffins and lattes. I can see you're sad. I don't know why exactly, although I could guess. You need soul food. So why not pack your bags for a few days? Take a drive down the coast and go and find yourself an adventure.'

Helen blanched, sitting back in her chair.

'I'm sorry, dear. I can see by your face that I'm interfering. But you've been here almost three weeks, managing so admirably. And I'm worried about you.'

'I've been painting,' Helen protested. 'You should see what I've already done. I've captured the colours and the light. You don't really know what that means –'

'You won't get better inspiration than along the West Coast. Or colours for that matter. Or light. It's only two hours away. You could head towards Langebaan, maybe stay a night or two.'

Helen changed the subject by flapping the newspaper to the next page.

When her coffee arrived, Helen found herself staring at the cup. The coffee tasted bitter after Madeleine's input ... Of course she meant well, but now Helen felt insignificant and put upon. Helen sank into her chair like a sack of wheat. To think her heartache was branded on her forehead – enough so that a complete stranger could read her hurt and advocate a cure! Madeleine didn't know a thing about her or her life! After a moment, Helen pushed the coffee away and stood up, leaving a twenty-rand note under her teaspoon.

Helen slogged her way back up the hill to hibernate in her humiliation. She wondered if she could feel any worse, a kicked dog retiring to lick her wounds. Madeleine had been trying to help her, she knew but oh…

The entrance hall shuddered as Helen slammed the front door behind her and slipped down onto her haunches, rocking herself, her arms around her knees. Who was she kidding? Certainly not Madeleine. Why didn't she just go home and get on with her non-life?

Her divorced life.

While George loved a new wife. A daughter on her way. In Helen's beautiful house. With *her dogs*, for Christ's sake.

And Helen, meanwhile, had nothing.

With her back against the wooden wall, Helen looked across towards the lounge, to that empty wall. The canvas was upstairs in the bedroom she'd chosen as her studio. There was nothing for it but to paint herself into oblivion.

♥

Helen didn't leave the house for days. Her fingernails became crusted with acrylic. She'd tried to scrub them clean at first, but then didn't bother. Her hair probably needed a wash but she avoided mirrors. Happiness's sidelong glances suggested that Helen was increasingly resembling the woman in the attic. Helen remembered to bath on Tuesday. That was before she got Olivia's e-mail.

Your turd of an ex is a daddy. God help that poor child. Saw the announcement in the paper. Elizabeth Iris Shaw.

Helen wanted to vomit. Elizabeth Iris. Had George at any stage mentioned to Rose that Iris was *her* choice? For God's sake: Iris was her grandmother! Did Rose know? Probably not, because George was a filthy liar. Helen of all people knew that. He'd managed to not make a baby and make one, all in the space of one year.

Standing in front of yawning kitchen cupboards and fridge, Helen realised she was going to run out of supplies soon. The food she was less concerned about, but the wine – well that was a crisis. She wasn't as inhibited after a glass of red … the white of the canvas was marginally less intimidating. It was always like that: the first stroke of paint across the surface dictated everything. The flow. The movement. The excitement or disappointment. How many times had she obliterated a germinating work with a white-dipped roller because something about it just told her it wasn't right? Sometimes she envied other artists who churned our variations on the same painting, month after month. It took the thinking away, paid the bills. But then, it also took away the joy. Of novelty. Discovery.

She reached for the last crust of bread. Toasted it would be alright, and she'd just scrape off the green frosting on the one side. The lone tomato in the fridge could be sliced thinly, the rotten side removed. She had salt. Pepper. It would do.

She would build up the courage to emerge from her cocoon when Alec's painting was done. Truthfully, it was already finished, but she found she was still too afraid to leave. And though she was craving a decent cup of coffee, she was too embarrassed to go back to the café. So she kept on dabbing and daubing.

Busy hands. Less thinking.

Perhaps Madeleine thought Helen had taken her advice. Her shame was ridiculous, she realised that. There wasn't anything wrong with being sad, except of course for how it felt. And the fact that she'd exposed herself like some flasher in a yellow plastic raincoat.

It was time for a swim, she realised. Give those locals somebody to talk about.

♥

Wet and bedraggled, Helen took the long way up the hill to avoid the coffee shop. She'd swum herself to ice and wished she'd brought a decent wrap. If she carried on like this, she was going to make herself sick – full-blown pneumonia and no one to take care of her. Helen tried to increase her pace, stubbing her toe in the effort. By the time she got to the front door she was bleeding and shivering.

A mess.

Madeleine was sitting patiently on a deckchair outside the house, auburn hair blowing in tight tendrils that bounced about her head.

'I thought you'd emerge eventually,' she commented, holding out a takeaway cup and a brown-paper bag. 'Just as you like it. And carrot-and-cream-cheese muffins – my latest invention.'

Helen took the coffee, her hands clutching at the warmth.

'Thanks.' Not knowing what else to do, she took a deep drag on the coffee.

Madeleine cocked her head, reminding Helen of Desmond. 'I'm sorry,' Madeleine said. 'Sometimes I shoot my mouth off.'

Helen shrugged.

'I'm a little sensitive these days. Happens when your husband has a baby with another woman.'

'Ouch,' said Madeleine.

'Oh, there's more ...' She sighed. 'Why don't you come inside? No one's seen the painting yet except for Happiness, and she just thinks I'm crazy.'

'Are you?'

'Not enough, or I'd have swum out and not come back.'

As they walked into the lounge, Helen was gratified by Madeleine's jaw dropping.

'My God,' Madeleine exclaimed, staring at the enormous Muizenberg landscape Helen had hung. 'I've only seen the sky like that once in my life, and you've captured it exactly. No wonder you couldn't leave the house.'

'It was finished days ago, really,' Helen admitted. 'I've been dabbling. Using up my supplies.'

Madeleine moved closer and reached out to the canvas as if tempted to touch it, but then stepped away.

'You should be selling works like these, Helen. I've never seen anything this wonderful.'

Helen laughed. 'Keep talking, Madeleine. I could do with an ego boost.'

But Madeleine was just beginning. Excitedly she gripped Helen's shoulders.

'You can put them on display in the café! I sell one, we put a new one up. They won't last a week!'

'This was my uncle's idea to keep me busy.'

'Clever man. You simply cannot waste this talent, Helen.'

'Funny,' Helen mused. 'That's exactly what he said.'

♥

But after finishing Alec's painting Helen was stuck again, uninspired despite the beautiful view. Sitting outside one evening, her wine glass filled, she found herself wishing she could *do something*. And perhaps she was ready. Perhaps Madeleine had been right – not that she'd suggested it again – that a drive along the West Coast would help.

Helen wandered into Alec's office to use the Internet. She couldn't recall the name of the town Madeleine had mentioned, but she clicked on images of flower carpets and coastline until she was able to devise a basic route. And she decided she would just go. She'd leave a note on the door of the coffee shop and in June's postbox, and leave first thing in the morning.

When she woke, Helen was strangely invigorated. For the first time in months, she had a real plan. An itinerary. She'd packed a bag the night before; her easel, sketchpad, paints and canvases were already in the car. Brushing her teeth, she took a long look at herself in the mirror. Her usually sallow skin had finally taken on a healthier glow. Though she was still feeling beaten, she was looking less like a ghost. The dark rings under her eyes had faded, and the collection of spots that had once congregated on her chin were almost completely gone.

Even with her prejudiced eye, Helen realised the escape was doing her good. And maybe this drive was the next step in her recovery.

Helen was by now used to the Opel, but people drove faster here than in England. She stuck tightly to the left lane so she'd be ready to turn off towards Milnerton and then Bloubergstrand. She'd never been all that adept at finding her way – the thought made her a little nauseous – yet here she was with a badly printed map, a tank full of petrol and an open schedule. She was following the coast, more or less, so she'd be okay as long as it remained on her left. Winding down the window, she breathed in the salty air.

She decided to stop in Bloubergstrand and fill her artistic well. Pulling off her shoes and rolling up her jeans, Helen walked along the beach's white expanse and stared over the bay to Table Mountain. This was the view one saw on postcards – the one you could sketch with a few strokes on a page. The flat-topped expanse dominated the sky, but today clouds were nowhere to be seen, despite the wind. A man down the beach was unrolling something in bright blue and yellow. He stopped for a moment, eyeing the sky thoughtfully. Curious, Helen sat down on the sand, wishing she'd bought a coffee.

What was he doing?

Further down the beach, a couple unpacked a bag and seemed to be waving their arms at each other, though Helen understood they were testing the wind, which she reckoned was fairly strong. By the time she looked again, the man with the yellow and blue was on the water in a wetsuit, the wind whipping up into the sky what looked like an arched glider. Attached to his feet was a small surfboard, and soon he was crossing the waves at a tremendous pace. Entranced, Helen watched him go, the glider or kite or whatever it was pulling sharply upwards. The man jumped, bouncing deeper out to sea. Helen wished she could see his face – at this distance she could only imagine his rapture.

After an hour, the original surfer had been joined by others, and she sensed their exhilaration as they emerged from the water, wet and winded.

How she envied them, but not enough to give it a go herself. What had formed in her mind, however, was a painting of twisting, spiralling kites and spraying ocean. She couldn't wait to begin it, so she pressed on and after an hour discovered Langebaan, the quaint fishing village that was her destination. She found herself a shady table at a restaurant near the beach, and opened her sketchbook.

The movement was easily captured. Arches crowning above the hardened lines of Table Mountain as they spun and dove. Figures facing the water on the beach carrying surfboards, others strapping on their boards or zipping up wetsuits. Helen was so entranced, she barely noticed the arrival of her spinach-and-feta tramezzino, and only sipped her Tab distractedly. Filling page after page, she realised she had enough material to do at least five paintings. Although she'd started in pencil, she began filling in with block colours using oil pastels. Image after image came alive as her fingers twisted and curled, rubbed and scribbled.

The dirtier her hands became, the more her heart soared.

♥

Helen didn't actually hear the man approach. In retrospect, he may have cleared his throat, but she had blocked that out, along with the noise of the restaurant. She had no idea how long he'd been standing there.

'I hope you don't mind,' he said, making her jump.

Helen looked up not out of politeness so much as irritation.

He was not someone she would have noticed normally. Nothing at all like George, who had both height and presence, and a crop of sandy blond hair that gave him a wilful, puppy-dog-needing-a-rescue look. (Rose must have sensed this too.) This man verged on stocky, with wide shoulders. Brown hair cut fairly short emphasised a square face and strong jaw. Helen noticed how he squinted slightly, as though the sun reflecting off her paper was too harsh for his partially hooded eyes. Only later did she notice that his irises were hazel.

'Can I help you?' Helen said, cringing at how thoroughly British and stuck-up she sounded.

'I'm sorry, it's just that I noticed you sketching and I wondered if you might let me take a peek.' Something about the way he smiled, perhaps the crease in the edges of his eyes, suggested that he laughed a great deal.

'I wasn't done yet,' she said almost petulantly, not really quite ready to welcome him into her world. But then she shrugged, pushing the pad over to him.

'May I?' He indicated the chair opposite her. 'Ah, Bloubergstrand. Those kite surfers would have chopped off an arm or a leg for one of these pictures.'

'I doubt that very much,' Helen replied, warming to his

compliment. 'They're just doodles.'

'They're really magnificent doodles. And from memory.'

'This morning,' Helen replied, nodding. 'Is that what it's called, kite surfing? It looked pretty tricky to me.'

'Oh, it is,' the man said. 'You need balance, courage and a talent for sucking up a lot of saltwater while still being able to breathe.'

Helen laughed, despite herself. 'Not your forte then?'

'Useless,' the man admitted. 'I'm not really a water baby.'

'I've swum every day since I came here just about. My neighbours think I'm bonkers.'

'And are you?'

'How could I possibly judge that if I were? Are *you*?'

'Mad enough to drive out here on a whim, I suppose,' he said.

'*And* on a work day.'

'Exactly.' He shifted. 'Well, I should get going,' he said, pushing back his chair. 'Thanks for sharing those with me. They're special.'

But Helen, thinking of Olivia's advice, if not entirely sure yet whether she should act on it, reached out and touched his arm.

'Wait,' she said, feeling herself blush. 'The least you could do is buy me a drink?'

CHAPTER FOUR

It turned out he was interesting. Self-deprecating. Intelligent. He ordered a bottle of wine, so it wasn't one drink, but two. And somewhere in the conversation he told her his name was Max. Not Maximillian – ever. (His parents, the only people who had ever called him that, were dead.) Just Max. Helen swirled the Merlot around her mouth – *A deep ruby*, Max said, *with garnet highlights on the rim.* Max could talk colours like she could paint them. And he identified each scent before she'd even imagined it. Blackcurrent. Red berries. Vanilla.

Helen's uneaten lunch was removed, and Max ordered olives and foccaccia with sun-dried tomatoes. Another bottle of Merlot. It slid onto her tongue and down her throat like velvet. Helen looked at Max, the wine buzzing into her head. It was four o'clock and she hadn't yet found somewhere to stay. But she kept sitting there, and Max didn't seem eager to leave either.

'I'm beyond driving,' Max told her, 'even by South African standards.'

He explained that his countrymen were rather less worried about driving drunk than hers. She smiled, a little self-consciously. *What was he suggesting?* Helen felt her flushed cheeks and touched her face. The bread had soaked up some of the wine, but she wondered if she could stand without tumbling over.

'I think I need to walk,' she said.

'Sure.' Max looked uncertain. 'Would you like to be alone?'

'Oh no,' Helen said, surprised by her own boldness. 'I was hoping you'd join me.'

They walked down Bree Street towards the lagoon. Helen had shoved her belongings into the car boot and now carried her sandals in her right hand. Max was in shorts, his muscular legs covered by a down of fine blonde hair. Tawny. Like a lion. Helen felt a giggle building. She *was* drunk. And with a man she barely knew.

'Careful there,' Max said, a firm hand grabbing her arm as she lurched forward. 'Easy now.'

His voice had a soft tone. Gentle, as though he was calming a horse.

Helen leant against him, feeling the solid weight of his body against hers. She'd missed this. The last time George had held her like this he'd been shagging Rose all afternoon. Guilt-affection, she realised now. She'd wanted to make love, but he'd held her instead. *It's not all about sex,* he'd told her jokingly. Except it was. Just not with her.

Helen let Max go, running fully clothed into the shallows, where she slipped and fell waist deep in water. She found she couldn't move, frozen in the cold water, sand welling inside her rolled-up jeans.

And she was crying. *Oh my God,* she thought, *I'm crying in front of a complete stranger and I can't stop.*

After a moment's hesitation, his forehead creased like badly ironed linen, Max smiled and then came to sit down next to her in the cold water. He slid his arm around her shoulders.

'Maybe I am bonkers,' Helen whispered, moving her hands to her face.

'Tell me about it, then, beautiful Helen.'

And so she did.

♥

Max chaperoned Helen to a bed and breakfast on one of the streets overlooking the water, and checked them into a room with twin beds. He dug into her suitcase for a nightie, then disappeared into the bathroom while she dressed. He put a glass of water next to her bed, and placed her suitcase on the rack so she could reach her clothes comfortably. He then guided her to the bathroom, and she liked the way he swung her round to place her feet in the bath and rinse off the sand.

She also liked the way he sat next to her as she drifted to sleep, heart wrenched and tears spent.

Waking in the morning, she could hear the soft drawing in of his breath. Not like George, nothing like George, who snored the moment he rolled onto his back, and who talked in his sleep. Helen looked across at Max, wondering if he had even held her hand. Her head ached. Her stomach threatened to heave, but lying chastely in her bed, untouched, she felt a vague warmth creeping through her. She wondered why she wasn't more embarrassed.

Maybe some good men do actually exist.

Helen had been more honest with Max than she had been with anybody in her entire life. Too honest probably. Considering her revelations, it occurred to her that she should repay his generosity by creeping out the room. Pay the hotel bill and disappear. Helen was, after all, a liability. She shifted, wanting more to cuddle up next to Max than to leave. But she wasn't that selfish.

Soundlessly, she crept out of bed. She wanted to kiss Max's cheek goodbye, but instead she left one of her sketches. A kite surfer reaching out to touch the crest of Table Mountain.

Reaching but not quite succeeding.

♥

Breakfast was a salmon omelette, a glass of orange juice and a large cup of black coffee. (She couldn't quite manage the milk.) She picked at the meal listlessly, moving it around her plate. Sitting alone on the other side of Langebaan, which actually wasn't all that big, Helen wondered if Max had woken up yet. Though her head throbbed painfully at the temples, despite the Nurofen, Helen felt unburdened. She decided that she'd drive to the West Coast National Park, on the banks of the lagoon, which she hadn't quite reached the day before.

She checked the sky, glad there were no clouds, since she'd read that the flowers were better on a clear day. Signalling for her bill, Helen scraped back her chair. It was already almost nine, and the gates to the park and the protected Postberg areas beyond the fence, had been open for a while. If she hurried, she might just be able to miss the hordes of tourists on buses, flocking in from Cape Town.

Compared to England, and even to her last few weeks in Scarborough, the landscape in which she found herself a few minutes later was dry and particularly rocky. Helen was more attuned to green fields and woolly sheep, clusters of yellow gorse against grey cobbles. Paddocks. Horses. The odd farmhouse or village with rows of red-brick houses. Yet there was something entirely decadent about this carpet of brilliant flowers spreading out before her: millions upon millions of blossoms gathered in tight formation in a kaleidoscope of pinks, whites and oranges. It almost took her breath away.

Wearing an odd-shaped straw hat she'd bought from a hawker on the side of the road in Blouberg, her face plastered with a thick layer of sunblock, Helen set up her easel. She didn't feel the same sense of excitement she had with the kite surfers, but she had a sneaky suspicion this may have something to do with some bottles of red wine … Still, she felt calm, unhurried and glad she'd remembered to purchase a few bottles of water – one for dehydration, but the rest for diluting paint and cleaning brushes.

The tourists did come, many of them peering to catch a glimpse of her work in progress. She tried to ignore them, but the voices of the tour guides carried above the chatter: *This area is one of six accepted floral kingdoms on earth. Known locally as fynbos, and internationally as the Western Cape Floral Kingdom, this one has more plant species than the whole of Europe! Eighty species of flowering plants are endemic to this region ... and that means they don't grow anywhere else in the world!*

Helen wanted to laugh. The guide's voice rose into a state of near frenzy, reaching a climax with every juicy fact. She'd also wondered about this bizarre display of succulent semi-desert plants, and now at least she could put a name to them.

Painting on a grand scale, Helen's canvas was quickly covered with colour. And beyond the canvas, to her left, clear purples verging on pinks grew more intense as the sun passaged higher into the sky. To her right, oranges and yellows with, on closer inspection, mud-brown centres. Close up they were fluffy, or frilly, star-shaped or prickly, dangly or dense – petals packed tight in rounded heads. In such small plants, the detail was really incredible.

Helen looked up at the queues of tourists that were building up outside the park. She could hear laughter and hooting, and once or twice she turned to watch students hanging out their cars or sitting on their roofs and bonnets. They seemed half-pissed or high on happiness. Her stomach growled, her omelette no longer filling the space left by her liquid dinner. As her canvas was already almost dry, she decided she would retire gracefully to the restaurant recommended by the B&B.

Parked at Geelbek a little later, Helen considered her supplies. Powder pastel seemed entirely too insipid to echo the colours she had seen from the road. She dug in her wooden paintbox, extracting a small pack of oil pastels to take inside with her.

The restaurant was set in a Cape Dutch building on the lagoon. She'd been told she may see flamingos but hadn't noticed any as she'd walked through the garden ...Were flamingos always pink, or did they come in other shades? She chose a table under an umbrella, then began to doodle while sipping a rock shandy. In her old life she would have felt self-conscious sitting alone. She didn't feel that now, but she recognised that it still wasn't quite as nice as sharing a meal with someone. She wondered what Max had done when he'd seen that she wasn't there. Perhaps he'd been relieved ...

Thinking back, she realised that he hadn't revealed much about himself. While Helen had spilt her life story in the shallows, he had been remarkably reticent. She didn't know his surname, where he lived or what he did for a living. How was it they'd managed to talk for so long?

♥

Helen accepted a basket of freshly made seed bread. It smelt delicious, and the pat of butter she spread onto it melted it immediately. With her mouth absorbing the delicious loaf and her eyes on her sketchpad, Helen was distracted enough not to notice his approach.

'I took a chance on finding you here,' Max said.

Helen swallowed quickly, her cheeks immediately red.

'Oh God,' she said. 'You must think me terrible.'

'Well, you did pay for the room at least,' he said with a note of mirth. 'And you didn't vomit.' He pulled out a chair, and settled himself down. 'These are great,' he said, drawing her sketches towards him. 'Especially this one. You've got this vygie perfectly.'

'Is that what it's called?'

'Golden Vygie or *Lampranthus aureus,* 60mm in diameter. Grows on granite outcrops.'

'You're a botanist?' Helen asked.

'I'm in the wine business actually, but I love plants. Thank you for the drawing. You gave me the best one, but I guess you know that.'

'I'm sorry,' Helen said. 'I made such an ass of myself last night, I thought I'd give you a break and vanish without us having to –'

'Hash it over in the morning? It's forgotten, Helen. I hope you feel better, though,' Max said.

'You know,' Helen replied, 'I feel more myself than I have in months.'

Max smiled, his hazel eyes crinkling at the edges, as he reached out to pat her hand.

Helen's lunch arrived, and while Max munched on the seed bread waiting for his own order, he told her a little more about himself.

'So, I live in Franschhoek, just near Stellenbosch,' he said. 'I have for most of my life, except for a brief internship in the Loire Valley in France. My father insisted on it. I didn't like it at first. I was terribly homesick. I missed Bourgogne.'

'Bourgogne?' Helen asked.

'Our farm. It's been in the family since the my ancestors arrived in May 1689, on a ship called the Sion. Although that may not seem so long ago by British standards, by South African it positively entrenches our family name into the country's history.'

'So, what's your surname?' Helen asked, glad for the excuse to ask.

'De Villiers. Of course, with the strong influence and force from the Dutch East India Company, the pronunciation has changed from the French. Nowadays we say the "s". It took less than three generations for the Dutch to eradicate spoken French from Olifantshoek, as it was then known. But enough of the history lesson.' Max studied Helen's expression, then smiled. 'You're far more polite than my brother. My conversation almost puts him to sleep.'

'Does he live at Bourgogne as well?'

'Oh, yes, dear old Jared and I are stuck with each other for life. We both love the farm far too much to leave ...'

'But you get along?' Helen asked.

'Oh don't get me wrong, I love my brother, but we're different. Sometimes I wonder how we can even be related.'

After lunch, Max walked Helen around the restaurant's garden and then past a bird hide that hulked over the water. He seemed quite content to identify each flower they saw, and then lie on his back in the sunshine as he waited for her to draw it.

'*Carpobrotus acinaciformis*,' Max said, 'Isn't the magenta beautiful? You must've seen these from the tarred road coming in.' Max had casually tucked his jumper on the ground under his head.

'I think so ...' But Helen was thinking about George. *George, who would never have let his clothes get dirty, and when had he ever been patient enough to wait for her to draw something? Usually he'd insist on her taking a photo and painting the image from that, so his precious time wouldn't be wasted. But he would buy her flowers. Beautiful bunches. Often just for the hell of it.*

'That was quick,' Max said, observing Helen moving to the next clump of fynbos. 'The mountain sour fig or *Carbobrotus edulis*. Those yellow flowers turn pink as the plant ages. Our housekeeper, Prudie, sometimes makes sour-fig preserve with the fruit ... Boy, can that woman cook.'

After an hour and a half, Helen's fingers were beginning to cramp. Max, almost comatose in the afternoon heat, hadn't moved for at least ten minutes, and she began to wonder if he'd fallen asleep. Standing up, she peered over at him, her shadow falling over his face.

'Perfect,' Max murmured. 'I've been shielding my eyes the whole afternoon, when you could've been standing right there.'

Helen smiled. 'My fingers are sore. I don't think I can draw anymore today.

'Does that mean I'm going to have to move?' Max asked. 'Because I'm not sure my body can stand it.'

'I'll help you up,' Helen said. 'It's the least I can do.'

♥

Despite their proximity, Max hadn't touched Helen the entire afternoon. She wasn't really sure if she liked this fact or not. Perhaps more than anything, she was attracted to his reserve. He was charming and gentlemanly, like George. But unlike George, he seemed aware of the space that she took up in the world, giving her a little more than she might have liked. Max deferred to her, but when she seemed uncertain, he made decisions. Like the fact that they should have seafood for dinner, and that he knew just the place, if she was interested.

Of course she was interested. She loved prawns and calamari. Helen had rarely had the opportunity to eat fresh oysters, and here they were in front of them, piled up in a silver bowl with Tabasco and lemon. The seafood came to the table sizzling in mini cast-iron frying pans. And the salad, piled high with feta and Kalamata olives, sat between them, the dressing slick and garlicy.

They drank white wine, Max seemingly untainted by the excesses of the night before, though Helen prepared herself with a bottle of sparkling water.

'You're not surely going to mix those?' Max asked, his expression a dead giveaway.

Helen hesitated, bottle mid-air, then poured the water into a fresh glass.

'Because that would be a travesty, wouldn't it,' Helen said impishly.

And Max laughed out loud. 'Years of training, I'm afraid. My parents gave us wine at the table as far back as I can remember.'

'And why spoil a good thing?'

'Exactly.'

But apart from that small slip of nonchalance, Max seemed so completely easy-going that Helen was beginning to wonder if *anything* stressed him out. And she was more than pleasantly surprised when he suggested that they share a dessert. She could hardly imagine George eating off someone else's plate.

'You choose,' Max said. 'I don't mind, really.'

They ate the lemon meringue pie slowly between sips of aromatic filter coffee, their pace evenly matched. Helen had enjoyed a *good* day, she realised.

'Are you happy?' Max asked her.

'You know what?' Helen said, smiling at this surprising realisation. 'I actually am.'

CHAPTER FIVE

Yet as dinner drew to a close, Helen began to feel a little nervous. Rubbing her arm distractedly, she realised that finding a place to stay had completely slipped her mind.

Max looked across at her, his eyebrows raised questioningly. 'Everything okay?' he asked, making a signing motion for the bill.

'Of course.'

'I kept the room,' Max said. 'In case you decided to come back.'

'That was nice,' Helen said.

He reached out, slipping his fingers between hers.

'Relax, Helen,' he said. 'I'm not a predator. They're just beds, and we don't even have to push them together.'

Helen blushed crimson. 'You make me sound like a vestal virgin.'

Max grinned. 'I haven't enjoyed myself so much for ages. Let's not complicate things.'

Following Max's car, her headlights scanning the quiet streets, Helen's heart thumped. Despite Olivia's advice, Helen hadn't even kissed a man since George, never mind slept with one. Though she'd have to take that step eventually ... She just didn't have the confidence right now to take the lead.

Over-analysis paralysis, Olivia would have told her, *don't think so much, Hellie, it just doesn't help.*

There was an open parking space next to Max's Land Cruiser. Helen reversed in, switching off the lights as her heart pounded.

'Let me get your case for you,' Max said, walking round to the boot. 'Do you want any of this other stuff?'

'I think I'll survive with just the suitcase,' Helen managed.

Max slammed the boot shut, waiting for the click of the lock.

'Think you're up to a nightcap?'

Helen nodded. Right at this moment, she would welcome just about any delay.

They sat in the lounge of the B&B. The air had chilled enough for a small fire in the hearth, and Helen breathed in the pungent aromas of burning pine. Max angled a new branch into the fireplace, and it popped and spluttered.

'Winters in Franschhoek can get quite cold and damp,' Max commented, 'but, the summers ... The heat is something else. Nothing you'd ever get in England. All you want to do is stretch out on a cold tiled floor and pant.'

'Like a dog?' Helen smiled at the picture.

'Exactly like a dog.'

'Does it work?'

'At forty-five degrees, anything is better than nothing. I've installed air-con in my study though. Jared was horrified – as if I was admitting some sort of defeat. You know, lowering the tone of the National Heritage buildings.'

'Is it beautiful there?'

'Every time I go away, I come back with new eyes. It's spectacular. We're hemmed in on all sides by the most magnificent mountains. But they never look the same. The seasons change. The plants. The skies ...'

'I love the skies here,' Helen said. 'They don't seem to end.'

'Come on,' Max said suddenly, 'I'll take you on a guided tour.'

♥

Helen gripped her jumper to her but Max, who was wearing short sleeves, seemed immune. Leaning in, he put his arm around her, drawing her against his chest. He'd grabbed two towels from their bedroom, and was carrying these over his other arm.

They found a sandy patch on the edge of the lagoon, and Max laid the towels out next to each other.

'Comfy?' he asked as she lay down next to him, her heart still pounding.

'Yes.'

When Max pulled her a little closer, it was more protective than suggestive. Helen tried to relax.

'So probably the most famous constellation of our skies is the Southern Cross,' Max said. 'You've heard of it?'

'Of course.'

'Ironically enough, the Southern Cross is one of the smallest of eighty-eight constellations, yet it includes some of the brightest stars in the heavens. Have a look up there. Which one do you think it is?'

Helen studied the night sky. There wasn't a single cloud marring its magnificence. But everywhere she could see, stars formed giant crosses.

'I don't know,' she said a little helplessly, 'maybe that one?'

'Perhaps the name is a little misleading. I often think it looks more like a kite than a cross. See over there, those bright stars trailing behind that formation? Those are the pointers, alpha Centauri and beta Centauri. They're really the key to knowing you've focused on the right spot.' Max moved his hands, tracing the lines of the cross. 'So, can you see it?'

'I can now,' Helen said.

'Of the two pointers, the one furthest away – that one, see? – that's the alpha Centauri. It's the third brightest star in the night sky and it's earth's nearest known neighbour beyond our solar system. The alpha Centauri isn't actually just one star. It's made up of three stars travelling together. The two brightest ones take eighty years to orbit around each other, can you believe?'

'Wow.'

'Of those two stars, the one alpha Centauri A is almost our sun's twin ... Anyway, so that's a little about the pointers. Would you like to see the Jewel Box or the Coal Sack next ...?'

Max took Helen on a journey across the skies, from Uranus to Jupiter to Mercury. He pointed out how Helen could learn to find south, his fingers directing her as he extended the long axis of the Cross right across the stars.

'Now draw another line, see, halfway between the pointers and ninety degrees to the line joining them. Where the two lines cross is more or less the south celestial pole ...'

And Helen, who'd felt that she would never be able to find her way again, was overcome with a strange sense of peace, finally knowing which direction was which. She looked across at Max, who smiled back at her.

'Feeling chilly?' he asked.

Helen nodded.

'Let's go inside, then. We've done enough sky travelling for one night.'

Her stomach wrenched as Max unlocked the door, letting her inside.

He sat down on the edge of his bed. 'Don't be nervous, Helen,' Max said.

'Is it that obvious?'

Max laughed softly. 'Maybe not. Maybe I'm just highly intuitive.'

'I'm sorry,' Helen said.

'I've had a lovely evening.'

'Maybe another ...'

Max went over to her, putting his arm around her shoulders. 'I know how important trust is, Helen. And first you need to trust yourself.'

Max kissed her cheek with a tenderness she hadn't experienced from George in the three years of trying for their baby.

'Good night, sweet Helen,' Max said.

♥

When Helen awoke, Max wasn't there.

Her heart fluttered. Had he left without saying goodbye? She looked towards where his suitcase had lain open the night before, but it was gone. Helen stood up quickly, finding some clothes to slip on, so she could check for his car. Fear. Relief. Sadness. Anxiety. Slipping on some sandals, Helen opened the room door, wondering if it would lock automatically. It didn't matter. She could ask the lady from the B&B to open it again if it did.

Rushing through the reception area, she poked her head around the corner of the breakfast room.

'Are you looking for your young man?' the owner asked.

Helen nodded, mute.

'He said to start breakfast without him. He'll be back at nine. I think he went to a meeting.'

Helen smiled in relief.

'Well, if the omelettes are still on offer ...' she said, pulling up a chair in the sunlight, 'I would love to give one a try.'

An hour later Helen was sipping coffee, a sketchpad in front of her. A face had begun to appear in the scribblings, and she realised with a sense of gloom that it was George's. For goodness sake, what was she doing? She tore the page out, ripping it into little pieces.

'Not good?' Max asked her, watching her frantic movements.

Helen laughed self-consciously. 'You're back.'

'I am. Did Mary give you my message? I thought you might be worried that I'd disappeared.'

'Men do that, sometimes,' Helen said cynically.

'Not this one.'

'Good news,' she said a bit snippily.

Max shrugged, letting her off lightly. 'I'm not really a morning person either. What are you planning to do today?' he asked.

The truth was she hadn't planned anything. Helen was trapped in some sort of lethargy and even though she knew she was going to have to find a new path, she wasn't really sure where it was quite yet.

'I hadn't really thought about it.'

Max pulled up a chair next to her. 'Well, I've been thinking. And I think I may have an idea.'

Helen noticed how his hazel eyes twinkled. And despite herself, she found herself smiling. 'What *are* you up to, Max?'

'Come back to Franschhoek with me. It's beautiful. Quiet. And I need help with the illustrations on the book I am writing.'

'You're writing a book?' Helen said, buying time.

'I've been tracing my family's roots from the first Huguenots. And actually, there are more than a few skeletons in the De Villiers closet.'

Helen's eyebrows raised quizzically.

'I spoke to my publisher,' Max continued. 'She hasn't settled on an illustrator yet, and when I told her how talented you are, well, she said I could make you the offer. Although I must warn you, the pay isn't exactly what you'd be used to in London.'

Max sat back in his chair, as though the excitement of the idea had suddenly drained him.

'What sort of illustrations do you need?' Helen asked. 'And how could you know that I'd even be the right person?'

'I *know*,' said Max. 'I thought as much when I saw your sketches of the kite surfers.'

But thinking that this explained his interest in her, Helen felt stung.

Max leant forward again, catching her hands in his. 'Don't look like that, Helen,' he said. 'I *want* you to come. We'd make a great team. And don't worry, no strings attached.'

CHAPTER SIX

Back in Scarborough, Helen had once again packed her bags, and was loading the boot of Alec's Opel with blank canvases. Her finished works were hanging at Madeleine's; in the three days she'd been away, one had already sold.

'You'll still be painting?' Madeleine asked anxiously. 'I can't have these blank walls ... – I might just have to put the protea photos back up again.'

'God help us,' said Helen, shivered dramatically. The photos were probably taken in the 1960s and were so faded it took a bit of imagination to work them out. 'Don't worry – I still have a bit of spare time. Why don't you drive through and visit? You can fetch what I've done.'

'Well,' said Madeleine, primping, 'I might just have to come and check if your virtue is intact.'

Helen groaned. 'He hasn't even kissed me, except on the cheek.'

'We'll see,' Madeleine said. 'You've landed with your bum in the butter, Helen. One of the richest wine families in the whole of South Africa, and you're a house guest.'

'I'm singing for my supper,' Helen retorted.

'Just saying that's all I hope you're doing, unless, of course, anything else would make you happy.'

But Helen was surprised to find she was happy already. She drove along the coast, passing over the scrubby mountains to Simon's Town, then on to Fish Hoek and Muizenberg. As the towns disappeared behind her, she looked to her right, enjoying the sight of the waves rolling onto the beach. A little further on, a water amusement park hunched paint-bare and weather-beaten along the road, and beyond that, on the other side of the road, Khayelitsha shacks stacked close on sea sand, corrugated iron glinting in the already harsh sunlight. The shanties seemed to stretch on forever. On a day like this, they even seemed idyllic.

Curving along the coast, the road joined the motorway in an unruly landscape dense with woody plants she didn't know. Every once in a while a tree bursting with yellow blossoms dipped under the weight of its plumage.

Max had told her to head towards Stellenbosch.

'They're working on some of the roads en route. You'll just have to be a little patient. Sometimes you're lucky and you don't even have to stop. Don't worry – you won't get lost.'

Two months ago, she might have been nervous. But now she felt like she was on an adventure, armed with Max's hand-drawn map. She negotiated her way towards mountains that reached jaggedly into the cloudless skies, and began to see a change in the landscape. Large areas of land had been cleared, and vines tangled along wire supports extended, it seemed, for miles. But September had brought other growth: like newly fallen snow, buds dotted bushes in the fields that she passed, making her think of cherry-blossom season.

And as the road rose in front of her and the Groot Drakenstein mountains became clearer, Helen gasped. She'd imagined something beautiful, but not like this. Lush and green, she passed wine farms sign-posted by 'Route de Vignerons' signs. Max had told her that only the most robust candidates had been selected by the eighteenth-century governor to set up their farmsteads on the formidable slopes of Hell's Height.

'You'll see what they saw all those years ago,' Max had told her. 'On the right, the Groot Drakenstein massif ascends steeply; to the left, the Simonsberg. Beyond, you'll see the Wemmershoek Mountain peaks, and below is our gorgeous valley.'

And he was right. How rich the valley looked in contrast to Scarborough, its thirst slaked by the constant flow of the Berg River.

'My family came in the first wave of Huguenots,' Max had gone on. 'And even when we're not physically in the valley, we never really leave.'

Looking at the views around her, Helen could understand why. She was drawing closer to the town and it was already a flurry of activity. A tour bus slowed in front of her car, and holidaymakers sat in coffee shops and cafés enjoying brunch as the day beamed brighter.

Helen checked the map, holding it up against the steering wheel while simultaneously watching the road. She was obviously on Franschhoek's main road and knew she needed to turn off at Bordeau Street and then towards the mountain foothills.

'Some of the road is dirt, but the Opel will handle it,' Max had said.

Helen changed gears, and dropped the map back onto the passenger seat. There seemed to be a lot of construction work going on beyond the town's pristine façade as houses were in the process of being restored to their former glory. Helen picked up the signs for Bourgogne, following them through an avenue of oaks.

Soon the car was passing through curlicued wrought-iron gates that swung open for her.

Helen's stomach dipped. Now that she was here, she didn't know in the least what to expect. Despite this, she was resolute. Here she was and she might as well get the uncertainty over with. She unclipped her safety belt in a single swift movement.

Leaving all her bags except her handbag in the car, she

walked up towards the house.

♥

She hadn't recognised the voice on the intercom at the gate. It wasn't Max.

Helen looked up at the homestead, its gables whirling and decked with fuchsia bougainvillea. She could make out the year the edifice was constructed: 1691. Not one of the first buildings to go up here then, but old enough. At both sides of the closed front door, wine barrels were stacked, seeming as venerable as the house itself. She stopped to listen, hoping to hear Max's voice. Instead from outside came the growling of what she assumed was a lawnmower.

Helen ascended the stairs and, feeling self-conscious, knocked.

With no reply after three attempts, she decided to walk into the backyard to find the person who was cutting the grass. If she had no luck, she reasoned she could go back into town for a latte and return later.

But it was as she turned that she noticed an approaching cloud of dust and the roaring of an engine. A quad bike skimmed over the dirt, drawing to an undignified halt below the stairs. A man stepped off, a smile lighting up his face.

'Helen?'

She nodded.

'Well, Max said you were talented, but he never mentioned how gorgeous you are!'

Helen hoped her face didn't give anything away, but she felt as if she'd been hit in the stomach with a sack full of stones. This man wasn't just attractive; he was sensational. Tall, with beautiful olive skin, green eyes, full kissable lips. And when he walked towards her, he did so with an arrogant swagger that left her breathless. Helen hoped she wasn't staring.

'Jared,' he said. 'Max's younger and *better* brother.'

Helen wondered if they should shake hands, but Jared kissed

her softly on the cheek. She might have found this presumptuous, but she simply swooned, weak at the knees and all the places that count.

Jared held her as if to study her face.

'You're quite, quite beautiful,' he said. 'Max really is getting sly in his old age. He had to run off to the auditors, by the way. Something to do with a late tax payment.'

'Oh,' said Helen.

'Now don't be disappointed, Helen. I'll take good care of you until he comes back. Promise. First things first, let's get you unpacked. We've put you in the main house, but if you hate it, there's a guest cottage you can escape to if you're tired of us. We're not easily offended.'

'I'm sure the main house will be lovely.'

'It is. But those wooden floors can get on your nerves. Corridor creeping is a mean and impossible feat.' Jared smiled at a youthful memory and Helen found herself smiling back.

'I guess your parents had a hard time keeping two boys in check.'

Jared grinned. 'Max was terribly good and responsible. I was always the tearaway – I think I singlehandedly turned our parents grey.'

'Er, well done?' Helen said, catching his mood.

And Jared laughed uproariously. 'Helen, I think we're going to get along just fine. It's so wonderful you've come.' Grabbing the suitcases and three of Helen's canvases out of the car, he led her back up the stairs.

As they walked inside the house, Helen was assailed by the smell of floor polish and window cleaner. In the entrance, on what looked like an old travel trunk, stood a basket of flowers – all kinds of proteas and pin cushions, many of which Max had identified for her in Langebaan.

Jared nodded at the arrangement. 'He's an old romantic, our Max. They're specially for you.'

Helen felt herself glow. 'How sweet.'

'Yup,' Jared said. 'Sweet. Not a word you could use to

describe me, I'm afraid. But I have other excellent qualities ...'

Despite herself, Helen felt herself blush. Jared smiled rakishly and turned away, his boots echoing on the yellowwood floors.

♥

Helen's bedroom was at the end of a long, high-ceilinged passage.

'It's not en suite, of course,' said Jared. 'The Heritage Foundation would have a coronary if we bashed down any walls. But never fear, the bathroom is just two doors down. Treat it as your own – no one else is using it.'

'Thanks,' Helen said.

'Your room. Wardrobe. Light switch. Fan – you'll probably be needing that. Bedside lamp. Bed.' Jared walked around the bedroom and then bounced experimentally on the enormous old bed. 'Max moved in this desk for you this morning,' he continued. 'He said you might want to set up an easel, but suggested you paint in the drawing room or on the porch so you don't poison yourself on fumes.'

'It all looks wonderful,' Helen murmured, noticing a small pile of books on the bedside table – one entitled *Stargazing in the Southern Hemisphere* – and a small vase of fynbos flowers.

Jared followed her eyes. 'That's why Max watches our accounts. I'm big picture. He's detail.'

'Right,' said Helen, nodding.

'Well, it's much too beautiful a day to stay inside,' Jared said, standing. 'You must be hungry And I have something in mind that will tempt you.'

'Lead on,' Helen said laughing. 'I'm tempted already.'

♥

Jared led Helen into a huge country kitchen. It was square, more or less, dominated in the centre by a huge railway-sleeper table. Above it, pots and pans hung from extended copper hooks. Benches made from wooden planks and wine barrels stood on either side, with mismatched wicker chairs on the short sides, two alongside each other. In the middle of the table was a bowl of fresh fruit: oranges, apples, bananas, grapes and avocados. A SMEG fridge and freezer in vanilla hummed in one corner of the room, an antique wine rack silently brooding in another.

'Pull up a chair.'

Helen expected him to offer her lunch, but he disappeared out the back door.

'Prudence!' he yelled. 'Prudence!'

Helen heard a soft reply before he emerged again, his arm around a hefty African woman. She must have been well into her sixties, if not older, her heavily lined lids drooping over soft caramel eyes.

'Meet the most important woman in our lives. This is Prudence, our second mother. Chief housekeeper. Chef extraordinaire. Beauty queen.'

Prudence slapped Jared lightly on the shoulder, but Helen could tell she was pleased.

'He only says that when he wants something,' she said, taking in Helen in one appraising glance. 'Welcome to Bourgogne.'

Helen smiled, then stood up to shake Prudence's hand.

'Did Max tell you when he'd be back?' Jared asked Prudence.

'Mr Jared,' Prudence cocked her head, a warning note creeping into her voice.

'I'm asking, dear Prudence, so I can have Helen back in time to greet him,' Jared said cheerfully. 'I'm taking her on a farm tour. Helen has to see the vineyards if she's to draw them.'

After a few yanks, Jared moved to a tall cupboard. It had several shelves and the cupboards on the left and right had large diamonds punched in them, filled with chicken mesh. It took a few yanks on the stiff handle to open the door, but when it did, Jared pulled out a picnic basket. Prudence's eyes narrowed.

'Prudie, Helen would love some chicken sandwiches. You're not a vegetarian are you, Helen?'

'No, but I don't want to cause any trouble.'

Prudence clapped her hands, and pulled out a red-chequered

ceramic jug from the fridge. 'Nonsense,' she said. 'Now, Mr Jared, you take Helen onto the porch with this lemonade. I'll call you when I'm ready.'

'Don't you think she's an angel?' Jared said. 'Max and I would be lost without her.'

'Out!' Prudence waved a dishcloth at him, her eyes twinkling.

♥

Helen had expected a walk to the vineyards; she hadn't anticipated a basket strapped to the quad bike, and Jared kicking the machine into gear.

'Hop on,' he said with a cheeky look.

'No helmet?' Helen said.

'Living dangerously is much more fun.'

Helen hesitated, remembering the uneasy skid as Jared came to an abrupt halt in front of the house.

'Come on!' Jared cried.

What the hell, Helen thought. She slipped her leg over the leather seat, feeling herself slide up against Jared's back.

'Ready?'

They skidded over bumps, avoiding pot holes and churning up mud. The bottom of Helen's jeans were soaked by the time Jared finally stopped. And rather than being afraid, Helen found she was exhilarated. 'Not everyone gets the Grand Tour!' Jared laughed and held out his hand to help her off.

She took it, shocked at the surge that pulsed through her as they touched. Jared angled his head, holding onto her fingers a little longer than was strictly necessary. 'Everything okay?' he asked.

Helen pulled away, as she tried to compose herself. 'Of course, why shouldn't it be?'

Helen thought about Max, not really sure what he was expecting from her. She remembered his gentleness and care when she wasn't really in a state to manage anything. But here she was with Jared, and for the first time since her divorce, she actually felt something; something long hibernated was stirring inside her and she just couldn't help herself. She liked it.

Jared hadn't moved away. He was still exceptionally close to her. Close enough for her to see the flecks of dust caught on his eyelashes, the tiny mole above his top lip. His eyes caught hers as he smiled, lifting his finger to trace the contours of her face.

Helen knew she should turn away, feign interest in the vines or the view. Make conversation. Ask for something to drink. Focus on how she'd been hurt by George to balance out the pressure building inside her.

Instead she stood still, feeling the soft touch against her cheek. A small sigh slipped out, a rising tide catching in her throat. She didn't know this man. And he didn't know her; her problems and her insecurities. Here in the vineyard in this country she was just beginning to know, she was completely new.

So when Jared cupped her face in his hands, she let him. And when he kissed her, she didn't melt. Her body surged with a newfound feeling of power, and for the first time in years she was the woman she was meant to be.

CHAPTER SEVEN

They returned from the vineyards just before dusk. Helen leant into Jared, feeling his back against her breasts. The closer they got to the main house, the more Helen's stomach began to churn.

She hadn't slept with Jared. Not yet. But she wanted to. Jared had held her hand, walked her through the vines. He'd laid out a picnic blanket and made her feel like she was the only person in the world.

And if he'd pushed a little harder, she'd have willingly succumbed. And not to prove Olivia right. Not to get that *post-George shag over and done with* or to *take back her femininity*. But quite simply because Jared made her skin sear. Feeling him now in front of her, she wanted to clutch him closer, drop her lips to his neck. She pulled her arms tighter around him.

'Hello, tiger,' he said softly, his right hand catching one of hers for just a moment.

♥

Max was sitting in front of the house under one of the oak trees. Though he was nursing a beer, Helen read an expression she hadn't seen in him before: anxiety. He stood up as soon as Jared switched off the engine.

'Hey, boet,' Jared said, almost bouncing off the quad bike.

'You're back,' said Max, a level of reserve just distinguishable in his tone.

'We are,' said Helen. 'How did it go with the tax?'

Max frowned.

'Jared said you had to go into town to sort out some tax thing?' Helen prompted.

'Oh, right,' Max said. 'Easy. Done.' His eyes trailed down her legs to the cuffs of her jeans. 'Where'd you take her?' he asked.

'Up to Elephant Rock.' Jared's voice was bright. 'We should all go again tomorrow, Max. You should see how the peach blossoms have opened since last week.'

Max nodded. 'Are you okay, Helen? Jared can be a little impetuous sometimes. And he drives like a lunatic. If I'd known ...'

'That's me,' Jared interrupted. 'Irresponsible as always. I had you quaking in your shoes, didn't I, Helen?'

Helen laughed to ease the tension. 'I'm perfect,' she said. 'And I'm braver than I look.' She jumped off the quad bike, and walked towards Max. 'I'm fine, Max, really. And hello.'

As Max kissed her on the cheek, his strong sandalwood smell engulfed her. Helen hugged him to her. She was, she realised, so glad to see him. He felt solid and strangely familiar. She felt him relax into her arms as though her touch had eased him.

'It's so good to see you,' Helen said. 'I missed you.'

Max smiled. 'You too.'

Jared stood slightly away from them, his face untroubled. 'What about a braai tonight?' Jared suggested. 'It's a perfect evening.'

♥

Helen watched the men trying to coax a fire.

'Come on, Jared,' Max said. 'We won't cook a thing on those puny flames.'

'I could pour some diesel on it ...'

'Ja, and burn off your eyebrows like last time. Just stoke it, boytjie.'

'Oh, right, make me do all the hard work ...'

While the brothers shared certain mannerisms, they looked quite different from each other. Jared was leaner, more angular, his skin a deeper, more even brown. Max was stockier and stronger, and his hair was at least two shades lighter than his brother's, with a distinct wave. And Jared seemed to do everything at double Max's pace. Jared talked faster. Moved quicker. Like he was constantly in fast forward. Jared seemed to throw his boerewors and lamb chops onto their communal pyre, while Max arranged everything with obvious thought.

Helen picked at the bowl of crisps Prudence had brought to tide them over. She'd tried to help the older woman lay the table outside, but Prudence had waved her away. Helen had watched her bring out the plates. She'd come back a few minutes later with a Greek salad and a baguette, and the next trip had resulted in a tray with a bean salad and two lidded Corningware dishes, which now sat ready at the table.

Helen stood up and approached the men at the fire. 'How is it coming along?' she asked.

Max put his arm around her, drawing her to him. 'We're getting there, aren't we, Jared?' He sniffed. 'Don't you love this smell?'

Helen nodded. 'It smells of sunshine. On rare good days my father used to pull out his barbecue and fan the flames with my mother's hairdryer. It was quite a ritual. He always burnt the meat, but he was so happy watching the flames.'

Max laughed and let her go to retrieve some tongs. 'Well, we'll try to keep this edible. Are you hungry?'

'Starved.'

Helen glanced at Jared, who acknowledged her with a smile Max seemed to miss. But Jared's jade eyes drilled into her, making her knees weak.

'Your glass is empty,' he said. 'Let me take you to the cellar so we can choose a bottle for dinner. What do you want, Max, red or white?'

'White,' Max said. 'Too hot for red. I can go if you like?'

Jared studied his ramshackle display of meat. 'I actually think you might spread those chops out more evenly, Max. I don't think I did a great job.'

Max laughed. 'I'll see what I can do. Don't be long now.'

♥

It didn't take long.

By the time they were halfway down the stairs, Jared's lips were on hers, his hands up her shirt. He unbuttoned her quickly, cupping her breasts and sending her nipples into peaks of ecstasy. Helen kissed him back. He tasted of beer and vinegar, his tongue exploring her mouth urgently. With each probe, she felt the heat draining between her legs. She throbbed everywhere, and pulled at his T-shirt to lift it over his head.

'God, you're hot,' Jared said, as his shirt dropped to the floor. 'I've been wanting you all night.'

Helen felt for his belt, his zip, her hand slipping inside his jeans. He strained against her fingers. She heard the echo of his buckle hitting the floor, jeans and scants following. Emboldened, Helen looked at him, saw him nod. Her mouth closed over him, sucking gently, then harder.

'Christ,' he said, holding her head, his hands knitted in her hair.

She moved back and forth, the sound of their breathing hollow. Then Helen felt his hands at her face, lifting her gently away.

'I might have a condom in my wallet,' he said, 'if that's –'

'Hurry,' she said. She unzipped herself, discarded her clothes until she wore nothing but her bra.

He took her on the stairs, pulsing inside her until she thought she would scream. His fingers, light and insistent, massaged her until she couldn't hold herself back any longer. She came in a flood, an almost animal cry escaping from her. Jared smiled, his body shuddering just after hers and his breathing heavy. Touching her face, he softly kissed her eyelids.

'This is not what I thought I'd be doing this evening,' he said.

Helen smiled. Confessions of love meant nothing to her just at the moment. But confessions of great sex ... now *that* was what she needed.

Jared stroked her face. 'Max will be wondering where we are.'

Helen felt her stomach twist into an almost instant pretzel. 'You go ahead. Give me a few minutes to collect myself.'

Jared grinned. 'Red or white?' he asked.

'What?'

'Red or white wine?'

'Oh, right,' she giggled. 'Red. Why not a bit of red?'

♥

Staring into the bathroom mirror, Helen pulled a brush through her hair. Her cheeks were a little flushed, but she still looked herself. Just not the old Helen.

Thinking of Jared's body made her legs feel as though they would cave. Perhaps Olivia had been right: *You know the old adage of getting over a man by getting one onto you ...* Except that Jared wasn't just any man. He made her heat up.

Helen checked her buttons. A good thing – she'd missed one, and another was in the wrong hole.

Max didn't have a claim on her, did he? He'd brought her here to work on the book – she hadn't made any other promises. He was a gentleman, so he wouldn't expect her to make any. Some beautiful scenery, a historic farmhouse, and perhaps something else might fall into place. He didn't have it in him to push or predict. He was far too nice to do that.

Helen brushed the dust off her jeans. She could do the book, couldn't she? After the interlude in the cellar, she felt capable of anything. Creative. Potent. Why complicate things? If it upset him, he didn't actually have to *know* about Jared.

The truth was her body was finally awakening from a long

and miserable hibernation. Tuning back into a world without George.

And it was amazing.

CHAPTER EIGHT

By the time Helen returned to the fire, the brothers were talking about an upcoming rugby match, betting on a predicted score, and Helen felt a strange admiration for Jared's composure: his side of the conversation didn't falter. They were so engaged that they barely noticed her return, or so she thought, until she saw Jared's eyes roving her body with a sense of ownership that made her blush. He held out her glass, letting their hands touch for just an instant, and a jolt of electricity darted up her arm.

Helen wasn't nearly as capable of subterfuge – her eyes were so dangerously locked on him that he only broke her stare when he went inside to fetch the salt.

'You're quiet, Helen,' Max said. 'Everything okay?'

Helen smiled. 'I guess I'm a little tired, that's all. All this country air.'

Max cut up the cooked sausage. 'So, what do you think of Bourgogne?'

'It's magical,' she said, and not just to make him happy – Bourgogne was everything Max had described and more. 'I can see why you know so much about the stars.' She pointed up to the clear skies. 'Two nights of the most perfectly clear evenings I've ever experienced, and both with you,' she said.

Max's face lit up. 'Well, I hope we'll have lots more. Are you happy with your room? I wasn't sure whether to put you in the cottage or the main house.'

'It's lovely,' she said.

A silence fell between them, but it wasn't one of those companiable lulls they'd shared in Langebaan. She felt the need to make an effort.

'Will we start on the book tomorrow, do you think, Max?'

'I'd like to, if that's alright with you.'

'Of course. I'm looking forward to it.'

Max offered her a piece of boerewors on a fork. 'Have you tried this yet? Traditional South African sausage. This one is extra special, though – Prudence makes it with my great-great-grandmother's recipe. She wasn't a De Villiers by birth; she came from the Dutch side of the family. A brilliant cook by all accounts.'

Helen bit into it identifying some familiar flavours: coriander, allspice and nutmeg. 'Delicious,' she said.

'Of course, recipes like this are closely guarded secrets.'

Helen smiled. 'I can see why,' she said.

'Here.' Max cut her another slice of meat. 'Sometimes the best bits are the ones you steal straight from the braai. My dad used to call them "cook's spoils".'

She opened her mouth, enjoying the mix of tastes on her tongue. Max was as gentle as always, caring for her in a way no man ever really had. Not even her own father.

When Jared returned from the kitchen with the Cerebos, she and Max were sitting side by side, sharing a piece of boerewors between them. Even to an outsider Max's stance would have seemed territorial, like a dog guarding a beloved mistress. Jared, however, appeared unperturbed, taking a seat on the other side of the table. He watched Max slicing and piercing the sausage, then helped himself to a plate.

'For some reason,' he said, looking directly at Helen, 'I'm as hungry as a fox. Helen, please pass the pap?'

'The what?'

'Just next to your left hand, yes, that dish. It's ground corn, another South African staple. We grew up on the stuff, didn't we, Max?'

'If Prudie had anything to do with it, sure,' Max replied. 'Try it with a bit of that sauce, Helen. Here, let me hold the plate for you.'

And Max, at ease in both their company led the conversation from there. When Jared's phone rang, they were almost all finishing second helpings. Jared held the phone in his palm, calmly checking who it was before he stood up and walked away from the table to answer it.

'Bugger,' he said, when he came back from a brief conversation. 'That was Heinrich. I forgot I was supposed to meet up with him tonight. He's sitting there at Reuben's wondering where the hell I am.'

'You'd better go,' said Max. 'We can clear up, can't we, Helen?'

'Yes, of course,' Helen said, wondering a little selfishly why Jared would want to dash away.

'Well, don't wait up,' Jared said. 'Heinrich's been planning this *skop* since Evan's bachelor's. It's not going to be pretty.'

Moments later, Helen heard the sound of a shower, a toilet flush. Remembering his body against hers, she reluctantly wondered how it would feel to wash him all away …

Max leant over to fill her glass. 'How's the wine?' he said. 'I forgot to ask. This was one of our better vintages.'

'It's lovely,' Helen said, trying to focus. 'Er, tastes like cherries.'

Max nodded encouragingly.

'And plums, and maybe a touch of oak.'

'You're a natural,' he said, smiling. 'Jared must like you. He doesn't bring this out for just anybody.'

Helen took another sip, then a gulp. 'I need to use the bathroom,' she said suddenly. 'Will you excuse me a moment?'

'Sure. I'll start taking in the plates –'

'Oh, please don't,' Helen said, surprised by the pleading in her voice. 'If you do, dinner will be over and it's still so early ...'

Max shrugged. 'You got it.'

Jared was in the entrance hall retrieving his keys. His jeans hung beautifully, and a light blue shirt emphasised his tan.

'You got ready quickly,' Helen said, making him jump. She wanted to reach out to him, but something about his expression told her not to. 'You look great,' she said.

'Thanks.'

'Listen, Helen, I've got to go,' he said, his voice clipped. 'Sorry.'

She was being dismissed.

'You have a fun time tonight,' she said in her most light-hearted voice.

'It's just one night,' Jared said, jangling his keys.

Helen felt herself go cold.

See you,' she said.

'Helen,' Jared called.

She turned. 'Yes?' she said.

'I'll be back later.'

She didn't bother responding.

♥

By the time she came outside again, Jared's car had already roared down the driveway. Helen sat down next to Max, and reached for her wine glass.

'He keeps a hectic schedule,' she said casually.

'Jared? That brother of mine doesn't sleep. Most nights he gets by on three hours. Sometimes it's like he's on a mission to exhaust himself.'

'Does it work?'

'I don't know. Probably. Jared's always one step ahead.'

Helen stretched. 'So what's the plan for tomorrow?' she asked.

'Well, I thought I could go through some of the family archives with you. Show you some of the photos. Then maybe we could go into Franschhoek and have lunch. Stop off at the

Huguenot Museum.'

Helen nodded. 'That sounds lovely.'

'I'm not really sure how you work, but I thought at least I could give you a feel for what I'm trying to achieve. And also for the atmosphere around here. That's what caught me about your kite-surfing sketches – you really know how to capture a mood.'

Helen smiled. 'And *you* really know how to flatter a girl,' she said.

'It's not flattery. Just the truth.'

A mosquito buzzed softly between them and Helen instinctively rubbed her arms. Max clapped his hands together.

'Damn it, missed,' he said. 'Shall I get an insect-repellent candle? Seems a shame to go inside.'

Helen finished the last of her wine. 'You know, Max?' she said. 'I'm actually not up for a late night as I thought I was. Let's go inside and make some coffee.'

If Max was disappointed, he hid it remarkably well. 'I'll show you how to use the espresso machine, in case you need to whip up a latte when Prudie or I aren't around,' he offered.

Seemed it was just like Max to remember. Helen touched his face, kissing him on the cheek.

'Thank you for a lovely evening, Max. And for inviting me here.'

♥

By the time Helen had dressed for breakfast the next morning, Jared had already disappeared. She wasn't sure if she was glad or disappointed. In the light of day, she wondered if the hours she'd spent tossing and turning were even worth it. Even if it was just one night, wasn't she the better for it? She wasn't the sexless, frigid ice queen George had moaned about. And it had taken a fumble in the cellar to show her that. Well, more than a fumble, actually ...

Olivia would have told her to grow up and enjoy the afterglow, so that is what she resolved to do. She felt like an idiot for cornering Jared against the entrance hall table. As if she could force him to ravish her! No, she'd wait for that feeling to fade in its own good time. And when she had to face him again, she'd thrust the memory of their encounter far from her mind.

'Knock, knock,' Helen said, as she approached the kitchen door.

'Good morning, sleepyhead,' Max said. 'Come on in.'

She sat down in one of the wicker chairs.

'Did you sleep well?' Max asked.

Helen wondered if Max had seen the light under her door. For someone who'd professed exhaustion, she'd taken an awfully long time to fall asleep. And even then she hadn't heard Jared come home.

'I did eventually,' she said. 'I don't know. For some reason, as soon as I was actually in bed my mind woke up. I ended up reading some trashy novel until one.'

'If you do that every night, we'll have to take you to the bookshop to stock up. Louis will be delighted you've moved in.'

Helen laughed. 'You're always full of good ideas, aren't you, Max?'

'Solution-driven,' Max smiled, 'what can I say?'

'But wouldn't it be better to solve the sleep problem?' she persisted.

'Oh, there are lots of ways to do that, but I'm not sure you're ready to discuss them.'

Helen felt the colour rise to her cheeks. 'Is this coffee mine?' she asked to change the subject.

'Just made it,' Max replied. 'But if it's cold, I'll drink it and make you a fresh cup.'

She sipped from the mug and sighed dramatically. 'Delicious,' she said. 'Careful, Max – I think I could get used to this treatment.'

'I was hoping there were easier ways of keeping you here than tying you up.'

Prudence bustled in from outside. Beside her was a younger woman in her early twenties.

'Good morning, Helen,' Prudence said.

'Morning,' Helen replied cheerfully. Last night she had begun to sense that Prudence didn't trust her – and granted, the notion was not ill-founded. Now she sensed her scrutiny, as if Prudence was a mother hen standing over her brood. 'This is Gladys,' Prudence said. 'My granddaughter.'

'Hello, Gladys,' Helen said. 'I'm Helen Shaw.'

The younger woman smiled.

'Gladys usually cleans your room first,' Prudence said pointedly, 'but she's not sure if she can go in there now.'

'Oh, please carry on. Don't let me stop your routine.'

Gladys retrieved a vacuum cleaner and a bright purple feather duster from a cupboard. Her steps echoed as she walked down the wooden passageway. Prudence hadn't moved.

'Anything I can do?' Helen asked.

Prudence huffed, then turned to follow Gladys.

'Since my mother's death,' Max offered, ' Prudie has taken her responsibilities to heart. And for reasons I can't understand, Jared encourages it.'

Helen drank the last of her latte and tried not to think about Jared. 'I hope I haven't offended her.'

'Don't worry,' he said, 'she'll come around. Now what can I get you? Toast, an omelette or muesli?'

♥

Max's study was on the exact opposite side of the house from her bedroom. Helen had guessed how it would look, and found she was wrong and right in equal parts.

She'd expected it to be neat: a perfectly clear desk with no sign of any paperwork whatsoever. She thought there'd be files on a shelf, lined up in date order or alphabetically, probably in height order. On this she was wrong, because Max's desk and bookshelf was an array of paper, and though the piles weren't filed, she could tell by the coloured dividers and Post-its that the heaps were aligned with some care.

She'd thought Max's desk would be an antique Victorian affair, or even older. It would be traditional, in walnut or mahogany with an original dark-green or burgundy leather writing surface embossed with some sort of pattern. Instead he was working at a desk of transparent tempered glass, with bright stainless-steel metal legs. It was probably Italian, clearly custom-designed and valuable. And instead of some modern, ergonomic, high-back executive chair, his was a heavily built mahogany antique, with clawed feet and black leather upholstery.

What surprised her most, however, was not the modern bookshelves or the AppleMac screen. Not the De Villiers hall of fame on the one wall, showing black and white faces through the centuries. Not the air conditioning unit humming above them, which she remembered he'd told her about. What caught her off guard was the kite-surfing sketch she'd given to him in Langebaan already hanging in pride of place above his desk.

Max caught her appraising glance across the room, and the way it lingered on the picture.

'I did tell you it was the best one,' he murmured.

Helen smiled. 'You framed it quickly,' she replied. 'It suits the room.'

'I like it,' he said. 'It makes me happy.'

Helen recognised another of Max's unique qualities: he was comfortable enough not to care that she might think him desperate or foolish. And she was glad that this wasn't her reaction anyway. She was chuffed. Thrilled that Max liked her work enough to want to look at it every day. And that there might be a little more to it than that.

Max offered Helen a seat opposite him. 'So let's talk about the book,' he said. 'I've been interested in De Villiers genealogy for years. It started in my late teens, actually, when I did a school project for my history class. Jared, of course, doesn't have the patience for the sort of trawling that family trees involve. He thinks it's much too intangible to be worth the effort.'

'Well, you and Jared don't seem to be cut from the same cloth,' Helen commented.

'You'd be surprised. In some ways, we're more alike than either of us would care to admit.'

'The book?' Helen prompted, not really wanting to be caught up in a discussion about Jared. It was far too distracting.

I've been collecting these bits and pieces for over a year. I've met up or corresponded with family members both in South Africa and internationally. We're quite an interesting bunch, even if I say so myself.'

'Well, *I'm* interested.' Helen hoped immediately that her comment wouldn't be misconstrued.

But Max continued. 'I started writing the book. At first it was terribly factual – accurate drawings of family trees done with genealogy programmes, that sort of thing. But I realised immediately that it was dull. Only a De Villiers would be prepared to labour through all of that, and then only the most enthusiastic and dedicated ones.'

'And?'

'So I stopped, and thought about what makes a story interesting. The plot. Sure. The setting. Of course. But really what most people tend to be interested in is other people. So I changed my focus to include chapters on key De Villiers members who had a specific story to tell. Scandal. Achievement against the odds. Tragedy. All set against a South African backdrop, almost as a means of showing South Africa changing at the same time as the family develops. One of my ancestors, Marthinus de Villiers, wrote *Die Stem van Suid-Afrika*, our national anthem.'

'The project sounds great.'

'My publisher saw the first few chapters and commissioned it based on those.'

'No mean feat,' Helen said smiling.

'I was pleased,' Max said modestly. 'I've had to fit it in between my other responsibilities at Bourgogne, so it's taken a little longer than it might have, but I'm happy with where I am now.'

'Where do I come in?'

'At first I was going to use the photos that I'd collected, which are available in the Huguenot Museum archives. They've been very helpful, offering to let me use of any images in the archive as long as I acknowledge them.'

'But?'

'But the photos lack vibrancy. When I show you you'll see what I mean. I'd like you to make the pictures come alive. Like your sketches of Bloubergstrand.'

Helen's brow crinkled.

'You don't think it's possible?' Max asked, concerned.

'Anything is possible, Max. I just hope I'll be able to pick up the atmosphere from the photos.'

Max smiled. 'Ah, but it won't just be photos. I'll take you around. To the homesteads. The mountains. The cemeteries. And of course you can read the stories from local accounts and my interpretation of them.'

Helen looked at Max. His face glowed with triumph and enthusiasm.

'We should get started then, shouldn't we?' she said. 'How many images do you think we are going to need?'

♥

They spent the morning paging through transcripts and information collected by other members of the De Villiers family that Max had sourced over the years. He laughed when Helen pulled out a comment he'd highlighted: 'Brilliant people the De Villierses – unfortunately all of them are not quite all there.'

'Needless to say,' Max said, 'that comment did not come from a family member.'

'But is it true?' Helen asked, giggling.

Max shrugged. 'I guess I'll have to let you decide, but don't judge us too harshly. Every family is bound to have a little melancholy, don't you think?'

Helen nodded. 'I think that's probably true.'

'Anyway,' Max said, 'the De Villiers family has an incredible legacy. They've been represented across most professions. As we go along, you'll find we weren't just ministers, although of course faith is what brought us from France. My first ancestors in the Cape, three brothers, Pierre, Abraham and Jacob (or Jacques as some remember him), were forced into hiding by the Edict of Nantes, which actually outlawed being Protestant. But I digress. There are all sorts of De Villierses in the bag: architects, authors, poets, engineers, farmers, scientists, you name it.'

'And winemakers?' Helen asked.

'We can't forget them, that's for sure. Funnily enough, Jared and I are the few remaining winemakers in the family – most people moved on centuries ago.'

'So how did your family get the farm?' Helen asked.

'Although the brothers were Huguenots, they weren't the part of the first influx. They seemed to arrive a year later than the others, but from the records we can find they were already involved in the community around Franschhoek. From what we can tell, Abraham was officially assigned his bit of land in 1711. He called it Champagne. Jacob got La Bri in 1712, and Bourgogne went to Pierre in 1713.'

'So he bought it?'

'No, it was granted to him by the Company. And Pierre was loaned 91 guilders and his brothers something similar to buy stock and materials from the Company. Believe me, it wasn't charity – the Company made seventy per cent profit. But the brothers paid off their debts by 1719, and bought more land.' Max shifted. 'You know what? I think we've had enough of a history lesson for the moment? Why don't we drive into town? I'll buy you lunch and then we can stop off at the Huguenot Museum if you think you can stand it.'

CHAPTER NINE

For somebody who'd been an integral part of the family picture the day before, Jared seemed remarkably absent. All day, Helen's encounter with him had flashed through her mind; its intensity still fresh. When she and Max came back from town in the late afternoon, Jared's quad bike was parked under the carport, but his canary-yellow Audi S4 convertible was missing.

Max helped Helen carry her sketchpad and portfolio bag into the kitchen, where Prudence was cooking at the stove.

'I'm not cooking for Mr Jared tonight, Mr Max,' Prudence said.

'Oh,' said Max, walking to the fridge to fetch tonic for their G&T's. 'Where's he off to this time?'

'He has a meeting in Cape Town. He said if it gets late he'll sleep at the Camp's Bay flat.'

Max nodded, then pushed a glass at a time into the fridge's ice dispenser. He pulled a bottle of Tanqueray off the booze shelf, adding a healthy tot to each glass.

'Looks like it's just you and me tonight, Helen. Do you want to sit on the porch or in the living room? I can burn some citronella candles to keep the bugs away.'

Although she was disappointed to be missing Jared, staying alone with Max was far less complicated, and she was in some sense relieved at the simplicity of being with him.

'Outside is lovely,' she answered. 'I've had a lifetime of living rooms. I'm not really sure why you South Africans ever stay indoors.'

'Well, winter does come eventually.'

'Winter!' Helen sniffed. 'You call that winter!'

Max laughed.

'Oh alright, so you get a bit colder where you come from,' he said.

As they moved outside, Helen watched the clouds gathering above the mountains. The sun filtered through them, transforming the whole range into a dusty peach glow.

'You'd think these mountains had been here forever,' Max said. 'But actually they've been formed by rainfall and glacial action on the sedimentary rock. One day, not in our lifetimes, of course, they'll be worn away completely and the whole area will be flat.'

'Hard to imagine,' Helen said, before a gentle silence fell between them.

'Do you ride?' asked Max suddenly. 'Horses, I mean.'

'Of course, what self-respecting Englishwoman hasn't donned jodhpurs and riding boots? What would our neighbours have thought if we hadn't?'

'Maybe one of these days we can go for a ride. It will give you an idea of the landscape, and it's really quite liberating seeing the area the way the pioneers did. We'll have to use a little imagination though – every tree you see here was planted. The wattles, the willows, the oaks, the yellowwoods. Even the Cape beeches. The area used to be covered completely in fynbos. Those settlers really made their mark on the valley. They even managed to chase away the last elephants.'

'You're kidding.'

'I'm actually not. This valley used to be an elephant breeding ground, hence its original name Olifantshoek – Elephants' Corner.

Local legend has it that in 1836, the last elephants, a mother and calf, were seen leaving here on what came to be the Franschhoek Pass.'

'That's sad,' Helen said.

'I guess it is. And it wasn't just the elephants who were disappointed with the new settlers either. This area was originally inhabited by the San, or the Bushmen, and the Khoi. The Khoi in particular were used as indentured labour – much of the wine farms' success was dependent on slavery.'

'You don't feel the weight of all that history sitting here, do you?' Helen commented.

'Jared certainly doesn't. He can't understand why I need to document the facts I discover. He's much more able to live in the moment, although, of necessity, he is able to plan ahead in terms of the plantings.'

'He's responsible for the wine-making?'

'Well, it was certainly his suggestion to rip out all the old vines about ten years ago and replant. I thought he was crazy, but he was convinced we were growing the wrong wine for our soil type.'

'What did your parents think?'

'It was just after they died, actually. I thought it was his way of grieving. But Jared isn't stupid. His research was impeccable. And he has a feel for the land that's almost instinctive.'

'So you let him do it?'

'It wasn't so much about letting him. When Jared believes something, you can't stop him. And he was right. The general quality of the vines had been declining for years.'

'And now?'

Max shrugged. 'We're exporting all over the world. Estate wine, which means that all our grapes are harvested here. Jared's been working on a new wine from this year's harvest. He's getting new labels designed, the works.'

'Yet he seems so –'

'Carefree? Happy-go-lucky?'

'Yes, both of those things. But also a little undisciplined.'

'Don't make that mistake about Jared. He may be my little brother, but he's a powerhouse, touched every once in a while by the De Villiers blues.'

♥

They ate a dinner of chicken à la king and rice, home-grown peas and a green salad. Although Prudence had cooked it, Gladys came outside to take the dishes away.

'Do you ever just do-it-yourself?' Helen asked. 'Where I come from, we had a char in twice a week to do the ironing and clean the bathrooms and kitchen. No live-in help unless you were super-wealthy.'

'Wait until the weekend comes,' Max said. 'Both Gladys and Prudie are in the church choir and you won't see them for dust. I'm quite a competent cook, I'll have you know.'

'And Jared?'

'God no, he'd rather starve. Jared is the family Hoover. He'll survive on leftovers, or charm one of his many love interests to rustle up something for him.'

'Ah,' said Helen, wanting to ask if there was a current girlfriend, but failing to get up the courage.

'He's in between women right now,' Max said thoughtfully, answering her unspoken question. 'Which is unusual. But it won't last long. For all we know that's what he's up to tonight.'

Helen picked up her glass, sipping the last of her sparkling water. 'I'd like to work on my sketches a bit,' she said as her heart quickened.

'Tonight?' Max asked, surprised.

'Just a few scribbles. I'm scared I'll forget some of the faces in my mind.'

Max nodded. 'Did you want to set up an easel in the drawing room?' he asked. 'I can move things around for you if you like.'

'Could I sit in the kitchen? I thought you might stay with me a bit. Ply me with coffee.'

Max laughed. 'If I didn't know what a self-sufficient woman

you were, I might suspect you were using me. I'll make you coffee, but on one condition.'

'Oh, and what's that?'

'You try a little glass of Bourgogne Muscadel first.'

♥

Helen turned in bed, realising that after all those liquids with dinner, she was going to have to tiptoe to the toilet. Slipping on her cotton gown, she groped for the light switch, then made her way to the bathroom. When she was finished, she wasn't sure whether to flush or not, but her sense of propriety overruled her desire not to wake Max up. Besides, it was the middle of the night and he'd gone to sleep ages before.

Feeling better, she moved softly back to her room. She slipped off her dressing gown dropping it at the side of the bed.

The knock was so faint at first that Helen thought she'd imagined it. She looked towards the door, and started to climb back in the bed. But the knock came again. Curious, she stood up, then walked to the door and opened it.

His hair was wet as though he'd just showered, and he was wearing a simple white T-shirt and a pair of shorts. No shoes.

'Jared,' Helen said, wishing her stomach hadn't thudded into her feet at the mere sight of him.

'If you want me to go away,' Jared said, 'just say so and I'm gone.'

'What are you doing here? I thought you were staying in Camp's Bay.'

Jared smiled, his emerald green eyes drilling into hers. 'I was lonely.'

Helen considered him for a moment. 'I don't think you're the sort of man who knows what lonely is.'

When Jared stepped forward, into her space, she could have stopped him or stepped away, but she didn't.

'Has Big Brother Max been talking about me?' he asked.

'Max and I might just have things other than you to talk

about.'

'Might you?' Jared said, his lips breathing softly on her neck. 'And do you think *we* might have things to talk about too?' He kissed her just below her ear, sending a shudder through her. 'It's just that between you and me, I think talking is a little unnecessary.'

'Really?'

Jared nodded, moving his lips to her cheek. His hands moved up to her chin, cupping her face so she couldn't look away.

'Are you wearing anything under that nightie?' he whispered. 'Because if you are, I think we should take it off.'

'The door,' Helen said hopelessly.

Jared edged the door closed with his foot and it clicked shut.

And then his hand moved up her leg and over her knee. And gently, ever so gently, his fingers moved up her thigh. By the time they reached the soft silk of her panties she was already wet. Jared curled the flimsy material back, plunging his finger into her. Helen gasped.

'I've been thinking about you all day,' he said, as he buried his head under her nightie.

'You've a funny way of showing it,' she groaned.

'I'll make it up to you.'

Helen could feel the slow then insistent movement of Jared's tongue.

'You taste amazing,' he said, standing to sweep her clothes over her head.

He lifted her, cradling her against him before arranging her on the half-opened quilt.

'Now, where was I?'

She strained against him, unable to take the intensity of his touch. His mouth. His tongue.

'Oh,' she whispered, as Jared moved along her body, his lips caressing her navel, travelling up to her breasts.

'Were you thinking about me?' Jared asked.

'I can't help thinking about you,' she said, almost angrily.

'Were you thinking about this?' he said, his hand between her legs.

'Yes!'

Helen pulled at his shirt. Wanting the feel of his naked skin on hers, she couldn't get close enough. Jared let her slip off his shorts, his underpants, until his naked body covered hers entirely. Helen pushed her groin against his, feeling him hardening.

'Did you bring something?' she asked.

And then he was inside her, rocking her in a frenzy of adrenaline and lust. Every cell in her body was on fire. When they came, Jared's eyes were locked with hers.

She felt as though she was seeing into his soul.

♥

'Why were you awake?' Helen asked, as she massaged Jared's scalp with her fingers.

'I don't sleep much.'

'Why?'

'I don't know. Too many ideas. Too many thoughts,' Jared said. 'They don't switch off.'

'I know what you mean,' Helen said.

'I doubt it. I don't think *anyone* really understands how it feels.'

'I could try,' Helen said.

'Don't try too hard,' Jared said. 'I'm indecipherable.'

Helen felt the rejection, but decided not to focus on it. Jared hadn't made any promises and she hadn't asked for any.

'So where've you been all day?' she said to change the subject.

Jared stiffened against her, the tension draining straight into his shoulders. 'Out,' he replied.

Helen didn't ask any more. But she withdrew her hand from his head.

Jared turned on his side to face her, his lean, almost hairless body tightening as he leant on his arm.

'I'm sorry, Helen. I just don't think much of conversation.' His hand dipped to cup her breast. 'So why don't we just focus on not talking?'

Feeling his taut body against hers, Helen nodded, her self-control draining away. 'Not talking is also good,' she agreed.

CHAPTER TEN

She hadn't heard him leave, but somehow Helen wasn't surprised not find Jared lying next to her the next morning. Helen hadn't even sensed him falling asleep.

Now she needed a shower; her body still held traces of their lovemaking. And the tossed-up sheets – well, they would surely to give Prudence something to think about, and offending Prudence's sensibilities was the last thing she wanted to do. She thought about stripping the bed, bundling the sheets into the wash with some excuse of spilt coffee, then realised that she'd only draw attention to herself. Maybe she would just make the bed.

So much for the uninhibited sex kitten: in the light of day, she was still worried about what other people thought.

Unlike Jared. Betraying his brother's trust under his own roof didn't seem to faze him in the least.

Helen washed quickly, dressing herself in a pair of denim cut-offs and a lacy white top. She checked her neck, and although Jared's lips had branded her last night, the traces of their intimacy had disappeared into her memory.

Walking into the kitchen, Helen expected Max, but it was Jared who greeted her this time.

'Morning,' Jared said, undressing her with his eyes.

'Hi.'

He sat down, helping himself to Corn Flakes. It took him some moments to register Helen's hesitation.

'Don't stand on ceremony, Helen, just help yourself. I'd make coffee, but Prudence always does it for me. I can't work out that stupid machine.'

'It's okay,' Helen said as she propelled herself forward. 'Max showed me yesterday.'

'Ah, Max.' A mocking tone crept into Jared's voice. 'He was waiting anxiously for you to wake up, but for some reason you overslept.'

Jared's gaze penetrating her, and the sensation went straight to her groin.

'Yes,' she said softly. 'I didn't sleep very well last night ...'

'What again?' Max said, coming in behind her. 'You poor thing, you must be exhausted.'

'Max!' Helen turned as Max kissed her on the head.

'Why don't you sit down while I sort out your breakfast?' he said. 'You do look tired.'

'I can –'

'But I *want* to.' Max guided her forward.

'Listen to the man, Helen,' said Jared. 'He wants to make you breakfast.'

Helen nodded, then sat down at the kitchen table opposite Jared. Too close and she was scared she'd give herself away. 'Well, I can't refuse an offer like that,' she said.

'No,' Jared commented, grinning. 'You should never refuse a good offer.'

Underneath the table, she felt his foot slip up between her legs. She stood up, knocking the chair over in her haste, her face turning pale.

'Here,' Jared said, standing up. 'Let me do that.' He picked the chair up with one hand, the other brushing against her bottom.

Max turned from the espresso machine his expression

unreadable.

'I need a tissue,' Helen blurted. 'Hay fever. Excuse me, I'll be right back.'

When she returned a few minutes later, Jared had vanished and she was relieved.

'Are you okay?' Max passed her a cup of coffee.

'Absolutely.'

'Good, because I thought we'd go out on the horses a little later, if you're up to it. I just need to work on the accounts for an hour or two, and then we can leave.'

Helen nodded, accepting the mug. 'That would be wonderful.'

♥

The stables, located beyond the garage, stood under a grove of oak trees. Sunlight dappled through the leaves, creating patches of green of such luminosity, they made Helen blink. A horse neighed from beyond the stables, and the pungent smell of hay and manure rose to meet them. Of all the places that Helen had visited so far in the Cape, this was the one that reminded her most of home. Saturday morning rides with her sister in tow. Dressage and show jumping on weekends, her father's car following the horse trailer pulled by their riding instructor's bulky and beaten white pickup. Then, when they finally returned to the stables, those endless hours of obligatory post-mud grooming that she'd always endured, with what she now recalled, was terribly bad grace.

Helen had lost interest in riding, and mucking in, long before her sister had. But that didn't mean the sight of the Arabs emerging from behind the stacked hay bales wasn't evocative. Holding out his hand, Max moved towards a chestnut horse, whose slightly curved-in ears pricked as Max whistled softly between his teeth. She nuzzled against him, clearly used to his presence.

'This is Star,' Max said. 'Terribly original, I know.' He

indicated a white patch on her forehead.

'She's gorgeous.' Helen reached out slowly to pet her.

'A real lady,' Max agreed. 'She's so dainty, and equally proud. You won't often find her at the back on a trail. She doesn't like to lose.'

'My kind of girl,' Helen said.

'Really?' asked Max, a look of surprise crossing his face.

'I don't strike you as competitive?'

'I don't know. I guess I hadn't seen you in that context.'

'Well, wait until you take me on at Scrabble. I'll try to annihilate you with no thought to your feelings or sensibilities.'

Max laughed. 'Actually, Helen. I think you may have me terrified.'

Helen smiled. 'Damn right,' she said. 'Now who is this?'

Another horse had edged in next to them. She was grey with a blond mane. She held her tail, also blond, erect and high, flicking away the odd fly.

'Hello, Pinotage,' Max said, placing a hand near her muzzle so she could sniff at him.

Pinotage arched her neck, then shook her head softly from side to side.

'They like you,' Helen said appreciatively.

'They should. Before you woke up, I plied them with sugar cubes and carrots so I could impress you with my incredible prowess.'

'Cheat,' said Helen.

Max chuckled. 'Yes,' he said, 'but are you impressed?'

'Of course. Just no such foul play when we get to that Scrabble game, or I might get defensive.'

'I'll take that as a warning.'

From inside the stables, Helen could hear the sound of voices, then an anxious whinny.

'That's Clare,' Max said. 'She's been a bit off colour. Eddie, the groom, told me she didn't want to leave her stall at all yesterday. The vet's coming later to check on her.'

'Poor thing,' Helen said.

'Ready to saddle up?' Max asked. 'I thought we'd cross between some of the farms, stop for a wine tasting or two, and lunch when we're hungry.'

'And you're expecting me to be sitting upright after that?'

'Oh, don't worry about that. Star once found her way back with Jared passed out cold after overindulging in brandy. Wine is one thing, but brandy ...'

'Let's go then, shall we?' said Helen, mounting Star with little effort.

Like most Arabs she was short, at most fourteen hands; Helen had ridden much bigger horses before. She looked down at Max, who was standing sheepishly next to Pinotage.

'I think I'm about to be outridden,' he said. 'You're full of surprises, Helen, did you know that?'

♥

It was about ten o'clock when they left. Clouds still hovered like wedding veils over the mountains, and looking across the valley, Helen could see a burst of blooms, dew-dotted spider webs and newly unfurling leaves.

They switched between cantering and galloping, stopping whenever the view called for it. At a stream a few kilometres from Bourgogne, they dismounted to allow the horses to drink.

'There's water all the way along the valley,' Max said. 'It's actually quite wet this time of year.'

Helen patted Star's rump, then bent over to throw a leaf into the water, watching it float downstream. Standing up again, she pointed to beyond where a wire-mesh fence marked the start of another property.

'I didn't expect so many fruit trees,' she said. 'Everything I read about Franschhoek was about wine. That, and of course, the fact it's supposed to be the gourmet capital of South Africa.'

'All sorts of fruits have been grown in this valley: pears, plums, apricots, peaches and even lemons. Some of the farms only changed to wine twenty years ago,' Max said. 'Some farmers grow both fruit and grapes for wine. And as for the food, you ain't seen nothing yet.'

'Is that a promise?' Helen asked.

Max looked at her, the shade of his hat hiding his expression. 'If you want it to be,' he said, then sipped from his water bottle. 'A little piece of trivia for you. Did you know that no matter the colour of an Arab's coat, all have black skin except under a white marking like Star's? It originates from when they were desert animals needing protection from the sun.'

'Do you always do that?' Helen said, moving closer to him. She tipped up his hat. 'Hide behind facts?'

'Is that what you think?' His eyes met hers with a directness she wasn't expecting.

And now that he was gazing at her, Helen realised she was the one who needed to look away. She needed to, but she couldn't. Max touched her face. Not in the possessive way Jared had, but gently. Reassuring.

'Right now,' Max said, 'I don't know where I stand with you …'

Helen's hand felt the late-morning stubble on Max's chin.

'… and I'm afraid that I'm going to be the one to lose out. While I hold back, denying myself to help you heal, someone else is going to snap you up.'

♥

They were moving again, Helen galloping ahead on Star as Max's words echoed through her mind. His openness had touched her, but the guilt was nauseating, a bitter taste at the back of her throat. She'd wondered if he suspected something, but his words showed that he was too trusting to think ill of her. Or of Jared.

The melding of night-time bodies in the room down the passage was so far beyond his natural goodness that it hadn't even occurred to him. Max had been thinking in the abstract, foreseeing something that might happen, not that had happened already.

If he only knew.

Helen wasn't a wicked person, at least she didn't believe she was. And she didn't know Jared well enough to judge him one way or another. *Wasn't that ironic?* She felt torn, and things weren't any easier now that Max had stated his intentions. She didn't know what to feel. And she especially didn't know what to do. So what had she replied when Max had spoken? Nothing. She was a coward; she hadn't said anything at all.

'Wait up, Helen!' Max said. 'What mission are you on?'

'Sorry.' She slowed the horse to a trot.

'No, *I'm* sorry,' Max said. 'I shouldn't have said what I did. No pressure. You don't have to run away from me. I'm perfectly aware of your boundaries.'

Maybe that was the fundamental difference between Jared and Max: Jared didn't care about boundaries.

Helen looked at Max. 'I'm not running away,' she said firmly. 'But you'll have to be patient with me, Max. I'm all mixed up. And to be honest, I'm not so sure of my own boundaries yet.'

'Let's forget about it for now,' Max replied, turning up a beech-lined avenue. 'There's somebody I'd like you to meet.'

The entrance road they followed needed resurfacing; where the tar was worn away in places, it was inexpertly and unevenly patched. Star and Pinotage's hoofs clip-clopped up the drive, Pinotage's tail swishing continually.

Helen watched Star's ears prick as a dog barked. 'There, there,' she said, putting her arms around the horse's neck and feeling her calm under her touch.

'Le Cadeau,' Max announced. 'One of the best-kept secrets in the whole of Franschhoek. Entry by special invitation only. Pieter Blignaut is what we call a *"garagiste"* in our circles. He only produces about two thousand bottles of wine a year, but the results are always spectacular.'

'Has he been in the area long?' Helen asked.

'All his life, and mine. Pieter is well into his eighties. He may even be ninety by now. He has some great stories to tell. His mother was a De Villiers, but from Jacob's line. That makes us relations, but only distantly. You might have to speak up when talking to him – he's a little hard of hearing.'

They approached a fork at the main entrance. To the left, a sign indicated 'Wine Tastings and Tours' and to the right, 'Private. Trespassers will be prosecuted.' Helen followed Max to the right, noting how the homestead had been cordoned off with a hardy green hedge, alternated with the odd cerise or white bougainvillea.

'We'll take the horses to the paddock first,' said Max, leading the way.

They dismounted and tethered the horses, and were checking if there was enough water for them in the trough when a child of about five appeared from one of the nearby staff houses. She wore a torn Hello Kitty T-shirt, a bright pair of pink frilly shorts and no shoes, and a toddler trailed behind her. She grinned, so Helen could see she'd already lost her bottom two teeth. Then, thrusting the tiny tot onto her hip, the little girl approached Pinotage.

'Sien jy?' she said to her sister, putting out her hand to the horse. 'Mooi perdjie!'

Max smiled and spoke in a soft, even voice to the little girl, although Helen couldn't decipher the Afrikaans. The little girl stared at him, then nodded, putting her baby sister on the ground.

'Come, Helen,' Max beckoned. 'We're going to give these little tykes a ride on Pinotage. This is Nadia,' he pointed at the older girl and then the toddler, 'and this is Priscilla.'

'Hello.' She pointed at herself. 'I'm Helen.' And when she reached out to pick up Priscilla, the tiny child reached confidently for her, cuddling her like a little monkey. 'Oh,' said Helen, feeling the slight hands gripping her neck, holding her so tightly she could feel the pressure of individual fingers. The little girl smelt of baking. Of new bread. Weirdly, she also smelt of paraffin.

'You okay?' asked Max.

'Of course…' her voice faded.

Max lifted Nadia onto Pinotage, then held his arms out to Priscilla so he could put her on too. Helen felt the little girl clutch her more firmly.

'I think she wants *you* to put her on,' said Max.

Helen lifted her towards the horse, and felt her neck being reluctantly relinquished. But as the little girl reached upwards, their eyes met. And, very slowly, Priscilla touched Helen's face, tracing her nose, her cheeks, her mouth. Suddenly, she beamed.

'*Pragtig!*' she said.

'She's right, you know,' Max said as Priscilla settled on the horse. 'You *are* beautiful.'

♥

The front door was opened by an old lady wearing a dress that could have been made from a pair of curtains. She wiped her hands on her apron, beaming when she saw who had knocked.

'Max de Villiers! *Kom binne, kom binne!*' She waved them both into the hallway. 'Pieter! *Ons het gaste.*'

The shuffle of approaching feet revealed an elderly gentleman with a craggy face, piercing blue eyes and a bow-legged gait.

'Pieter, Magda,' Max said, 'this is my friend Helen, from England.'

Magda clapped her hands together, almost curtseying. '*Welkom.* Welcome. You must be hungry ...' And with that, she dashed away.

Pieter smiled at Helen. 'I was in England once,' he said. 'After the War. I bet it doesn't look anything like it did then.'

'Where were you?' Helen asked.

'What?' the old man said, cupping his palm to his ear. 'This blasted hearing aid. It buzzes. Can't hear a darned thing most of the time.'

'Where were you in England?' Helen asked again.

'Oh, Cornwall. King Arthur country. My grandmother on my mother's side lived there. That was before I met the lovely Magda and put down some serious roots.' He pointed to the vineyards, then winked at Helen. 'In all senses of the word.'

'You planted here yourself?'

'Replanted, like young Jared and Max. Still got my fruit trees for Magda's *konfyt.*'

Helen looked at Max, a question reaching her eyebrows.

'Jam,' whispered Max.

Smiling, Pieter gestured towards a room off the entrance hall. 'Come inside. It's always so nice to have visitors.'

Helen and Max settled down opposite Pieter on an inflated sofa covered with what resembled supersized crochet doilies. Glancing round the room, Helen saw it was dominated by a gigantic fireplace, with wood stacked in neat piles on either side of the grate. Above it was an oil landscape of a vineyard, the eye drawn in by neat lines of cultivation. It was painted with flicks of complementary paint colours, giving the scene an unusual vibrancy that Helen loved.

'That's a beautiful painting,' Helen said.

'My grandson,' Pieter replied. 'He's immigrated now to New Orleans. Makes a fortune through his own gallery.'

'Helen's an artist too,' Max said. 'She's working with me on my book.'

Pieter turned his complete focus to Helen, and his face took on a faraway look. 'Are you really? But how wonderful! Max doesn't often bring guests to see us, so he must think highly of you. I'm not surprised though.' Pieter leant forward conspiratorially. 'Beautiful and talented. Quite a combination, and I'm sure Magda won't mind my saying so.'

Helen felt herself grow warm. There was something touching about this person sitting opposite her. His words seemed to carry an undeniable weight, and when he looked at her, it was as if he understood her perfectly.

Pieter acknowledged her with an incline of his head that said everything. When Magda scuttled back into the room bearing an enormous tea tray laden with scones and other pastries Helen didn't recognise, Pieter sat back to retrieve some handiwork from a bag next to his armchair. Arranging skeins of wool on his lap, he picked up a needle and began to thread it.

'The devil finds work for idle hands,' Pieter said, beginning to sew what Helen realised was a tapestry.

Max leant over to pass Helen a plate. 'You have to try Magda's *koeksusters*; the best in Franschhoek,' he said.

As Helen bit into the dough plait, the syrup oozed into her mouth, filling it with sweetness. 'That's got to be fattening it's so delicious,' she said.

'You don't have to worry about that,' Pieter said. 'You're just a slip of a thing.'

The conversation was light, though sometimes a little stilted. Magda clearly understood English, but seemed shy moving away from the comfort of her mother tongue. Max tried to draw her in but often failed, responding instead with a look towards Pieter, who filled in for her.

Helen wondered a little why Max had brought her here. The homestead was beautiful, certainly, and the couple charming, but it was though Max was expecting something to happen. As Magda collected the teacups to return to the kitchen, he stood up with her.

'Magda,' he said, 'let me help you.'

Despite her initial hesitation, Magda nodded and they both disappeared to the kitchen. Helen didn't quite know what was expected of her, so sat quietly, her hands in her lap. She thought of asking about the tapestry. What was he going to do with it? How did Pieter start? But Pieter, humming under his breath, seemed so totally absorbed in what he was doing that she wasn't sure he'd even noticed she was still there.

'My first wife,' Pieter said suddenly, looking up over spectacles that had slid down his nose. 'That's where my grandson gets his talent from. She could sketch a rabbit as it was hopping across the front lawn, and capture it perfectly. Like a photo.'

'Oh,' said Helen, not wishing to interrupt the flow of his story.

'She was a fine woman. You remind me a little of her. You have the same shaped face and eyes. But where she was defiant, in you I see something else. Loss, maybe? A little sadness?'

'You said she was defiant?' Helen deflected the attention from herself.

'She died in a fire in the 1950s. Christine didn't need to be there that day, but she thought it was all so unfair. Of course, she could have thought about how losing a mother would affect our daughter, but she didn't think that far ahead.'

'She was impetuous,' said Helen.

'Impetuous or stupid. All these years later, I still can't decide which.' Pieter picked up a length of cobalt blue wool and sucked the end to a point.

'What happened?' Helen asked, not able to contain her curiosity.

'She had coloured friends. Both of us grew up in the area, so we all knew each other well. Some of those farm lads I'd known my whole life. When the forced removals began, she swore she was going to take a stand. If she couldn't stop it, she was going to make a spectacle of it.'

'I don't understand,' Helen said.

'Well, the apartheid government had decided the coloured community couldn't live in a certain section of Franschhoek any longer. Our friends and their families were booted out of their own homes, moved off to Groendal, through the Group Areas Act.'

'My God,' said Helen.

'Christine decided they shouldn't go quietly. She said they should resist. And her friend Petronella said it was alright for her. She had a home and a husband and child to go home to when she was finished fighting. Christine watched Petronella leave, then set the house on fire from inside, so nobody would see her in time and stop her. A symbol. If Petronella couldn't live there, nobody else could.'

'But something went wrong.'

'Everything was already wrong. The house went up like a tinderbox. I wasn't there at the beginning, but Petronella turned around. She could see Christina near the window, and she couldn't understand why she didn't try to break out. She was leaning forward, trying to unbutton her jersey.'

'But why?' Helen asked.

'It must have caught alight. We'd always laughed about that jersey – pretty, but not practical. Not for an arsonist anyway. The buttons were tiny. She tried to rip at it. Petronella called her brother. Told him to go back and help Christine. By the time he got into the house, her whole outfit was on fire. He smashed the window with a brick, trying at least to get some oxygen to Christine, but that only fed the fire. He couldn't get in. When the fire engine arrived, Christine had already died from smoke inhalation and third-degree burns.'

Helen's face dropped. Though Pieter's storytelling was unwavering in its delivery, his eyes sent a shock of pain through her. Half a century later and she could feel his suffering. But then the old man smiled, his eyes twinkling once more.

'So,' Pieter said. 'She was beautiful and defiant, but that didn't help her at all. And now I have Magda and she's my whole world.' He stood up, offering his arm to Helen. 'Come, my dear. There's something I'd like you to see.'

♥

Leaving Le Cadeau, Helen was silent. The bottle of Le Cadeau Syrah pressed on her by Pieter was packed in Max's haversack. Pieter and Magda had walked them to the paddock, and had waved as they trotted back down the driveway. Helen looked at Max, who looked back silently.

'Why did we come here?' Helen asked. 'Did you know he would tell that story?'

'I don't know. The first time I met you, I thought you reminded me of someone. I was looking through some of the De Villiers photos the other day and found a wedding picture of Pieter and Christine with my grandfather.'

'That doesn't explain anything.'

'You're right,' Max said, 'but Pieter has always been good to me, especially when my parents died. I wanted you to meet him.'

'And the fact that I resemble Christine?' Helen persisted.

'Well, I thought he'd like you. He'd approve. Seeing you would make him happy.'

Helen's face took on a troubled expression. 'Except that I stirred up memories that should be left in the past. I don't think I made him happy in the least.'

'That's where you're wrong. Pieter's had his share of suffering, but he has a good life. He's contented. He's accepted his past and dealt with it.'

'Unlike me, you mean?'

Max sighed. 'I just wanted to show you that moving on from tragedy is possible.'

'I'm not an emotional pawn, Max.' Helen was suddenly angry. 'I don't work according to some timetable, and especially not yours.'

'I didn't say you did. I just wanted to give you hope.'

'Can we go back to Bourgogne now, please? I think I've had enough life lessons for one day.'

CHAPTER ELEVEN

'What's it with you two?' Jared said, helping himself to salad. 'Lovers' tiff?'

Max glared at Jared, then stabbed his sirloin with uncharacteristic menace. 'Mind your own business,' he said. 'You really can be such a smartass if you want to be.'

'I'm only trying to ease the mood,' said Jared, moving his eyes to Helen's.

She found herself looking away. She actually didn't feel angry any longer, just raw, but making up after an argument had never been her strong point. For all his faults, George had always been the one to apologise, looking hangdog and suitably contrite. Of course, that was one of the first things to change; apologies that might have been forthcoming in his pre-affair days were remarkably absent once he hit the tennis circuit and discovered *Rose*.

The irony now was that Max's stony face now hinted at passions she hadn't been aware of. That easy-going Max could be so stirred up was something of a surprise, a *good* surprise. Though just then, with his expression hidden under the hoods of his eyes, she found him unreachable. And this was the part she didn't like.

And then there were her old worries coming to the surface. Helen thought back to that tender moment when they'd lifted Priscilla and Nadia onto Pinotage – the first direct contact she'd had with children since her last failed IVF. Perhaps it was this memory rather than Pieter's message of healing that had bothered her. This physical touch had made her realise, almost viscerally, that, rather than dealing with her loss, she'd simply been blocking it. When she'd felt that child's hug, the feeling of actually being *held* by a child, the devastation had been almost overwhelming. How was she meant to pretend that she was whole and happy, when her life's path was so far from what she'd wished for?

Across the table, Jared picked up a piece of cucumber in his fingers, biting into it noisily.

'Well, I'm out tonight,' he said. 'Heinrich's having a party on his farm. Trying to impress some new bird on the scene.' Jared checked his watch. 'Actually, I should have left ten minutes ago. I said I'd help mix cocktails.'

'Well, don't let *us* stop you,' Max said.

Helen studied Jared, wondering if he ever included Max in his whirlwind social life. Or if it occurred to him that she might want to join him.

Jared stood up. 'I'll crash at Heinrich's place. I'll be far too drunk to drive,' he said in his matter-of-fact manner. 'Then I'm back to Cape Town about those labels – Angelique wants to show me final drafts. But thank God I'm getting out of *here*. You can cut the atmosphere in this room with a knife.' He left with a tog bag in one hand and two bottles of sparkling wine wedged under his arm.

Helen waited for the squeal of tyres to subside before she spoke again.

'I don't want to fight,' she said. 'I hate fighting.' She wondered if she had the courage to say sorry. Surely, in this new stage of her life, that was something she could do?

Instead, she reached out for Max's hand, expecting him to withdraw it.

Except that he didn't; he gripped it with unexpected ferocity.

'I'm sorry,' Helen said with surprising ease. 'I guess I'm just questioning everyone's motives … And those kids, it was just –'

'I'm sorry too. It was supposed to be a good day. I didn't realise being near Priscilla and Nadia would upset you so much, or I wouldn't have offered them a ride. And I'm not George, Helen. I don't *want* to hurt you.' Max was silent for a moment. 'I'm going to say this and maybe you won't like it. But there are other routes to motherhood, and maybe you haven't considered them. And maybe, one day, you'll be ready to.'

Helen sighed. 'You say that, but what kind of prospect would that be for a future partner?'

Max shook his head. 'Oh Helen, you can't have looked in the mirror much lately or you would know the answer to *that*.'

His gaze was so intense and warm that Helen felt herself blush. Their hands were still entangled but Helen sat back in her chair, feeling overwhelmed.

Then Prudence walked into the dining room, carrying a tray. Sensing Prudie's eyes on her, Helen attempted a smile.

'That was delicious,' she said. 'The steak was cooked to perfection.'

Prudence acknowledged this with a curt nod, then took most of the remaining dishes, her retreating bottom undulating like a massive wave.

'That Pieter Blignaut. He must have been a charmer in his day,' Helen said, trying to reclaim the mood.

Max laughed. 'I wouldn't be surprised.'

'How did he meet Magda?' Helen asked.

'Two years after Christine died, they were set up at a Christmas Eve party.'

'A blind date?'

'Something like that. Anyway according to my grandmother, Magda always treated Christine's daughter, Juliet, like her own. She and Pieter had twin boys after that.'

'Lucky him,' Helen said. 'A second chance at love. And a family.'

Max seemed pensive. 'Yes. And there's really no such thing as a typical family anyway.' He seemed about to say something, but then stood, picking up the last dishes. 'Maybe it's time to hit the sack.'

Helen folded her serviette. 'I haven't got very far with my sketches,' she said. 'Perhaps I should apply myself for a while.'

'In that case, maybe I'll sit with you.'

And Helen realised that she liked that idea – now that the silences between them were comfortable again.

♥

Jared didn't return for three days, but when he did he was unshaven and a little wild-looking, his lack of sleep evident in puffy red eyes.

'Met someone?' Max asked as Jared swung his tog bag onto the kitchen table.

'What makes you think that?' Jared returned, then beamed wickedly. 'Had a blast. Friday, we parked all night on the beach. Bonfire, the works. Heinrich scored some pot in Groendal. Good stuff. Fucking awesome. It was like some camp out from school with all the crappy things like discipline and Reginald Esterhuizen excluded.'

'Who was Reginald Esterhuizen?' Helen asked, trying not to show any reaction to Jared's arrival.

'Headmaster,' said Jared. 'God that man was a tyrant. Nothing got past him.'

'Yes,' agreed Max. 'Not even Jared. And *that's* saying something.'

Prudence walked into the kitchen, her eyes alighting on the prodigal son.

'Prudie,' Jared said, jumping up to dance her round the kitchen.

Laughing, she tried to pull his arms from her waist as he dipped and tipped her ample frame, humming some wild tune that Helen didn't recognise. When he finally stopped, giving in to Prudence's protestations, he did so rather majestically, spinning her under an arched arm before bringing her to a sudden halt.

'Miss me?' Jared asked Prudence. 'Won't you be an angel and run these clothes through the wash? Got to give them back to Heinrich when I see him later.'

'You're going out *again*?' Helen said, but immediately wished she hadn't. 'Why not?' Jared asked. 'Got a better offer?'

Max raised his head, clearly noting something in her voice.

She forced a laugh. 'Clearly neither of us can compete with Heinrich, eh, Max?'

Max smiled, and seemed to relax. 'I guess not.'

♥

Over the next few days, Helen was relieved that the tension between her and Max eased. But she couldn't help wonder about Jared – there was something about him that jarred. More than once she'd wanted to raise the subject but hadn't thought it either the right time or the appropriate subject.

On the work front, she and Max had created a routine that seemed to work. They'd start with a morning of discussion, during which they poured through the manuscript and accompanying photographs or the family tree, which Max kept open for them to study. After lunch they worked separately, Max on his Bourgogne responsibilities and Helen on her sketching. She liked sitting outside on the porch. Max had lent her a radio, so she listened to music sometimes, or she drew while taking in the sounds of farm life around her. Sometimes they didn't see each other again until close to four in the afternoon.

There were distractions though. The wine estate was often busy, with busloads of tourists or individuals in cars pulling in for wine tastings, or the odd estate tour. Though the tasting area was nowhere near the main house, the sounds often resounded to where Helen sat as well, and she listened for the noises of different nationalities and accents, guessing, often correctly who had just visited.

It was on one such afternoon that Helen found herself

growing restless. Her hand, which was accustomed to gripping paintbrushes and pencils for hours, cramped up. And though she was often able to concentrate and maintain a pattern of creativity for several hours at a time, her mind seemed to seize.

Helen put aside her easel, and stood up, rubbing her fingers on her plastic apron. She'd leave everything as it was for now – that is, apart from placing the lids on the tubes of Winsor & Newton. She untied her apron, leaving it to dry in the sunlight, and went to the bathroom to wash her hands. She could hear Max talking on the phone, his voice rising and falling – it seemed it was someone from the mobile bottling unit trying to raise the prices for a small order. Deciding not to disturb him, Helen wondered away from the house in the direction of the tasting room.

Several cars and buses were parked outside, and some of the coach drivers were standing next to their vehicles, puffing on cigarettes to pass the time. Helen waved vaguely, then strolled towards the sound of laughter that echoed from the stone-floored room, and slipped in via the back door.

Jared didn't see her. Dressed impeccably in a pair of chinos and a black Bourgogne golf shirt, he had taken full charge of the space. His smile, as irresistible as the first moment she'd met him, lit up his whole face as he charmed his audience through the history of the vineyard. And what he lost in inconsistent information and a poor memory for dates, he more than made up for in delivery.

'You see,' he said, 'as any good oenologist will tell you, the soil, the vine and man (or woman!) are the pillars needed to create a good wine. A good wine will dance with your food, and I'm sure you'll take my word for that. I've also been told you don't have to finish the whole bottle in one night. But take it from me – a whole bottle is a hell of a lot more fun!'

Jared moved to a map to point out the wine areas around Cape Town.

'So of course every region will produce a different wine. While I would obviously prefer Franschhoek wine – and with good reason, I make it! – Paarl wines are more voluptuous and rich. Stellenbosch produces New World wines – they're upfront and bold, with a little bit of competition between the elements. But I'll tell you a little secret: Franschhoek farmers *really* know about wine. My family has been in Franschhoek since the 1680s; we've had more than enough time to perfect the art. And just so you know, every time I'm forced to taste from the barrels during the process, it's for completely philanthropic reasons ...'

The group laughed and followed Jared through to the production area.

'... And I bet most of you would like to know how we establish that our grapes are ripe. Well, we have a family of baboons that live on the property. When they come down from the mountain, sit on the post and shake our vines, then it's time for the harvest. A baboon knows a delicious grape when it sees one. So we really believe in science at Bourgogne – in this case – natural science.' More laughter. 'But seriously, folks. Nature is pretty organised. Different grape varieties never actually ripen at the same time, so we always have enough time to harvest each cultivar before the next one is ready. Harvesting starts in January and usually ends around March, depending of course on the year...'

Helen hadn't been near the giant vats before. Giant metal containers dominated the entire area, and a strong smell she didn't recognise tickled her nose. Perhaps she'd expected something a little less clinical, but Jared certainly wasn't describing a process that happened without the occasional creative insight.

'So, once the grapes are harvested, the real work begins. It takes a ton of grapes to produce six- to seven-hundred litres of white wine. With red wines, you get a little more because you keep the skins. Either way, you're looking at a lot of grapes! And wine grapes don't look anything like table grapes. They're about the size of a pea and very juicy. We use this machine to separate the stems from the fruit, because stems are very bitter and affect the taste of the wine ...'

Helen noticed how Jared met the eyes of the people listening to him. And she was pleased to see it wasn't only the young beautiful women – and there were quite a few of them. He bent down to acknowledge some of the kids, helped an old man on a Zimmer frame down the corridor, and manoeuvred a short woman to the front so that she could see. At first, she didn't think Jared had noticed her hovering on the edges of the crowd, but as he described the fermentation process with cultured yeast, he looked directly at her, sending blood flowing straight to her cheeks. Their glances may have only locked for a second, but it was enough to make her wonder what on earth she was doing there.

Jared smiled, then turned.

'Right, ladies, gentlemen and children, let's continue on to my favourite place: the barrel room. You'll know that most white wines are not stored in barrels, except for chardonnay. All our barrels are imported from France, and we can only use them a maximum of three times. Hopefully that goes a long way in explaining why a bottle of wine is *never* too expensive ...'

As the group sipped and spat and ticked off their wine orders back upstairs, Helen turned to leave. She hadn't seen Jared approach, so his hand at her elbow startled her. She jumped, dislodging his hand.

'Leaving already?' he asked, putting his arm around her to pull her to him.

'I was just taking a little break...' she muttered.

'Ah Helen,' Jared said. 'You haven't even had a taste. The Syrah is not to be missed.'

'I really should be going,' she said. 'I didn't even know you'd be here.'

'Good surprise or bad surprise?' he asked, his eyes burning into her like a laser.

'I don't know,' she said honestly.

Jared grabbed her hand, pulling her behind the bar counter, where he chose her a glass and placed it in front of her. 'You can't do a book about a wine family without knowing about the wine,' he told her. 'Here. Our Sauvignon Blanc. When we rebranded it, we called it Emily, after our mother. It's gentle and elegant, like she was, but something determined lurks beneath the surface.'

Helen sipped. 'I think I know what you mean,' she said.

'See, I'm not the Big Bad Wolf.' Jared grinned mischievously. 'Unless, of course, you want me to be ...'

'Not here, Jared,' Helen said. 'Please.'

Jared threw his arms out, admitting defeat, but then he caught the eye of one of his guests and went off to play host again. Helen watched him chatting to the man, nodding vigorously as they gazed at a wine glass filtering light from the window. So unlike Max, she thought, who seemed so reserved about himself and his capabilities. In contrast, Jared seemed completely without inhibitions. He *expected* people to like him, and without any apparent effort of his own, they did. She was no exception.

Gradually the tourists trickled away in their little groups, boxes of wine and souvenirs sold to them through Jared's easy-going charm, stowed carefully in their boots and onto the coaches. Until it was just the two of them sitting alongside each other at the bar, and Jared was working through the Bourgogne repertoire of wine and anecdotes. He had a way of making her laugh despite her best intentions, a condition that worsened the more wine she tasted ...

'I was thinking about the other night,' Jared said under his breath as he poured some dessert wine.

'Were you?' Helen tried not to meet his eyes, but failed as usual. She was drawn to him in a way she couldn't explain. This, despite knowing that his every action over the last few days told her she should be wary.

Jared leant a little towards her, his breath against her cheek. 'It isn't easy keeping away from you,' he said softly.

Helen's face must have given her away.

'I like a bit of secrecy, but I know that's my bag, not yours.'

'Max,' Helen said.

I know there's Max, but I can see the way you look at me.'

'And how is that, exactly?' Helen challenged.

'Hungrily,' Jared said.

From anyone else that would have seemed arrogant, but Jared stated it like a simple fact.

Helen sighed, looking away.

'There's nothing wrong with following your instincts,' Jared said. 'You're sexy as hell, and I don't think you even realise it.' He put his hand on Helen's thigh, and it smouldered.

'I'm not good at this kind of talk,' Helen whispered.

'So, let's not talk. Let's just see what happens.' Jared glanced at the tasting room's entrance. The cars and buses had all left.

'It's closing time.'

Helen felt her heart tighten as Jared came closer. He lifted her onto the bar counter, started unbuttoning her jeans.

'Stop me,' he said. 'Any time you want ...'

♥

'Helen? Helen?'

A male voice echoed down the path towards the tasting room. Panting, Helen felt the imprint of Jared's body on her, inside her. She pushed him away, watching the slow curl of a smile crease his lips. Jared stood up, neatening his clothes. Then he sauntered to the back room to retrieve another bottle of Syrah.

Flushed, Helen slipped back down onto her bar stool, edging her tasting glass towards her.

'Helen? You there?' Max sounded worried.

'Max,' she called after a pause, 'I'm down here.'

He burst through the door. 'Oh, good,' he said. 'Your car's still here and Prudie didn't know where you were.'

'I tried to tell you where I was going, Max, but you were on the phone –'

'Christ, yes. Underhand bastard has upped his fees for the mobile bottling units. And he knows he can do it too, with Gerhard's plant being on the blink for three weeks.'

'Supply and demand,' said Jared as he reappeared. 'I might do the same in his position. He's probably run ragged.'

'He's run ragged because he has lots of work. *That's* where profit comes from.'

Jared sat down behind the bar. 'So you see, Helen. Our business ethics are a little different. Max keeps me on the straight and narrow.'

Not all the time, Helen thought. 'Well, I agree with Max if that counts for anything,' she said.

Jared raised his eyebrows, then laughed uproariously and pulled another glass from under the bar counter. 'I see I'm outnumbered. We'll have to agree to disagree. Max, are you joining us for a tipple? You can't expect Helen to understand the De Villierses until she's tasted all our wine.'

'And have you?' Max addressed Helen as Jared poured the Syrah.

'Have I what?'

'Tasted *all* the De Villiers wine?'

'Not if I plan on walking back to the house,' Helen said lightly. She reached out and patted Max's arm. 'So,' she said. 'Did you win the argument?'

Max nodded. 'I appealed to his humanitarian side,' he said.

'And that worked?' Jared said incredulously. 'I wouldn't have thought Mike had a humanitarian bone in his body.'

'Oh, he didn't,' Max said. 'Until I mentioned my connection with the Wine Board.'

This only made Jared even more cheerful. 'Max, my boy, I don't know what we'd do without you. So when is he coming?'

'Tomorrow,' Max said. 'At nine o'clock. You did remember to order the extra bottles we needed?'

Jared downed the rest of his wine. 'I may not be good for much, my brother. But for once I actually did remember to do that.'

CHAPTER TWELVE

elen thought that their afternoon interlude might have changed Jared's mind about going to see Heinrich, but in that she was mistaken. Jared swung out of the house shortly after six, giving Prudence a departing slap on the rear as he passed her in the kitchen. Prudence jumped and squealed, but still watched Jared's departure with an expression of affection.

Helen was hungry at dinner, and ate quickly in between sipping sparkling water in an attempt to dull the effects of the afternoon's wine. But Max picked at his lasagne, forking it around his plate. Their conversation began in fits and starts, until eventually Max put down his fork, pushing his plate away.

'I don't think I can do this,' he said.

'Do what?' Helen's heart sank.

'I'm not a complete dolt, Helen. I can see that Jared intrigues you. For all I know you've already slept with him.'

Helen looked away.

'Being the good guy really has very little value, it seems to me,' Max continued. 'Perhaps I should have tried to seduce you in Langebaan when I might have had a chance. I was a fool to bring you here – how could I possibly have thought you wouldn't be attracted to Jared? I should probably warn you that his attention span is shorter than a baby's. When he's with you, he's completely with you. And when he's not, it's as if you never existed. I can't tell you how many of his girlfriends I've had to comfort while he's nailing somebody else. And how, when I tell him that, he shrugs and says I should have taken the opportunity ... Distraught woman. Shoulder to cry on. Who knows where it could lead?'

Helen's mouth dropped.

'He doesn't understand how he hurts people. Myself included. I thought there might be some sort of level of trust between brothers. Keep away from Max's girl. It's not like he can't get someone to drop their knickers just by looking at them from across the room. God, I've seen a seduction in play. Thirty seconds and he's left the building, with the prettiest woman at the party. Married. Engaged. But he doesn't actually give a toss.' Max turned his knife on the table. 'I thought with you, maybe it might be different. I love my brother. And I know he loves me. But God, Helen, he knew how I felt about you.'

'I do care about you, Max,' Helen said.

'Oh, come on, Helen. I'm no competition for my little brother. So, let's just keep it platonic, which is obviously what you want. But do me a favour. No sneaking. No lying. I just can't do that. I want to do this book together. Maybe I'm a masochist, but I don't want to see you go.'

'I'm not in love with Jared,' Helen said firmly.

'No, but you will be. God, even Prudence is in love with him, and she changed his nappies!'

Helen's eyes filled. 'You're giving up on me,' she said.

'I'm not. I'm giving you what you want. At least Jared has had the courtesy of pursuing you with a little secrecy. I'll tell him we're not happening. We're not going to happen. I haven't even kissed you, for Christ's sake. Not that I haven't wanted to a hundred times.' Max stood up, pushing back the chair roughly. 'No guilt, Helen. I know you're not a cheat. Maybe it's time for you to fall in love again. Just not with me.'

'I'm not actually a piece of merchandise you can calmly pass on,' Helen said. 'And how do you know that Jared is even interested?'

'Oh, he's interested, all right. He hasn't been out of the house so much in months. That's his vague sense of conscience talking; giving us time alone,' Max said, picking up the salad bowl to carry it to the kitchen. 'I'm setting you free of any obligations you might feel, Helen. The rest is up to you.'

♥

Angrily, Helen slapped acrylic on canvas, and found she was painting her first impression of Bourgogne.

Brookie lace and gables, ivy clinging determinedly up a wall. That impressive bougainvillea, and the Cyprus trees, thick and tall, planted too close to the house. She managed to capture the look of the paint peeling just under the gutter, now rusted. The weather vane she'd found so quaint as it twisted in the breeze, though it was depicted, she realised, slightly larger than it should have been.

Helen had thought of leaving. Packing her unimpressive belongings and returning to Scarborough. To England even. It was November, and she'd been in the Cape for just over four months. With a few meaningless shags to show for it, some paintings sold for much less than they would have fetched in England, and a book commission she wasn't sure she should continue with.

And where did Max fit into all of this? Surprisingly, his attention towards her didn't seem to have changed, and the latte delivered as she painted suggested no hidden agenda.

'Goodnight, then,' Max said, placing the steaming mug on her bedside table.

Helen wanted to catch his hand but Max retreated, not even glancing at her work.

'Goodnight, Max.' She attempted a smile.

He'd smiled back, but with a smile that didn't reach his eyes.

Helen went to bed smelling of soap, her hands raw from scrubbing the paint from her fingertips. She fell asleep half-listening for Jared, and at four she thought she heard the slam of a car door, keys in the lock and the squeak of footsteps on the wooden floor. But not in the direction of her room. Down the passage the shower squealed; there was the battering of uneven water pressure as she became more alert. He didn't come, and she fell asleep, head half-cocked, waiting.

When she awoke, her head ached. She felt as though she'd been crying, but she didn't remember any tears, not even in her dreams.

She dressed quickly, pulled on a pair of trainers and slipped out the front door bearing a bottle of mineral water and an apple from the kitchen. She wasn't much of a runner, but she liked to walk. She ended up strolling through the vineyards and up into the mountain foothills, and she didn't return for four hours.

♥

'Where in God's name have you been?' Jared's trousers were muddied, and he'd gouged out a chunk of skin from his arm.

Less forcefully but equally dirty, Max made a move towards her, but then stopped.

'I went for a walk,' Helen said.

'A walk?' Jared asked quizzically, as though he'd never heard of such a thing. 'But you didn't leave a note.'

'I'm sorry, Jared. It was a spur-of-the-moment thing. I needed to … clear my head.'

'Are you okay?' Max asked.

'I'm fine. Well, apart from a bit of sunburn and an attack by rampant fynbos of some sort.'

Helen walked past inside, making her way towards the bedroom passage. She could sense their eyes on her, a silent exchange that had passed between the brothers.

It was Jared who followed her inside. 'Helen,' his voice caressed her back. 'We were worried about you. *I* was worried about you.'

'I already told you I'm sorry,' she retorted.

'Max told me what happened last night.'

'Well, what *did* happen? Perhaps you can help me out?'

She felt Jared's hands on her shoulders as he spun her around, gazing at her with his emerald eyes. His touch was rough and insistent and when he put his lips on hers, it was all she could do not to lose her balance completely. Jared's mouth parted slightly, his tongue touching hers. Head spinning, knees weakening, she realised she was kissing Jared back, and with a hunger she hardly recognised.

'Well, that's settled then.' Jared sealed their kiss with a pout. 'What are we going to do for the rest of the day?'

But her pleasure was interrupted by the soft entry of Max's shoes in the hallway. Self-consciously, she stepped back a little.

'So,' he said. It came out like the sound of a throat being cleared. His face was inscrutable.

'Helen's going to stay,' Jared said. 'Aren't you, Helen?'

She nodded.

'That's great news.' The cheer in his voice either real or very well enacted. 'So we'll finish the book.'

'Of course,' Helen said. 'We were doing so well.'

'Have you seen her drawings, Jared?' Max asked. 'You won't believe how's she's captured Grandpa.'

Jared nodded, but Helen wondered if it was with interest or dismissal. Either way, the comment reached a dead end.

'Well, anyway,' Max said. 'I was coming inside to tell you that I've got to go into Cape Town to see the auditors again. You'll be okay taking the day off, I think?'

Without warning, Jared thrust Helen over his shoulder. Seemingly oblivious to her shrieks and Max's dismay, he charged with Helen down the corridor.

'Don't worry about us, Brother Max,' Jared called. 'I'm sure I'll be able to entertain her until you get back.'

♥

It wasn't just the sex, although the sex was phenomenal. Jared made Helen feel like she was completely captivating. When she spoke, he lay on his stomach, leaning his head on his hands to focus entirely on her. He made her laugh and his endless energy didn't just mean stamina in bed, but also gave her a refreshing outlook on what life was like as an eternal optimist. While George had been the sort of man with a solid foot on the ground at all times, Jared seemed to be in a continual bounce. *Like Tigger*, Helen thought, giggling. *So George was Eeyore.*

Jared was also extremely tactile. Even out of the bedroom, he always had a point of contact with her: a hand on her thigh, a foot against hers, fingers laced. She was in a constant state of ecstasy. That afternoon they made love in the vineyards (Merlot grapes, T4577) as the sun was just beginning to set.

'Do you always bring your girlfriends here?' Helen asked, straightening the picnic blanket he'd brought along.

'Every relationship is unique,' Jared replied, evasively.

And perhaps she didn't really want him to answer. Jared slapped away a mosquito. 'Maybe we should get back to the house,' he said. 'Rustle up something to eat.'

He drove them home through the vineyards as shadows began to dance. Helen liked the speed. It gave her an excuse to push against him, feel the solid contours she was getting to know. The fumes from the quad bike rose from the exhaust, but somehow this was not unappealing. She knew later, this would be a smell with totally new associations.

'Good day?' Jared asked her as he helped her off the bike.

Helen smiled. 'You know, despite the fact you're digging for compliments, I'll have you know that you've totally lived up to my expectations.'

'You had expectations?' asked Jared, grinning. 'You could have let me know a little sooner. Think of all the time we've wasted.'

Though it was meant to be light-hearted, the comment made Helen think of Max. She looked for his car as they walked past the garage. Silent and still.

I'm going to let myself be happy, Helen thought. *I deserve to be happy.*

As Jared slipped his hand into hers, she neither flinched nor pulled away. *I deserve to be happy,* she told herself, repeating it like a mantra. *I deserve to be happy… I deserve …*

CHAPTER THIRTEEN

It had felt to Helen that Jared had curled around her for most of the night, but by the time she awoke his side of the bed was cold.

In the kitchen, all she could make out was Prudie's solid bulk as her flapping biceps stirred something on the stove. Helen was intimidated; she couldn't deny that. There was something about Prudence's eyes that drilled into her, making her feel decidedly small. She turned to escape back to her bedroom, but Prudence whirled round and gave Helen an all-knowing look.

'Mr Max said to tell you that they're at the mobile bottling unit.'

No 'good morning' then.

'Mr Max left a pot of coffee for you. I was going to bring it to your room, but you were still asleep.'

Even that sounded accusatory.

'Thanks, Prudence.' Helen tried a smile on the older woman. 'I really appreciate it.'

Prudence snorted, her back once again to Helen. Resigning herself to the glacial treatment, Helen pulled a banana from the fruit bowl, then cut it into some muesli, adding a dollop of plain yoghurt on top. Sitting at the kitchen table, she pulled a magazine in front of her and tried to read. She wondered if she should try to make things easier between her and Prudence. The way things had turned out, Helen wasn't planning on going anywhere soon. But the wall of uniform kept her at bay. She just didn't have the nerve.

♥

The sound of activity drew Helen closer.

She heard bottles shattering, following by a torrid hurl of abuse. It didn't sound like Max, and she couldn't really picture it being Jared. She turned the corner as Max approached from the opposite side, his forehead crunched in a worried frown.

'Helen!'

'Are you okay?' Helen replied, seeing his expression.

'I'm just going to check the bottle stocks up in the warehouse. Simon ...'

Helen nodded. 'I heard glass breaking. Do you want me to come with you to count?' It was the least she could do, she reasoned.

'Sure, but don't you want to say good morning to Jared first?'

She shook her head. 'I don't think he's going anywhere,' she replied.

They walked side by side to the warehouse. Max was silent, as though their once amicable conversation had become a chore. Helen again was aware how unalike he and Jared were – even the way they walked was different. Jared took large, quick strides, getting everywhere as fast as possible. Max's set his pace to match hers, and he never seemed to be in a terrible hurry – despite what she now imagined was a crisis with the bottling.

'Is it serious?' Helen asked, as Max bent to unlock the warehouse door.

He bent to examine why his key wasn't inserting smoothly into the lock. He jiggled it and twisted the handle simultaneously. The door creaked open.

'With a small range like this, there's a chance that bottling on different days could make a huge difference to the taste of the wine bottled later. Not to mention the fact that we'd have to get the mobile unit in again – the additional cost would be enormous. Come inside.'

Helen followed Max, who peered into the darkness, feeling for a light switch.

'Damn it, Jared,' he muttered tensely. 'I told you to order extra.'

'Where do the bottles come from?' Helen asked.

'Cape Town. I could have picked up more yesterday if I'd known. Simon doesn't have a licence, so he only drives on Bourgogne. And they'll never deliver today. Shit. Shit. Shit.'

Looking at Max, Helen realised that this was the first time she'd seen him in a state. He rubbed his neck, pulling slightly on his ear.

'I could go,' Helen said brightly. 'You guys watch the bottling here, and Simon could come with me and show me the way, right?'

'You won't fit the bottles in your car.'

'So I'll take yours, with a trailer if necessary. I used to pull a horse trailer when my sister was competing. As long as I don't get lost, I'll be fine.'

Max still seemed hesitant.

'Look, Max. What other options do we have? It's either that, or you go and I help Jared. It's not like I know anything about bottling, but I *can* drive a car. I'll just go slowly.'

Max studied Helen. 'I'm not worried about the car, Helen. I'm worried about you. That's an awfully big responsibility to put on your shoulders.'

'I can handle it. I'm a big girl. Besides, I want to help. '

'Okay,' Max said.

'Okay?'

'We'd better hitch the trailer then, and get you on the road.'

♥

Half an hour later, Helen waved goodbye to the brothers,

affecting a cheerful look.

In the Land Cruiser's rear-view mirror she saw Jared wave and then immediately turn and march back towards the bottling plant. Max stayed watching them a little longer. Was she imagining his hesitation? Jared hadn't even contested her going to Cape Town, and she wondered why her feelings were hurt. He'd given her a good-morning peck when she and Max had come back from the warehouse, but he was obviously distracted. After the night they'd spent together, she found this vaguely insulting.

She'd noted the way Max's nostrils had flared slightly, the way he'd pulled his mouth into a smile before giving Simon his instructions in Afrikaans. She hadn't understood a word, of course, but the message had nevertheless been clear: Simon was responsible for getting them to the factory and back, and if the bottles didn't match exactly, Simon would be in a world of trouble. Simon had nodded furiously, taken the sample from Max, and indicated to Helen that she should follow him to the garage. She hoped for the sake of the journey that he spoke a little English at least.

This was not the morning she had expected, but she was rather proud of herself. She was going on a mission. They were making wine, and she was going to be part of it.

♥

By the time Helen returned, it was well after lunch time.

Though she wasn't normally one for greasy takeaways, she and Simon had eaten burgers at a roadside Wimpy, and that had hit the spot. The trip had been pleasant: the vineyards on either side of the road were green and luscious in the early-summer sunshine, the Winelands breathlessly still and undisturbed. There'd been carol services and Christmas fairs promoted on placards along the way, and that had felt rather odd to her: Christmas in this heat? And despite the aircon in the Land Cruiser, a trail of sweat had clung to her neck.

Max had phoned as they were passing the Spier Wine Estate.

'You're a lifesaver, you know that?' She'd noted the relief in his voice.

No, she'd found herself thinking before ending the call, you're the lifesaver around here.

It was true. Without Bourgogne, Helen would have been out on a limb. It wasn't exactly as if she'd forgotten that her wedding anniversary was the following week, but it didn't cause the stab of pain she'd thought it would. A winter wedding had been her idea. She'd loved the thought of fur-trimmed capes and a long, flowing winter gown. Glühwein and mince pies. In this environment, with the sun beating down and the clouds mere flecks across the blue, their 'special' day seemed just too distant a memory.

And now she had Jared to get back to. She pictured him shirtless and tanned in the vineyard, his total disregard for the glass of red wine knocked over on the picnic blanket, seeping pink as he moved closer to her. Even the memory of how he'd looked at her made her stomach twist. Helen's foot pressed down heavier on the accelerator, and Simon threw her a questioning glance.

'Max needs us to hurry,' Helen said, and the name 'Max' seemed explanation enough as far as Simon was concerned.

They parked as close to the cellar area as Helen could manage. Reversing carefully, she eyed the trailer in her rear-view mirror. Max had emerged at the sound of the car, indicating with a swinging motion that she could back up even further.

When she stopped, he opened her car door.

'Impressive,' he commented. 'A woman of many talents. Why don't you come and see what all the fuss has been about.'

Inside the warehouse, Helen realised she hadn't even had time to study the mobile bottling unit: a truck loaded with all sorts of metal tubes and mechanical parts.

'It's Italian. It can bottle as many as three thousand bottles an hour ...' Max began to tell her, but Helen's eyes had already flicked towards Jared, who bounded over and embraced her, swinging her around in his strong arms.

'You're back!' he said happily, putting her back down on her feet and kissing her with firm yet tender lips. 'Come, let me show you!'

Grabbing her hand, he led her to where Simon was placing the newly arrived bottles.

'That's the in-feed table. It can unscramble one hundred bottles at a time and feed them into the machine. From there, each bottle is rinsed upside down with sterile water. The water is drained and the bottle is placed upright on the track ...' Jared pointed. 'Now, as winemakers we have a choice: to purge the bottles with carbon dioxide or nitrogen oxide. We've left that step out this time – Pieter did last year and the results were great.'

'Pieter from Le Cadeau?' Helen asked.

'Yes.' Jared pulled Helen towards where the bottles were revolving under individual spouts or pumps. 'Can you see the bottles over there? Those are being filled to a height that we have pre-agreed. We call this process gravity filling for obvious reasons. It's all completely sterile – the filling heads and header tanks are sealed to the atmosphere, but we take four control samples at the beginning, middle and end of the bottling run, just in case there are issues later on. Max and I have to take full responsibility for the quality of the wine, so we like to be sure. The bottling company will take two of each of those bottles and keep them separately for quality control. That's their "insurance policy". We keep the others.'

Helen watched the turning machinery. 'What about sealing the bottles?' she asked. 'Do you use cork?'

'Today we are,' Jared told her, pointing to a collection of filled bottles. 'Stainless-steel cork jaws and dust blowers remove the dust before the corks are compressed. The machines create a vacuum in what we call the bottle headspace before the cork is pushed in – pretty nifty. Some of our wines are screw cap, though. And then of course our sparkling wine is closed with a crown seal, but we're not tackling either of those today.'

Jared pointed to a collection of filled bottles.

'So that's the out-feed tray. Simon and the team will take those bottles and pack them into trays. We apply all our labels by hand, but that will only be done next week.'

'So what happens when all the wine is bottled?' Helen asked.

'It depends. Some days we are bottling more than one wine, and then we need to do a wine change – that takes about half an hour because everything would have to be cleaned out, and sterilised. Today, we'll simply finish up and leave the plant company to use nitrogen to push the last of the wine through.'

Jared squeezed Helen's hand. 'So that's it really. Max and I will be here for most of the day, but for you it might be a bit dull.'

Helen looked to the door of the cellar as Prudence arrived with a tray of sandwiches, fruit and juice. 'Lunch!' she said to Jared.

'Prudie, you're a wonder!' He strode over and picked up a thick wholewheat sandwich, biting it with gusto. 'Max! Grub's up.'

Max poured himself a glass of fruit juice. 'Want anything, Helen?'

Helen noticed there were only two plates and glasses. 'No, no. You guys go ahead.'

The brothers perched themselves outside on a shaded wall, the sounds of the bottling plant clanking and whirring inside the cellar. Jared's plate was already empty by the time Max had only eaten half of his food.

'You need me to make you some more, Mr Jared?' Prudence asked, but Jared simply wiped his mouth with the back of his hand and shook his head. 'Back to work,' he said, giving a half-wave. 'I'll see you later.'

And Helen, who'd thought of watching a little longer, realised she'd been dismissed.

CHAPTER FOURTEEN

As December rolled in, so did the tourists. The wine-tasting tours, Jared's chief domain, increased to twice, sometimes three times a day. Max knuckled down meanwhile, arranging end-of-year bonuses, VAT returns and other administration. In fact, since the bottling, neither Jared nor Max seemed to have had much free time.

Helen took to horse-riding on her own first thing in the morning. The book was progressing nicely on her side, and she revisited her artwork brief with some trepidation. There were very few images still to draw, and what would happen when she was finished? The thought worried her, and when neither brother mentioned it, she worried even more. At least if she had some time to plan ... get her head right, well, she believed she could cope with anything. Being at Bourgogne had brought both stability and uncertainty into Helen's life ... Not unlike the De Villiers brothers themselves. Max remained constant, but Jared was his own man – untameable, even if she had been so inclined.

Unlike Max, Jared seemed incapable of splitting his attention. He was with her entirely, or he was somewhere else. The moments that he was with her made up for everything. Although he'd told her Max was the romantic one, he brought her flowers and surprised her with visits when she least expected them. He held her possessively, even in company, insisting that they be seated alongside each other in restaurants when they went out with his friends. The first time she'd met Heinrich, he'd nodded thoughtfully.

'So *you're* Helen,' Heinrich had said in a way that made her flush.

Jared slipped his arm around her, drawing her in. 'I told she was beautiful, didn't I?' His touch had sent a shiver of anticipation down her spine.

In between book illustrations, Helen was working on another painting for Madeleine, who'd still not managed to get away from the café at Scarborough.

'I thought it'd be easy to come for the day,' Madeleine had told her on the phone. 'But I'm having to manage front-of-house and do *all* the baking ...'

'How about getting a temp?' Helen asked.

'Oh God, I can't face that, Helen. And I wouldn't trust a temp with my recipes. It's okay. I can do another few weeks of this, but I'm looking forward to when it gets a bit quieter. Thank goodness I close on Mondays, or I'd be working twenty-four seven!'

Helen cradled the receiver to her ear. 'I could bring the paintings to you,' she mused.

'Oh, would you?' Madeleine's voice brightened. 'I could do with a friendly face ... And you can distract me with your dirty secrets.'

Helen laughed. 'Monday, then? I'll finish this one before I come, then at least you have four new ones for your blank walls.'

'And I can pay you for the ones I've sold. You sure you've only got four? They'll be snapped up in a second.'

'Afraid so.'

'Better than nothing,' Madeleine grumped. 'I can't wait until Monday.'

♥

But when Jared heard of Helen's plan, she could see he wasn't happy. His eyes clouded and his hands, not normally still, seemed to grip at his knees as though to prevent him from standing.

'What's wrong?' Helen asked, fixing on his tense expression.

'Oh, it doesn't matter,' he said with a De Villiers shrug. 'It's just ...'

'Just what?'

'I'd kind of planned an outing.'

'What do you mean "an outing"?'

'It was supposed to be a surprise,' Jared pouted. 'If I told you I'd ruin it.'

'Do you want me to cancel?' Helen said, wondering what else to do.

'Postpone it a week, or even a few days,' Jared replied, running his hand along her leg. 'I'll make it worth your while. I promise.'

And that's what she did, even though she could hear the disappointment in Madeleine's voice.

'I'll come on Wednesday,' Helen promised.

'I'm working on Wednesday.'

'I can help you out at the café. Take some of the burden off you.'

'That sounds nice,' Madeleine said, with forced cheer.

'I *am* sorry, Mad.'

'I know you are. I know.'

♥

Helen sometimes wondered what Jared did all night.

He'd put her to bed in the most delicious of ways, but she could count on one hand the number of times they'd actually woken up together. She'd never known someone to sleep so little. When she woke, Jared had always conjured up some of the most grandiose and unrealistic of plans – for the vineyard, for them, for future holidays.

She spoke to Max about it, but he was dismissive.

'It's just hot air, Helen. Jared has always had a vivid

imagination. As a little boy, he could never just be himself, so he was always Man-cub, or Willy Wonka or Peter the Pan.'

'Peter *the* Pan?'

'That's what he called him.'

'It sounds like he was, well, a little ...'

'Hyper? Frenzied?'

'Well, yes, both of those.'

'That's just Jared. Don't worry about it.'

And Helen nodded, her mind temporarily eased.

On the Monday of her failed arrangement with Madeleine, Jared enthusiastically slipped his hand up her nightie before she was even awake.

'Thanks for the wake-up call,' Helen murmured as he slipped naked into her bed.

Through the slightly open curtains the sun had barely peeped over the mountains.

'What time is it?' Helen asked.

'Just before six,' Jared replied. 'Too early?' A rueful smile crossed his face.

'It is *quite* early ...'

'Time for another round, then ...'

By seven they were on their way.

'What's happening with the wine tours?' Helen thought to ask as they pulled out the car port.

'Max or Henriette.'

'The labelling?'

'Simon,' said Jared.

'Despatch?' Helen asked further.

'Max will do it.' Jared thumped the steering wheel with both hands. 'For Christ's sake, Helen. Do you want me to turn around and go back to work? What the fuck's the problem?'

Helen blanched.

'No problem,' she said quickly, patting Jared's knee. 'I just don't want to be the reason you fall behind.'

'Well, I won't fall behind. I've taken care of it. Now chill a bit, okay?'

Helen tried to laugh. 'You're the boss,' she said, trying to keep the edge out her voice.

'That's right,' Jared replied. 'So if I want to take a day of leave, I don't have to report to anybody.'

It took a little while before Helen felt comfortable enough to venture any conversation, and Jared, his knuckles white at the steering wheel, shoulders tense, didn't seem so inclined either. She wondered what she'd done to anger him. She was about to ask about the day's activities when Jared's fingers loosened, one hand raking through his hair.

He looked across at her, and smiled. 'Sorry I snapped, Helen,' he said. 'No excuse really.'

'It's okay.'

Jared moved his hand, resting it lightly on her thigh. The air conditioner was on full throttle. It almost felt like the wind through her hair.

♥

They were an easy walk to Camp's Bay beach from the family apartment.

Helen had guessed at the De Villiers wealth but 'the flat', as Jared referred to it, suggested money she could only have dreamt of. It was on several levels with marble staircases and kitchen tops. Each light fitting was a work of art; one that particularly caught her attention seemed to be made of paper mâché. It was shaped like a buffalo's head and as far as she could tell was life-sized. The cupboards were cherry wood or something similar (hard wood, not veneer), and huge stacking doors opened on three levels to balconies with the most spectacular views of the ocean she had ever seen. They even beat the views at Scarborough, which Helen had barely thought possible.

On the beach, Jared set up an umbrella and arranged two deckchairs under it. And Helen felt the sun seeping into her skin.

'This isn't the Med. You're going to burn without sun block,' Jared commented. 'Turn over, let me help you.'

His hands massaged above and below her bikini, along her back, the lengths of her legs, around her bottom. It felt so wonderful she realised that she might just fall asleep.

'Roll over,' Jared said softly, his lips at her ear.

She did, and when he kissed her, it was though they were melting into each other.

'If we carry on like this,' she murmured, 'we might just have to get a room.'

'I have a room,' Jared said. 'Luckily enough.' But he pulled away slightly to pour out some more sun cream, his hands gentle over her stomach, thighs and the curve of her cleavage.

'Now you,' Helen said, as she rubbed the lotion over his chest, feeling the hardness of his muscles and the smooth curvatures of his shoulder blades, the bumps of his spine, and the narrowness of his tanned hips.

The caramel tones of his skin made Helen wonder how much of the time he was in 'meetings' might have involved sun, sand and a laptop locked up where he couldn't see it. She recognised also that Max would have been stuck behind his desk managing the admin and making up for Jared's absence ... The thought was disloyal and Helen tried to push it away. It wasn't her business anyway.

Helen stretched out next to Jared, who was on his stomach. He'd balanced his sunglasses just above his fringe and was lying with his head on his hands in a sunlit stupor. She picked up the paperback thriller she'd found on a bookshelf in the flat, and tried to read, not really warm enough yet to brave the Atlantic. She thought back to her first swim on these shores, and how different she'd felt then. She'd been so consumed by the hurt she'd felt for George, and now here she was beginning to feel something more than just lust for the man lying next to her.

Leaning over, she kissed Jared softly on his exposed cheek.

'What's that for?' he asked.

'Happiness,' she said.

Jared turned his head slightly. His face had taken on a look of tenderness – and vulnerability – that she hadn't noticed with him before.

'You're getting under my skin, Helen,' he said. 'I can't stop thinking about you. I know I should feel guilty about Max, but I don't, not completely. No one could get this lucky without ...'

'Without hurting someone along the way?' Helen finished for him.

Jared sat up, taking her hands in his.

'I can't help it,' he said. 'I love Max. He's the only real family I have left. But that day I saw you coming up the drive ... I can't really describe it. I know I can be hard to live with ... but if you decide to stick around, my God, you'd make me happy.'

'The book's nearly finished,' Helen said.

'Don't you think I know that? That's why I'm asking you. Stay anyway. Work on another book. More paintings. I ... I could set you up in a gallery in Franschhoek.'

'But do you even want to know how I feel?' Helen asked.

'About the gallery? Of course I do! We could dream it up together. We could –'

Helen pulled her hands back. 'I mean about you.'

Jared caught her hands again, kissing each finger with such passion that it almost felt as though he was making love to her. 'Darling Helen, I don't think even you know that. So why rush things? We'll have great sex. A great partnership. One day, when you let yourself go, you might even fall in love with me.'

She was, Helen realised, well on her way to doing just that.

♥

Like Helen, Jared was a good swimmer, matching her even strokes with his own. When she'd suggested they get in the water, he'd seemed to expect her to dip in a toe. It certainly didn't seem to have crossed his mind that she might actually swim. He followed as Helen dived through the waves, until they were both in deep water, treading as they caught their breath.

'That's what I love about you,' Jared said, as Helen curled her legs around him.

Not quite *I love you*, but it still made Helen's heart skip.

'What's that?' she asked.

'No half measures. I can't tell you how many girlfriends I've had who wouldn't venture past calf height.'

'And how many girlfriends *have* you had?'

But he was evasive as ever. 'Doesn't matter. What matters is where you learnt to swim like that.' he said. 'For a Pom, you really aren't bad at all – this water isn't exactly warm.'

'Bracing,' Helen said. 'I was on the swimming team at school. And you're not too bad yourself.'

'Waterpolo,' Jared said. 'Vicious sport. We used to grow our toenails so we could scratch our opponents underwater without being caught.'

'Lovely.'

'I tore the cartilage in my knee during a match. Not enough for surgery, but it made me wary.'

Helen smiled. 'Not for very long if I know you, Mr De Villiers.'

Jared laughed. 'Race you back to land, Ms Shaw. You may not find this water cold, but my bits are beginning to freeze up.'

By lunchtime the sun was baking, and despite a slight breeze the sand was almost impossible to stand on without sandals. They'd thrown a Frisbee in the shallows and attempted a few rounds of beach bats, but both of them were thirsty and eager for something other than another ice-cream lolly. Swinging the umbrella over his shoulder, and nodding for the release of the rental deckchairs, Jared walked ahead to the showers. Helen watched him rinsing off, the water trickling down his back as he moved his hands through his hair. A little like a leopard preening.

Stepping from the shower, Jared rubbed himself down, then wrapped his towel around his waist, extracting his swimming trunks from underneath the makeshift skirt. He pulled his jocks and shorts up under the towel and slipped on a T-shirt. It had only taken a few seconds for Jared to get dry and fully clothed.

'Come on, Helen,' Jared said. 'I'm starving. Just dump your stuff over here while you rinse off.'

Helen showered and slipped a sundress over her bikini, which immediately left watermarks over her breasts and buttocks.

'Sushi,' Jared announced.

By three o'clock they'd shared a bottle of wine and enough California rolls and fashion sandwiches to lull them into comfortable oblivion. They strolled the few steps back to 'the flat', and fell asleep on the enormous bed, their arms around each other, the sounds of the sea mixing with the chatter of passers-by beneath the veranda on the street leading down to the beach.

♥

As always, Jared was already out of bed when Helen woke up. She could hear him outside on his phone. Slipping on her sandals, she found him standing facing the ocean.

Positioned behind Jared, she put her arms around him, listening to the tail-end of his conversation. He jumped, finishing it off quickly.

'Well, I'm sorry you feel that way. That's not at all what I meant, but it's up to you ... No, I won't be back this evening, not till late anyway ... I told you, I'm at the flat ... Fine. Why don't you call when you're ready? Bye.' He turned, pocketing his mobile phone. He kissed Helen, just a peck.

'Hello, gorgeous.'

'What was that all about?' Helen asked.

'I shouldn't have phoned her,' Jared replied. 'Never do business when you've taken the day off.'

'Is everything okay?'

'Brilliant,' Jared said, cupping her bottom. 'Because I have the sexiest woman in the world wearing nothing but a T-shirt standing right in front of me. What could possibly be wrong?'

'If you say so.'

Jared checked his watch. 'Although, unfortunately, we have to leave in ten minutes ...'

'Where are we going?'

'Well, if you think this view is beautiful, wait until you see the next one.'

♥

They skipped all the queues for the cableway. Helen didn't ask Jared how he'd managed it and he didn't tell her, but she suspected this was not the first time he'd bent the rules, nor would it be the last. Jared positioned them so that they were at the closest edge to the city. It wasn't dark yet, but the streets below were just beginning to flicker with evening lights.

The cablecar lifted, and the city bowl swept out below them. Then the harbour, the V&A Waterfront, and the ocean beyond. Soon the cablecar began to rotate, offering them a 360-degree view all the way up. Over a thousand metres, but it was ten short minutes and the ride was over. Jared held Helen's hand as they were buffeted by the other departing passengers.

'This way,' he said, leading her to a rocky outcrop just off the pathway.

Just next to them, little rabbit-like creatures bounded away to just beyond their reach.

'Dassies,' Jared said. 'You should see them in the middle of the day; they simply stretch out and absorb the sunlight.'

'Do people feed them?'

'I guess so, but we're not really supposed to.'

Sitting next to each other on a flat rock, both of them fell silent, their words stolen by the majestic colours of the changing sky and the city life below. Jared picked up his cooler bag and pulled out two glasses and a bottle of Bourgogne sparkling wine. The cork popped, and Jared poured generously.

'Cheers,' he said.

Helen shifted closer to kiss him. 'This is magical,' she said.

'No, ' Jared replied. 'You are,' and he kissed her back.

CHAPTER FIFTEEN

elen didn't know how to broach the subject. Jared seemed unconcerned as to Max's opinion and though she'd asked Jared several times, he'd made no effort to chat to Max on her behalf. She realised finally that she'd have to do it herself. Knocking on Max's study door, she waited for him to wave her in. Max nodded for her to take a seat while he finished his phone call.

'What's up?' he asked, plugging his mobile phone in to charge.

Helen handed Max a file. To protect them, she'd placed every illustration in a plastic, punched folder. They were all in order, tracing a three-hundred-year history in a mix of media, sizes and styles, a deviation from her normal mode. Usually, she stuck to one style throughout a book, but there was something about Bourgogne that had inspired more creativity than she'd ever thought possible.

'I think I'm done,' she said.

Max took the file from her. Though he'd seen many of the illustrations before, he hadn't seen them presented like this. As he flapped through, his expression was unreadable and Helen felt her stomach twisting. She knew she'd already let Max down once; she didn't want to do it again.

Max got to the last page, then closed the file.

'They're fabulous,' he said. 'Well done.'

Helen studied Max, and though his words were the right ones, his eyes said something she couldn't quite hear.

'Are you sure?' Helen said. 'Are you happy?'

'They're great. Really.' Max turned his back to Helen as he fiddled in a drawer behind him.

'You don't need me to change anything?' Helen prompted.

'No,' he said without turning around. 'I think we've covered it. Of course, my publisher will have an opinion, but I doubt there'll be much more to do.'

Helen couldn't stand it. She slipped behind Max's desk, forcing him to turn and face her.

'Max,' she said, 'what's going on?'

'Nothing, nothing,' he said gruffly.

But then his hand lifted to trace her face, his fingers raking gently through her hair, his touch as tender as a feather passing. Helen didn't move. Max stepped closer to her, touching his lips to her hairline, then traced her forehead with kisses. A surge of emotion passed between them.

'I'm sorry I've hurt you,' Helen said.

Max remained silent, kissing the bridge of her nose, then her cheeks, her eyes, as though he was worshipping her, memorising every inch of her face. He didn't have to say anything for Helen to know how he still felt about her.

To stay here with Jared was cruel. The gallery they'd found in town had a little apartment above it that Jared was planning to rent out. But rather than staying here and torturing Max, she should move in there. Her question was answered: it was impossible to talk to Max about staying on at Bourgogne. She couldn't even attempt it.

Max kissed her once softly on the lips, then let her go.

'I'll miss you, Helen,' he said.

And Helen smiled, then stroked his cheek. 'And I you,' she said.

♥

Jared stood by the bed watching Helen pack.

'I don't get it,' he said. 'You want me to trek into town to come see you? What's wrong with staying here?'

'It's five minutes' drive, Jared. And you can stay over any time you like.'

'Well, I *don't* like it, actually. Max is a selfish git and I don't see why we have to run our lives according to his timetable.'

'Max doesn't even know,' Helen said, trying to put her arms around Jared to pacify him.

'Well, fuck it, Helen, maybe I should march into his office and tell him what he's doing. Moping around like some love-struck teenager. He made the decision, and don't you forget it.'

'I don't think Max felt he had any choice,' Helen said. 'He already knew how I felt about you.'

'So now you're moving into that cramped apartment because of *him*?' Jared's eyes blazed.

'No, I'm moving there for you. I'm not going to be the cause of strife between you, and I'm certainly not going to rub Max's feelings in the dirt. We need to give him time. Having me in his kitchen every morning isn't helping things.'

Helen put the last of her things into her suitcase.

'What about the cottage?' Jared asked. 'You could move in there?'

'I really don't think Max needs to see me for while,' Helen said. 'The cottage is in his back garden.'

'It's also *my* back garden,' said Jared.

'I'm sorry,' Helen said. 'We just need to give him a few months.'

'Meanwhile, I'm schlepping out every time I want a shag.'

Helen's heart went cold. 'Is that all this is about?'

'It's not *all* it's about,' Jared said. 'You know I want to spend time with you ... preferably when you're naked.' He laughed, and even though Helen laughed too, she didn't think it was all that funny.

'Five minutes,' Helen reminded Jared. 'I promise you it will be worth the effort.'

Prudence emerged from the kitchen as Jared lifted Helen's suitcase into her car, a smile across her usually broody face. She was carrying a basket containing a few bottles of pickles that she'd made, some chicken sandwiches and a litre of home-made lemonade.

'In case you get hungry,' Prudence said, not unkindly. 'There's also a spare kettle, a few teabags, milk, sugar ...'

'Thanks, Prudie. And thank you for taking care of me so well.' Helen looked towards the house. 'Have you seen Max?' she asked.

Prudence shook her head. 'Not since this morning. He went out riding.'

'But he knew I was leaving this morning,' Helen said, trying to keep the hurt out her voice. 'Can you at least tell him I said goodbye?'

Prudence nodded.

'I think that's about it,' Jared said as he loaded the last of her canvases onto her back seat. 'I'll meet you there, Helen. Park under the shade cloth – I'll just park at the pub and walk across.' He smiled at Prudie. 'Guess it's just the three of us again tonight,' he said. 'Any chance you could whip up some oxtail? Tell Max I'll be back around seven.'

'Okay, Mr Jared.'

Helen felt a twinge – of what? Jealousy? Nervousness? Regret? She hadn't even left and Jared was making plans. Starting up the engine, she resolved to ignore any feelings she wasn't entitled to: this was her choice, after all.

As she drove down the avenue, she glanced towards the stables where she'd spent so much time over the last few weeks. Her heart shifted as she saw Max, still mounted on Pinotage. Their eyes locked. A nod from Max. There was just so much Helen still wanted to say to him, and she almost stopped the car to run back.

But she didn't.

♥

They'd rented the apartment furnished. It wasn't at all to Helen's tastes or, judging by his grimace, Jared's. Nevertheless it was convenient, and the gallery area down below was spectacular. Well lit. A clever use of space, and huge windows offering a backdrop of the Wemmershoek mountains.

Jared yanked her bags up the staircase.

'You're going to lock this off, right?' he said. 'When you're downstairs in the gallery, make sure no one can get in here.'

Helen was touched by his protectiveness. 'If you think that's necessary.'

Jared dumped the bags in the sitting room upstairs. 'It's necessary,' he said. 'Trust me.'

And she took him at his word, writing down 'locksmith' on her long list of to-dos.

Helen hadn't originally planned to open the gallery to the public until the beginning of January; she didn't have enough paintings yet. But Madeleine, hearing of her plans, was immediately supportive.

'Your own gallery, wow,' she'd said. 'Would you like to fetch the ones from the café? And maybe you could use the one in Alec's house. You wouldn't have to sell it, but it would make an impressive backdrop ...'

'What about the new paintings I've done for you, Madeleine? I was going to bring them through –'

'Keep them there, honey. I'll get by.'

Helen was amazed by the kindness she encountered. The florist across the road brought her a huge bunch of strelitzias to brighten the starkness of almost-empty walls. On her second day, her neighbour from the Huguenot coffee shop brought a latte and a muffin as she was scraping old flyers from the gallery windows. Jared organised a rush job on signage for the shopfront, and Gladys, Prudence's granddaughter, offered to come and help clean the day before Helen opened her doors.

But there was no real razzmatazz when she did.

No champagne and canapés. The whole of Franschhoek was a festival of Christmas fairs and company parties, and anything she might have attempted would have paled in comparison.

'We can do something official in February or March,' Helen said, and Jared agreed.

'You'll need to get business cards at the very least,' he said. 'I'm not sure who prints ours. I'll have to ask Max.'

Max.

It had been a week, and she'd neither seen him nor heard from him. Despite herself, she missed the way he'd so often offered to make her coffee, sliding it over without pulling her out of her creative zone. She missed his explanations of life on Bourgogne, filled with anecdotes and wry humour that kept her entranced for hours. She longed for the way he looked at her when she was talking, as though what she was saying was so valuable and interesting. However she felt about Jared, she missed Max.

And it wasn't as if Jared wasn't a star. He was tireless, and had done everything in his power to speed things along. When Helen was about to collapse from exhaustion, he'd scoot her upstairs so he could hang yet more of her paintings.

'I'm keeping you from Bourgogne,' Helen said.

'Bourgogne's been there for generations. It can wait.'

That wasn't exactly what she meant and Jared probably knew it. But she was mindful not to remind him of his responsibilities, remembering what had happened the last time she'd done that. And in some ways, Jared was bringing Bourgogne to her. He'd stocked the fridge with white wine, the cupboards with red, and had replaced the odd plastic furniture with more tasteful items.

Most of the crockery in the apartment had been fine, but Helen had missed a few essentials: a potato peeler, a grater, a decent bread knife. When she and George had first got married, they'd started completely from scratch, so they'd chosen every item together. George had never been one of those men who were only interested in drills, saws and a new set of screwdrivers; he'd fancied himself as a bit of a chef. So setting up here was a little different – she could chose a pink colander simply because it was something George would have loathed. The thought gave her a childish thrill.

And so the opening of the gallery was nothing more than an unlocking of doors, turning the 'Closed' sign to 'Open', and setting up an easel and paints near the back of the room. Jared had set up credit-card facilities … Well, she suspected Max had.

And Madeleine had been right about Alec's painting: it was the perfect backdrop, and by the end of day one, she'd already had three offers on it, all of which she'd refused. She had, however, sold two other paintings to an American tourist who'd recently bought a holiday home near Llandudno in Cape Town.

Until she could afford to get someone to come in and help her, Helen was going to have to sit in the gallery all day, between few brief forays upstairs for tea or coffee or a sandwich. She didn't mind; she was going to have to paint fast and with great dedication if she was going to keep up. She'd spoken to Olivia about couriering the paintings she'd put in storage when she'd left for South Africa. The mood and style were different, but therein lay their value: she didn't want to be stereotyped, fearing the kiss of death if she was only valued for one type of landscape.

And through it all, Christmas remained at the back of her mind. Helen was a family girl, and now she'd placed herself at the other side of the world; she realised this was going to be a holiday she was going to spend if not alone, then close to it.

Christmas was only a few days away, and Jared hadn't brought up the subject of where he'd be spending it. And because he didn't, Helen was afraid to. Madeleine had invited Helen to spend Christmas with her family in Scarborough, and Helen was tempted. She didn't want to be one of those people who kept others in reserve until a better offer came along, but it seemed that was what she'd been reduced to. If Jared hadn't brought up the subject by the end of the day, she decided, she would go to Madeleine's.

CHAPTER SIXTEEN

riving to Scarborough, Helen replayed the previous night's conversation, trying not to feel hurt.

'It'll just be awkward,' she'd said.

'Where's your Christmas spirit, Helen? You can't expect me to choose between Max and you?'

'Well, *I* had to,' she'd replied, trying to contain the resentment in her voice. 'If I just go to Madeleine's, then no one has to feel uncomfortable.'

Helen recalled the way Jared stood up, picking up the Audi keys. He'd tossed them from one hand to another, then marched towards the open gallery door.

'Well, you seem to have made up your mind, so who am I to stop you?' he said.

And that's what the entire debate had amounted to: Jared leaving the apartment without so much as a goodbye.

Helen didn't really understand Jared's moods. One moment he was high as a kite, truly invincible, and the next, it seemed as though he could hardly build up enough energy to speak, especially when it came to subjects he was uncomfortable with. She'd wanted so often to talk to Max about it, but nowadays that was impossible.

But where did Jared's sadness come from? Sometimes she

wondered if he avoided reality – which was why he'd left it to her to have the discussion with Max. And things had only got more complicated with the gallery. She'd loved the idea that he supported her art, but she didn't want to be beholden to him, which was why she insisted on paying at least half the rental. But judging by his reaction to Christmas, he didn't actually like it when she made her own decisions.

Helen parked outside Alec's house, this time carrying a bag just big enough for three days' clothing, and a small shopping bag of presents. She unlocked the front door, feeling the sense of familiarity and calm of her uncle's house. Looking across at the blank wall in the lounge, she realised how right Alec had been: the room needed that painting, just like she needed Jared.

Helen sighed. If she'd made a mistake in coming here for Christmas, it was too late now.

She walked into the kitchen. She'd die for a cup of tea, but she'd forgotten to pick up some milk en route. She wondered if she might have left some in the freezer ... As she opened the freezer door, there were footsteps outside. A loud knock.

'Open up, Helen! It's me.'

Helen's heart bounced as she ran to the door, flinging it open.

'I didn't say goodbye,' Jared said, 'and I missed you.'

He kissed her with such passion that her blood seemed to evaporate.

'It's only been a few hours,' Helen said, trying to hide her relief.

'A few hours too many. I'm not good at saying sorry,' Jared said.

'Is that what you're doing?'

He nodded. 'Am I forgiven?'

And Helen led him inside, closing the door firmly behind them. She began to unbutton his shirt.

'You might have to try a little harder than that ...' she said.

♥

It was a Christmas Eve unlike anything Helen had ever experienced before. For one thing, the sun was so harsh and hot that they dried within minutes of getting out the sea early that morning. The Christmas trees and lights seemed incongruous to her; the fake snow decorating shop windows made her want to laugh. Who would want snow when you had weather like this?

Although Jared hadn't said as much, she had a feeling he'd only stay until Christmas morning. And with a few extra hours together, she wasn't going to complain. They motored along Chapman's Peak Drive, only recently reopened after a treacherous rock fall, and with the wind through her hair, Helen felt like Grace Kelly. Jared drove too fast, but the exhilaration overcame her sense of fear. They zipped around corners and screeched perilously close to the turquoise depths with its billowing foam below, and she experienced a feeling of immortality.

Jared was so confident at the wheel, that she didn't think to doubt or caution him. Besides, with his hands at the wheel, and the smile of triumph glowing in every part of his face, he was so sexy she couldn't concentrate on much else.

For lunch, they ate calamari in Hout Bay. Jared ordered beer shandies, which they gulped down, needing another round almost immediately. Though Helen would have been content to sit and watch the world go by from their table, Jared couldn't sit still enough to have dessert.

'I'll have you for dessert later,' he said. 'Come on, let's walk.'

They kicked off their shoes, dipping their feet into the hot sand as people passed by with their dogs or chasing after children. Jared took Helen's hand and they walked into the water so that their feet wouldn't burn.

'Are you glad I came?' Jared asked.

'Of course I am,' Helen replied, amazed that he needed to ask. 'I didn't want to leave you. I just thought it would be best –'

'Let's not have *that* conversation again.'

Helen nodded, noticing how the mood had suddenly changed.

'Perhaps we should get going,' Jared said. 'Didn't Madeleine say we should be there at four?'

♥

Madeleine's festivities were to begin with Christmas Eve drinks, before the main event the next day. Helen had never been to Madeleine's home: apart from that time at Alec's place, they'd really only seen each other at the coffee shop. From the outside, her home was fairly typical of Scarborough – clapboard, with a corrugated iron roof and shutters in a rich, cheerful blue. Unlike many of the other houses though, it was well kept, with none of the deterioration of a seldom-used holiday home. Signs of everyday life pointed to permanent occupation: a bicycle lay toppled in the front yard, a dustbin waited for collection and a half-repaired boat stood on blocks under a carport.

'You made it!' Madeleine said, accepting a bottle of wine from Helen. 'And you must be Jared.'

Helen was grateful for Madeleine's quick summing up of their situation: that Jared was in town despite what she'd relayed on the phone.

'Come on in.' Madeleine waved them past her towards a patio. 'Colin's just bringing the Weber round from the garage. You're staying for something to eat?'

'I thought you were feeding me tomorrow!' said Helen.

'What can I say? I can't have hungry people on my watch,' Madeleine laughed. 'June's popping over later.' Madeleine looked at Jared. 'Shall we lay a place for you tomorrow as well?' she asked.

Jared smiled. 'Thanks for the offer, but my brother's on his own.'

'Fair enough,' Madeleine said, moving the subject quickly along. 'Let's crack open some of these bottles. Sure that's something you'll be able to help with, hey, Jared?'

Helen watched the easy way Jared integrated with the group. Having opened and poured some wine, he helped Colin set up the barbecue. When she looked again, they were engrossed in conversation with a few other men, loading charcoal from five-kilogram bags.

'What happened?' Madeleine asked when he was out of earshot.

'What can I say? He can't resist me,' Helen laughed.

But Madeleine detected a note of concern in her voice. 'Are you okay, love?'

'He apologised. We've moved on. It's not that big a deal.'

'But?'

'But nothing. We're fine. Other than the fact that I'm worried about Max. I haven't seen him since I moved into town.'

'What did you expect, Helen? Isn't that what you wanted?'

Helen bit her lip. 'I didn't expect to miss him so much,' she admitted. 'And my feelings are hurt, I suppose.'

Madeleine motioned Helen towards the kitchen. 'God, you're a complicated being, Helen,' Madeleine said, extracting tomatoes and lettuce from the fridge. 'You're just as confused as the men in your life. Colin may be a little predictable at times, but at least he's mine.'

'Jared's mine,' Helen said.

'You think so?' Madeleine replied.

'Actually, I don't know what to think.'

Madeleine handed Helen a cucumber and a few avocados, then pulled a bottle of olives off a shelf. They moved to the sink, where Madeleine had placed a few chopping boards and a big wooden bowl for the salad. Without any discussion, they washed and cut the vegetables. Madeleine fetched a container of feta cheese, cutting hefty white blocks and dropping them into the bowl. She looked at Helen.

'Does Jared love you?' Madeleine asked.

'I don't know. He's not so much a man of words as of action.'

'Do you love him?'

'What's with the twenty questions?' Helen asked, the pitch of her voice rising.

'I'll take that as a no.'

Madeleine's son, Kyle, ran into the room, still wet from the swimming pool. 'Mom, Dad wants to know if the firelighters are finished.'

'Look in the cupboard in the scullery,' Madeleine said. 'I bought some yesterday. And how many times have I asked you to dry yourself before you come inside?'

Kyle rolled his eyes. 'Only a thousand, Mom. I'm just helping Dad out.'

Helen watched Kyle vanish. 'I'm scared to fall in love, Mad. Think what happened last time. That doesn't mean I'm not crazy about him. What's not to like?'

Grinning, Madeleine looked out the window to the back garden. 'You're right of course, Helen. He's sex on legs, that one.'

Helen laughed. 'Madeleine,' she said, 'you don't know the half of it!'

As the sun dipped towards the ocean, couples stood outside chatting. The older kids had walked down to the beach, and the littlies were already fed and seated in front of a cartoon in the lounge. A baby cried, and a mother to whom Helen had been introduced but whose name she'd forgotten got up, glaring at her husband, who was on his third beer and had seemingly acquired a hearing defect. Helen looked at Jared and he gave her a lascivious grin. He walked over, placing his arms around her, and kissed her gently.

'Can I get you another drink?' he asked Helen. 'What about you, Madeleine?'

As they both sipped their G&T's, the smell of the braai billowed into the house and Jared went outside to play pool cricket with the children, who'd returned from the beach. Dancing around him, the kids yelped when Jared bowled, diving in all directions as Kyle swung the bat, hitting the ball with a solid thud.

'He seems like a nice man,' Madeleine commented.

'He makes me feel whole again.'

'And that,' Madeleine said, 'is nothing to sniff at.'

♥

They returned to Alec's house just before midnight, and Jared looked at his watch with a dramatic flourish.

'Have you been a good girl this year?' he asked.

'Well, if I haven't been good, then at least I hope I've been good *at* it.'

Jared smiled. 'I'll vouch for you,' he said, 'when Father Christmas comes down the chimney.'

'Don't you think you'll be asleep by then?'

'Asleep? I'm completely wired Helen. I don't think I'm much in the mood for a sleep.'

Helen shook her head. 'I just don't know how you manage.'

'Pure luck, I suppose,' Jared replied. 'Come on, tiger. Let's go and sit outside on the patio. I want to give you your present.'

'What about tomorr–' Helen stopped herself. *Go with the flow, Helen.* 'I can't believe the nights in this place,' she said instead. 'Who'd have thought I could be outside on Christmas Eve?'

'Christmas, actually,' Jared said, tapping his watch. 'Happy, happy.'

He handed her a cylindrical parcel wrapped in red tissue paper and tied with silver ribbon.

She shook it, smelt it, then held it to her ear. 'Any hints?' she asked.

'It might have something to do with your new venture.'

'A paintbrush?' said Helen.

'Not quite.'

Helen pulled off the paper, pulling out a tube that resembled the one that once contained her Fine Arts degree. Popping off the lid, she extracted a sheaf of papers, her forehead crinkling in confusion. She moved closer to the light to read it, and as understanding dawned, she felt a warm glow seeping through her.

'A whole hotel?' she said.

'I took Lars to the gallery when you were out last week. He was bowled over. With any luck, you've got enough work to support yourself for the next six months. And that doesn't even include anything you might sell in the gallery.'

'You knew about this and you didn't tell me?'

Jared pulled her closer. 'Don't you think I wanted to? With all this work, you're going to have to hire yourself an assistant. And the great thing is, Lars has given you free reign. Obviously he wants you to look at the hotel and the interior design storyboards to get an idea, but pretty much the whole project is entirely up to you.'

Helen couldn't believe her luck. No financial worries, and a man who cared enough to back her the way Jared just had.

'And that's not all,' Jared said, pulling out another wrapped box. The necklace was a shower of sapphires and tourmalines, more exquisite than anything Helen had ever seen. Jared fastened the catch at her nape, kissing her as he did so. 'Gorgeous,' he said. 'Like you.'

Helen looked at Jared, feeling tears of surprise and joy beginning to well. 'Thank you, Jared,' she said, embracing him.

'You're more than welcome.'

She stood up from the lounger where they'd been sitting, holding out her hand to him. 'And since we're exchanging gifts, mine for you is in the bedroom,' she said.

Jared raised an eyebrow. 'Darling Helen,' he said, a naughty look on his face. 'I thought you'd never ask.'

♥

It didn't matter that she woke just after five, the darkness still present but edging silently away as the sun began to lift.

Jared was gone. She knew it before she'd even rolled over to switch on the bedside lamp. Helen tried to block her disappointment, but it gnawed at her. She was still wearing her necklace and not much else, and though she'd felt sensuous and sexy last night, now she just felt abandoned. What was wrong with her? Jared hadn't said he'd leave so early, but she knew his habits by now. For all she knew he could have driven back to Franschhoek at three, crossing Cape Town at its most secretive and seductive.

Jared's holdall was gone; Jared was gone. But the painting she'd given him last night was still next to the bed, where he'd left it after thanking her. *He didn't like it,* she thought. *How humiliating.* Helen got out of bed and stretched. Subconsciously, she'd probably hoped to wake before Jared left, but she was not actually an early bird. Lunch with Madeleine and Colin was only at twelve thirty. She had a whole morning to kill on her own, but strangely enough, she didn't feel like sleeping any longer. *Especially* on Christmas Day, which was all about being with people you love.

As she passed the bedroom mirror, she looked at herself, studying her new necklace. So he'd left early. What did it matter? She'd stay in Scarborough just for today – she wasn't about to let Madeleine down, and she'd be lonelier spending Christmas in Franschhoek without either of the De Villiers brothers.

Resorting to what she always did to fill the void, Helen pulled out her paints to soothe her negative thoughts, and when her phone rang at eight, she was completely engrossed in depicting a stream where she and Max had stopped with the horses.

'Hello?' she asked, her fingers leaving brown streaks on her mobile.

'Good morning, sleepyhead; happy Christmas!'

'Jared!'

'I'm sorry I left without saying goodbye. I couldn't sleep.'

'That's okay. I missed you when I woke up though.'

'Well, I've had almost all night to think about you. So I might just have missed you more.'

Helen could hear the smile in his voice. 'Please come back to Franschhoek tonight, Helen. I know you'll be with Madeleine today, but I need to be with you.'

'Okay,' Helen said immediately.

'Okay?' Jared sounded relieved. 'And Helen, please bring my present with you? I didn't want to move it last night because I didn't want to rustle the wrapping paper – I thought it'd wake you up. Then when I was driving home, I realised how that might have seemed.'

'I'm not that precious,' Helen lied.

'Well, please bring it. I'm counting down the hours. Let me know when you're on your way and I'll meet you at your flat.'

And Helen's spirits lifted: this could still turn out to be the best Christmas she'd experienced in a long, long time.

CHAPTER SEVENTEEN

Jared left for Hong Kong towards the end of January.

In some ways, Helen was relieved. It wasn't that she wouldn't miss him – over the last few weeks they'd spent so much time together that when she wasn't with him, she felt unfinished. It was rather that she was behind on her deadlines and, if she was honest, completely exhausted. Jared kept a pace she wouldn't have thought she was capable of – certainly not since she was a teenager. A social animal, he wasn't content kicking back in front of the telly, or listening to music for an entire evening. When they spent an evening in just each other's company, there was always an event planned afterwards: *Heinrich's having some mates over to play 30 Seconds; do you think we'll make it by ten?* or *I promised we'd drive into Cape Town tonight; Susana says there's a really hip salsa bar opening this week.*

Helen had probably seen and experienced more in the last month than she normally would have in a year. But with this came a sensory overload: music pounded in her ears for days after an all-night dance session, her eyes hurt in the sunshine after too much to drink, and though she wasn't a prude, she wasn't sure she liked the casual attitude to drugs that characterised Jared's circle. Like the fact that 30 Seconds wasn't entertaining enough without a spliff or a sniff of something. Jared never pressured her into anything, but she knew very well what her choice was – either she went with him, or he went alone. And she preferred driving him home safely than letting him find his way wound up, inebriated or high. She tried a few new things, but not everything about this high-rolling lifestyle suited her.

Helen knew her work was suffering. She was grown up enough to view her painting critically, and the truth was that some of the canvases she'd produced recently lacked depth and warmth. Lars, the hotelier, had popped in yesterday to see how she was progressing, and had rejected two of her paintings outright.

'They're just not the same quality, Helen,' Lars had said. 'I can't quite put my finger on it.'

'Maybe if I change the skyline …' Helen had suggested. 'There's something about it that doesn't work, does it?'

Lars had looked at her. 'Are you alright, Helen?' he asked. 'I don't want to be personal or anything, but you're looking tired.'

Helen sighed.

'I'm fine, Lars. Thank you for asking.'

'Jared away?'

'He left this morning.'

'Well, don't be too sad. It's only three weeks.'

Helen smiled. 'I'm a big girl, Lars, I think I'll manage,' she said, remembering the last time that she'd used that phrase, she'd been talking to Max about fetching the bottles.

♥

She decided to catch up on her sleep: to be in bed by nine every night while Jared was away, despite a few invites from his crowd. On the fifth or so refusal, the invitations stopped, not that it worried her. She was on a full detox. No alcohol. No coffee … Okay, one in the morning, that was all. Lots of fresh fruit. Painting all day. A bike ride every evening up and down a few hills, past the Huguenot Monument usually. Sometimes she took her easel with her like she'd done in Langebaan, stopping at a scene that played with her imagination.

She rode past Bourgogne often, but hadn't stopped to see Max.

And Helen was surprised that she didn't feel lonely. Not at all. A week passed, and she felt fulfilled. Jared phoned or texted her every day: the sales trip was going well, he was lining up some opportunities and thought he might go to Florida for a wine fair in October. Maybe she could come with him. Boy, did they know how to party in Hong Kong. He didn't have to sleep if he didn't need to. The dim sum was to die for. Seriously. And he was going on a junk with some wine buyers and hoteliers. Did Helen like silk scarves? He'd seen some stunning ones. There was a stack of South Africans living there just dying for some decent SA wine. Wasn't that great?

Helen barely got a word in edgewise, but it didn't matter. She didn't have all that much to say, except that she missed him. *Love you*, he said casually as he signed off. He'd never said that to her face so she wondered if he meant it. Two weeks and he'd be back and she'd be able to tell for certain.

On Monday morning, she stayed at the gallery. Her assistant, Sally, had called in sick with flu, but Helen was happy to stay in and watch the tourists pass. She was surprised to see the bent figure of Pieter Blignaut peering in through the shop window.

Helen opened the door for him. 'Hello, Pieter.'

'Well, there you are young lady. I never see you here. Just stopped in to buy some droëwors at the biltong shop. You know what it is to have a craving ...' Pieter bit into the sausage, and sucked on it with loud slurping noises. '*Ekskuus*, I don't have all my teeth.'

'Where's Magda?' Helen asked, looking down the street.

'*Ag*, shopping at Pick n Pay. I told her the chutney she makes is much better, but she says she's not a preserve factory. Tired, *jy weet*? We're getting on, and she hates all that chopping.'

'Maybe I could help her some time?' Helen offered. 'But I don't know how to make chutney.'

'Well, there's a solution. Magda tires so easily these days. Can I sit down, Helen, *skat*?'

Helen gestured for Pieter to come inside and he followed her willingly. She indicated a couch at the back of the gallery, and went upstairs to fetch him a glass of juice. He took it with a tired smiled, and sipped thirstily.

'What's happened to Max these days?' Pieter asked Helen.

Helen shrugged. 'We don't see each other much, Pieter. You know, with Jared ...'

Pieter nodded, obviously not expecting any further elucidation. 'He seemed so happy with you at Le Cadeau. I was pleased for him. He's had a lot of responsibility since the passing of his parents. It's not easy being an orphan, especially not with the family business to run. Not to mention Jared's difficulties.'

'I don't really know what you mean, Pieter.' Helen looked at him, an uncomfortable prickling rising from the back of her neck.

'Nothing to worry about, Helen. I have a *groot bek*, and Magda says I should learn when to keep my mouth shut. It's none of my business. And you should choose for yourself. Nothing I have to say on this subject is of any consequence.' Pieter stood up and strolled around the gallery. He stopped at a landscape she'd painted of a vineyard in full blossom.

'Beautiful,' Pieter said. 'Max was right about your talent. Perhaps one day you'll come and paint at Le Cadeau. Jared's in the East, I understand. Magda makes a *lekker* snoek pie.' The invitation came out a little jumbled, as though Pieter was out of practice and Helen smiled, appreciating the man's hospitality.

'I'd love to,' she said.

'You would? Well, that would be very fine. You come tomorrow. Nine o'clock, so you've some time to paint. And you're welcome any day. I'll tell Magda to expect you.'

♥

Helen woke the next morning to a sense of anticipation, as though she was about to embark on some sort of cultural adventure. At seven thirty, she heard Sally let herself in downstairs, her heels clicking on the laminate floor, then the *sweep-sweep* of a broom. Helen got dressed, checking her phone for any messages that may have come in overnight from Jared – nothing other than his standard goodnight, but it made her smile.

In her eagerness to paint at Le Cadeau, Helen arrived at eight forty-five, but Magda, who was sitting crocheting on the porch, got up immediately to welcome her.

'*Welkom.* We are so pleased you decided to come,' Magda said formally. 'Pieter has been talking about nothing else.'

Helen smiled. 'I'm flattered.'

'He's even been around the farm this morning, finding places for you to paint.'

'Really?' Helen said. 'He didn't need to do that.'

'Oh, it's an excuse for him to see the farm with a new eye. It's *lekker* to see him *so opgewonde.*'

Helen picked up the tone, if not the exact meaning of her words.

'He's just on the telephone,' Magda continued. 'He'll be out soon. Let me get you some tea. Rooibos okay?'

'Thank you,' Helen said, although she hadn't yet got used to red bush tea, and actually didn't like it much – she wasn't keen on the smell. Nevertheless, when the tea arrived on a tray covered in an embroidered cloth with a hand-knitted tea cosy in the shape of an English country cottage, she took her cup and sipped gamely. She rather hoped, however, that Pieter might finish his call and rescue her from being plied with any more.

'Have a soetkoekie?' Magda held out a plate of biscuits.

So much for the detox. One couldn't hurt. And actually the sweetness of it masked the bitterness of the tea.

When Pieter arrived, he lost no time in taking Helen out in an old beige pickup with a dent down the left side, a broken headlight and a passenger door that could only be opened from the outside, and then with extreme force. Magda had thoughtfully packed Helen a small flask of lemonade and some fruit to tide her over until Pieter picked her up for lunch. He showed Helen one or two scenic spots that she thought too panoramic to capture well enough on the canvas; the view that spoke to her looked down on the farmhouse, giving a bird's eye glimpse of the dense thatch and high gables of the main building. Though Pieter's hearing loss had prevented them from talking much during their drive, now that the old diesel truck's drone had quietened they maintained a companiable silence, with Pieter nodding thoughtfully, his forefinger and thumb stroking his chin. Helen wasn't sure whether to set up her easel or to stand contemplating with Pieter, but then he turned to her and beamed.

'I think this is the place, ja?'

Helen nodded taking in the old slave bell that would have summoned the workers from the three-aisled barnlike building to the left. The main house – built in the shape of a double-H, with a gallery linking the two sections – was flanked by an orchard. Helen asked what sort of fruit might grow there.

'Figs, almonds, chestnuts and peaches,' Pieter said. 'I'll take you there after lunch. Some of the trees outdate the buildings by a few years. My first wife used to draw there. She found the silence comforting.'

'Christine?' Helen said, remembering.

'That's right.'

Helen walked to the vehicle, pulling her hat and other belongings from the seat. Pieter had loaded a plastic chair onto the back of the pickup, and he hauled it off for her. Then he slammed the doors shut, waving cheerily, and told her he'd return at twelve thirty, unless she called him earlier.

The time passed quickly, with Helen sketching different views and impressions in her pad, not yet decided on what to paint first. There were so many angles she could chose: as a series, enough for several representations. Yet somehow the vision of Christine sitting alone in the orchard awoke something in Helen, and that is what began to form on the canvas: a woman not unlike herself, lying on a blanket with her legs kicked up behind her, a look of concentration on her face as a rabbit hopped past. The main building lined the right-hand side of the painting, and a younger version of Pieter stood in a doorway, his hands cupping a pipe that he was trying to light. Something about his expression showed he was watching the woman, but though tempted to approach her was holding back. Instead he was angled toward a little girl of about three, who was digging in the herb garden with a small trowel.

As Helen painted, she was so absorbed in the scene that it didn't occur to her to think what Magda or Pieter might say about what she was creating. It didn't until Pieter drove up, and taking one glimpse at it, gulped, turning pale. *Just how insensitive could she be?* Flipping the canvas over, Helen showed Pieter some of her other sketches, but he was not to be distracted.

'You've got her exactly right. Untouchable. I always thought Jared was a bit like that, but you've proved me wrong.'

'I'm sorry,' Helen said. 'She's caught my imagination.'

'I can't really blame you, my dear,' Pieter said. 'Christine had a habit of doing that. Now let's go down to lunch. But if you don't mind, Helen, I'd rather you didn't show Magda. I don't want to upset her.'

♥

Helen didn't make the mistake of working on Christine's painting, as she started to think of it, at Le Cadeau. She did, however, stop at the Huguenot Museum to see if she could find a photo of her. And surprisingly enough, there she found the image Max had mentioned: Christine and Pieter's wedding photo, with Max's grandfather Adam de Villiers.

And Max had been right: she did resemble Christine surprisingly closely. Dressed in Dior's 'new look' with a full skirt, rounded soft shoulders, almost pinched waist and pointed bust, and crowned with a sophisticated beaded veil, Helen could easily have passed for Christine. But that was until she looked at Christine's eyes, which were guarded, despite the obvious joy of the wedding. And it was this look that made them different.

Helen sat flapping through the wedding album looking for

more images of Christine, other expressions she could echo in the painting.

'Do you see now what I meant?' a voice said behind her, and Helen jumped, slamming the album closed with a thud.

'Max!' she said, turning to look at him.

Helen realised her heart was pounding. It had been easier to keep Max out of the top of her mind having not seen him for a while, but now that he was standing right in front of her, she recognised she hadn't forgotten anything about him. As he looked back at her, his hooded hazel eyes were impenetrable. He smelt vaguely of the Bourgogne tasting room and the memories came flooding back.

'What are you doing here?' she asked finally, as their eyes locked.

'Fact checking for the book. My proofreader asked a few questions about spelling discrepancies.'

'Ah,' Helen said, 'the book.'

'Our book,' Max said, reminding her gently.

Helen looked away.

'How've you been keeping?' Max asked. 'I heard from Jared that your gallery's doing amazingly. Is that so, or is that just a Jared-ism?'

Helen noted a trace of bitterness. 'I've been lucky,' she said.

'Glad to hear it. Sometimes you just don't know ... Jared doesn't always portray things accurately, especially when it comes to ...' Max's sentence drifted away.

When it comes to you? When it comes to women? When it comes to how things actually are?

'Has he been in touch?' Helen said with a brightness she didn't feel.

'Once in a while. Usually when he needs something. You know Jared – the best delegator ever. Hopefully my workload will be considerably reduced when he gets back.'

Helen smiled, realising that Max was right. Jared had already emailed her several times with instructions: buy two birthday gifts (one for somebody she hadn't even met); follow up on missing post; pay an outstanding mobile phone account before he was cut off.

Max glanced at the wedding album, then Helen's open sketchbook.

'Those are great. Really great,' he said, stepping as if to move away.

'How's Prudence?' Helen asked quickly to draw him back.

Max stopped. 'She's clucking over me like a mother hen, waiting for her other chick to come home to roost. She's keeping busy making Jared's favourite dishes and freezing them.'

'Lucky Jared,' Helen said, trying to keep the irony out her voice.

'Oh, don't let her get to you. She does her best to chase every woman away. Prudie doesn't like to share her boys.'

'So I gathered.' Helen sighed. 'I bet she couldn't wait to see the back of me.'

With that Max pulled out the chair next to Helen, and sat down quickly. 'That may be true, but *I've* missed you, Helen Shaw,' Max said with an intensity that made Helen reel. 'I thought it would get easier if I avoided you, but I don't think it has.' He leant forward, and his proximity made Helen feel immediately warmer, safer. 'I know you're with Jared, but maybe we can still meet up once in a while.'

'As friends?' Helen said cautiously.

'Why not? Keep each other company till Jared gets back.'

And Helen smiled, holding out her hand. 'It's a deal, Max. I can't think of anything I'd like more.'

♥

Except that with each time they met up, there was something lurking below the surface. Uncomfortable pre-kiss silences that would have led to something had they let them. More than casual glances. Hellos and goodbyes tinged with longing, and which Helen realised were not one-sided.

But they didn't cross any lines. They drank coffee at

Calypso's, went riding, cycled to neighbouring villages and ate lunch in Stellenbosch, watching clusters of newly arrived students accompanied by bulging suitcases and nervous-looking parents.

When Max fetched Helen from her painting spot at Le Cadeau, Pieter and Magda remained tactfully silent, offering them a lunch of frikkadels with mashed potato and tomato-and-onion sauce, or tuna sandwiches with Roquefort salad. And on some afternoons they all sat on the porch, idling the afternoon away with talk of the 'Swallows' in from Europe who, occupying their summer homes, set to out-party each other with drunken debauchery fuelled by generous quantities of local wine.

'Have you been to one of their parties?' Helen asked, thinking they sounded a lot like those hosted by Jared's crowd.

'Once or twice,' Max answered. 'Not really my scene.'

And Pieter, who'd missed the question, patted his ears. 'I just thank the good Lord for my deafness. I used to hear music right across the valley, but now I'm lucky if I can hear the conversation at the dinner table.'

His comment made them all laugh, and Pieter beamed appreciatively.

Helen always arrived on her own at Le Cadeau, but after Max arrived on three consecutive days, she started to anticipate him. He never stayed much longer than an hour or two, and often brought gifts for the older couple to add to the lunch table. Onion marmalade. A milk tart made by Prudie. Potato salad with thick mayonnaise, chunks of egg and chopped parsley. He kissed Helen lightly on the cheek as he left, embracing Magda in the same way.

And she watched him go, trying to keep her emotions in check, trying to remain impassive to the void he left. Jared had been away too long, she decided. Soon he'd be back, filling up her life in a way Max couldn't. Besides, she and Max always met on neutral territory: he'd never even been inside the gallery, and she couldn't go back to Bourgogne – certainly not with Prudence keeping guard. So how could she even compare her feelings for these brothers?

♥

Later, when she returned home after her evening exercise, she didn't expect to see Max. But there he was sitting on her front step, next to a window with a spotlight on her most recent work of a labourer sleeping under a Le Cadeau camphor tree. Helen pushed her bicycle closer, pulling off her helmet.

'Hello there,' Helen said.

'Long ride?'

'Long enough. My legs and butt are so sore, I might just have ruined any chances of any exercise tomorrow.'

'You probably just need a hot bath, soothe those muscles,' said Max.

'I'm sure you're right ...'

Max pulled himself up from the step, moving aside so she could unlock the gallery. She checked the bicycles' tyres for mud, then pushed the bike into the storeroom under the stairs, leaning it against an old heater that had been left in the upstairs apartment. Helen pulled off her muddy shoes, leaving them on a floor mat. Then having hung her helmet on a nail she'd hammered into the wall for that purpose, she turned to Max.

'Do you want to come in?' she asked. 'You could take a look around while I bath.'

Max nodded, following her inside. 'I guess you're wondering why I'm here,' he said.

'Not really,' Helen said, then blushed. 'Well, maybe just a little.'

'I thought you might like to come swimming.'

'Now? At night?' Helen asked, a bemused look crossing her face.

'It's full moon. And I know I told you I'm not really a water baby, but a night swim in Africa – well, that's something special.'

'Well, I –'

Max put up his arms, as though admitting defeat. 'Just a thought,' he said. 'No pressure.'

'Oh, but you misunderstand me,' Helen said. 'I'd love to

come. It's just that I'm ravenous. I'll have to make dinner first, or I won't be able to think of anything else.'

Half an hour later, when Helen came barefooted from her bedroom in a pair of jeans and a cerise halterneck, Max had poured her a glass of wine. He was sitting in her lounge with the television on mute, but switched it off abruptly.

'Feeling better?' he asked, and Helen nodded, taking the glass. 'The furniture looks great here. Nice to see it being used properly.'

'Oh, that was mostly Jared,' Helen said. 'He has an eye for décor that amazed me.'

'Did he now?' An unreadable expression crossed Max's face. 'Well, that's our Jared, surprising us at every turn. Did he tell you where that sideboard comes from?'

'No, he didn't.'

'My maternal great-grandmother brought it into the family as part of her trousseau. It was made for her by her younger brother. Feel here, under the edge of this door.' Max took Helen's fingers in his, tracing the initials and date that were carved there. 'My mother used to let us trace that with pencils and paper, although Jared never really showed an interest. I have an old exercise book of the patterns and initials I traced as a child. I can't actually remember any longer where they all came from.'

Helen sipped her wine. 'But doesn't it bother you that this stuff is here, then? I thought I was borrowing cast-offs, not family history,' she said.

'Of course not,' Max said. 'Why should it? At least you're enjoying it. That sideboard's been under an old sheet in one of the barns for at least twenty years.'

'Oh,' said Helen. 'Jared said he took it out of the cottage.'

'Did he? I guess I must be mistaken then, although...' Max retrieved his glass. 'What about some music while you're cooking?' he asked, changing the subject. 'That is, if you still want to cook.'

'My iPod dock's over there.' Helen indicated some speakers on a shelf.

'Anything in particular?'

'You choose,' said Helen. 'Linguine carbonara okay?'

'Delicious.'

Max chose Louis Armstrong, whose voice crooned like gravel across the small apartment, alternating with the imaginative twists and turns of his trumpet.

'Good choice,' Helen said.

'Satchmo always said, "If you have to ask what jazz is, you'll never know."'

'You like jazz?' Helen asked as she cracked the eggs.

'I like Big Band. One day I should take you to a concert at Kirstenbosch Botanical Gardens. It's the most breath-taking setting, almost like sitting in an arena, but you're on the grass with your picnic, overlooking Cape Town.'

'Sounds wonderful.'

Max pulled up a kitchen stool, seating himself on the other side of the counter where Helen was cooking. She'd pulled out some lettuce, tomatoes and green peppers, and without any discussion, he began to cut up some of the salad stuff, turning the chopping board at an angle to slide it in. As *What a Wonderful World* filled the room, Helen found that they were both singing along, and where George might have sounded like he was barking, Max's voice was pure velvet. She looked across at him and smiled, pouring more wine into his empty glass.

By the time their dinner was over, they were on their second bottle, with Helen having knocked back a great deal more than Max. She was happy; they'd danced around the room, laughing as they bumped and turned in the tiny space. And later Max would be taking her to the swimming pool of a friend whose house he was sitting in town. Helen opened a bar of chocolate, snapping off a few blocks, which she slipped into Max's mouth before popping some into her own. She hadn't meant to be provocative, but the expression on Max's face changed. It was a kind of hunger that she recognised. And as his feelings burnt into her, she felt an internal jolt in response.

'So, how about that swim?' she said carefully, stepping back.

Taking her cue, Max nodded.

♥

They'd thrown their stuff into the boot of the Land Cruiser, but as Max was reversing he suddenly stopped.

'Actually, are you okay to walk? Not too stiff? It's only a few roads down, but parking can be tight. And I shouldn't really be driving.'

'Sure,' Helen said. 'Why not?'

Helen steadied herself against Max as they strolled. Dogs growled on their approach, their yelps only fading again as they moved on. There were no street lights, so the roads were dark, the only illumination coming from the moon and the houses, where lamps glittered beyond half-closed curtains. Some of the homes had televisions blaring, in others they could hear the sounds of raised, angry voices, a baby crying. Beyond a hedge two cats hissed and spat. The darkened streets smelt of just-cooked dinners – curries, roast chicken, and fried fish that reminded her of the corner shop near her home in Dulwich. To Helen, the atmosphere was both eerie and seductive, a raw slice of life. Another avenue and then Max released her, extracting a set of keys from his pocket.

Inside the dark house, she felt the flicker of fur against her ankles and squealed.

'It's only Tammy.' Max laughed softly as a silver-dipped Burmese made figure of eights between her legs. 'Xssss, xssss,' Max clicked, and the cat followed him to the kitchen, where he filled one bowl with Whiskas and a second with water.

Another Burmese with large expressive eyes, descended on them, talking to Max in a soft sweet voice that made him pull out and fill another bowl. 'Come outside,' Max said to Helen, swinging open the back door to a reveal a swimming pool surrounded by a potted garden of hanging plants, ferns and palms, all decked out in fairylights.

There was a heady collision of scents: something floral,

buttery, then lime, jasmine and frangipani.

'It's exquisite,' Helen murmured, conscious that the air was still turgid with the day's heat.

'I thought you might like it.'

Max disappeared inside, returning moments later with two glasses of Amarula on ice.

'We left our bathing suits in the boot,' she said, her eyes meeting Max's.

He looked back at her with an almost guilty stare. 'Do you want me to go get them?'

Helen shook her head. 'Turn around.'

She lifted the halterneck and unclipped her bra. In the silent garden, they could both hear the sound of her jeans unzip, the flutter of material falling. And then she was standing outside under the moonlight, the air caressing her naked skin.

With his back to her, Max's T-shirt was soon tossed aside, then his shoes, his jeans ... And Helen, who'd promised herself she'd look away, took in the figure in front of her. Max's shoulders were wider than Jared's, his buttocks more square and his well-proportioned legs covered in a blond down.

'Can I turn around now?' Max asked, and Helen realised that she wanted him to.

When he did, she could see that he was already aroused. He stood there making no attempt to cover himself.

'Just no touching,' she whispered.

'You're even more beautiful than I imagined,' Max said.

'You imagined?' Helen teased.

'From the first moment I met you.'

'I thought you were admiring my sketches ...'

'Your sketches are fantastic, but they don't compare ...' Max moved slightly forward.

'No touching?' he said. 'Are you sure about that?'

'Your brother –' Helen reminded him.

Max groaned. 'I know, I know. I think I'd better get in the water then, cool off.'

Helen watched him walk to the pool and dive neatly into the

deep end, making hardly a splash.

'Are you coming in?' he asked re-emerging. 'Or are you just going to stand there making me horny?'

Helen laughed, then slid gently into the shallows. The water against her skin was like silk, and warmer than the icy Atlantic. Not bathwater warm, but warm enough not to chill her immediately. An underwater light gave the water a blue, almost electric quality, broken only by the movement of their shadows as Helen flipped onto her back, floating like a snow angel in powder. The moon shimmered above them, and in the sky, as Max had once taught her, she could make out the Southern Cross. The memory of that night made her tingle.

How had things turned out like this?

Even here, with nothing between them but sheets of water, she was keeping her distance. But Max was swimming towards her – she could sense his approach through the ripple of the water.

Helen opened her eyes, to find Max's face within breathing space of hers.

'This is not a good idea,' she said.

'We're just swimming,' Max reminded her.

And Helen closed her eyes, trying to picture Jared's face, Jared's voice, Jared's body. They were all there in her mind, but fuzzy and overlaid by Max's face, Max's voice, Max's body.

'I'm crazy about you, Helen,' Max said, his slow strokes lap-lapping against her. 'I think you know that. I'd care for you in a way Jared never will.'

And in the soft stillness of the water, she could hear his unspoken words. *Choose me, Helen. Choose me.*

'I'm sorry, Max. I don't know what ... I'm just so ...'

Helen dipped down and swam for the shallow end, feeling the heaviness as she lifted herself out, as if the water was trying to suck her back in.

'You're leaving?' Max asked.

'I have to go.'

She used her halterneck to dry herself as much as possible,

then dressed, shivering.

Max had followed her out the pool, but made no effort to put on his clothes.

'I'll walk you back,' Max offered, and Helen wished she could read his eyes in the darkness.

'I'll be fine, Max. It's not far. I'll text you when I get home.'

'I'm sorry,' he said. 'I can't help how I feel.'

'I know you can't, and I don't know how I feel,' Helen said, wishing she could take Max in her arms, but knowing that they'd both be lost.

'Can I call you tomorrow?' Max asked.

'Let's just not,' Helen said. 'For now. I need to think. Just give me some time, okay?'

And Helen walked away, leaving Max standing with his arms folded against his chest, lost and forlorn like a small boy, his teeth chattering from the cold.

CHAPTER EIGHTEEN

ared was flying in on a direct flight to Cape Town from Singapore, arriving just after seven thirty in the morning. He'd told Helen he'd catch a taxi, but she couldn't wait, especially after what had happened with Max.

Helen stood anxiously outside the arrivals hall. With the airport still under partial reconstruction, she'd arrived early, worrying about parking. And now, pacing up and down as passengers rolled suitcases through the automatic glass doors, she wondered if she should have dashed to the loo. *Too late*, she thought. She couldn't risk missing Jared, especially since he wasn't expecting her.

By the time he finally emerged, wearing a pair of Levis and a plain black v-necked shirt, she'd coaxed herself into a frenzy. What if he wasn't glad to see her? What if this wasn't a *happy* surprise? What if he noticed something different about her, even if she wasn't sure that there was? He strode forward casually, carrying his laptop bag easily over his shoulder. His hair was shorter, spikier, and streaked with blonde highlights, his skin darker than when he'd left. And he looked relaxed. Actually, he looked sensational.

'Jared!' She noticed how her body shook at his sheer

proximity.

'Helen.' He smiled, dropping his bags, and picked her up and kissed her with his soft, insistent lips. 'Hello, tiger,' he said gruffly. 'You smell wonderful. And you're much sexier than a taxi driver.'

'I couldn't wait to see you,' Helen said. 'I hardly slept last night thinking about you.'

'Now that was silly,' Jared replied, kissing her fingers, 'especially since I'm not planning on letting you sleep tonight.'

Helen led Jared out the building, paid for parking at the automatic machine.

Are you happy for me to drive?'

'Sure,' Jared said. He lifted the luggage into the Opel, shutting the boot with a thud. 'As long as you go fast.'

He pushed back the passenger seat so he could stretch out his legs. Before long, they were racing back onto the highway while Jared chatted away.

'Singapore's a bit characterless,' he said. 'Overpriced and plastic, despite the government's attempts at tourism. Raffles has a bit of history. Joseph Conrad, Noel Coward, Rudyard Kipling ...'

'So you were in good company, then,' said Helen.

'Not,' Jared said, 'as good company as I am now. But I really preferred Thailand. Bangkok is raw. Real. Just a few days there and you know it'll take a lifetime to penetrate the Thai psyche. Which makes it so much more exciting.'

'And what about sales?'

'Oh, brilliant response. The Dusit Group, Baan Krating Resorts, Imperial, Amari ... We should expect some hefty orders from those who haven't yet signed on the dotted line. I had a translator, thank God. Being a *farang*.'

'*Farang?*'

'Foreigner. It's all about etiquette, respect. I would have got it so wrong.'

Helen glanced across at him. Despite the distance, he didn't look jetlagged.

'Are you tired?' she asked, touching his thigh.

'Not too tired,' Jared said, pulling her hand between his legs. 'I missed you more than I expected. Visions of Helen Shaw kept popping into my head. '

'I'm glad,' said Helen, trying to concentrate on the road as he stirred under her fingers.

'Are you now?'

'Especially as we'll be able to do something about it the moment we get back.'

'Promises, promises,' Jared said. 'And we'd better be ruthless about it. I told Heinrich we'd meet the crowd for lunch. I hope that Sally woman is guarding the fort.'

'Lunch today?' Helen asked, hoping the disappointment wasn't noticeable in her voice.

'No time like the present. Now, don't be selfish, Helen,' Jared chided. 'I promised you my attention all night, but we still have to eat. And I'm dying for a decent steak.'

♥

Wedged in between Heinrich and Susana, Helen wondered why she'd even bothered to come. Jared had insisted on sitting opposite her, but the table was wide, and the conversation had splintered into little groups.

'You've been quiet, Helen,' Heinrich said.

'I've had all those commissions to work on,' Helen replied. 'The only way I could catch up was by keeping my nose to the grindstone while Jared was away.'

'And did you?' Heinrich asked.

'Did I what?'

'Catch up?'

'Oh, yes. Just about.'

'Good, because you know how Jared is. Not sure how he'd feel trapped in that little flat of yours. The man's a prowler. He needs his space.'

Helen felt her hackles rise. 'Jared has *space*,' Helen retorted. 'He's just been away for three weeks!'

Across the lunch table, Jared's eyebrows rose and Heinrich, blocking his face with his hands, pretended to ward off her blows.

'Please don't hurt me,' Heinrich whined, sending Susana into fits of giggles.

'Ha, ha, very funny,' replied Helen, trying to curb her irritation with a deep slug of wine.

'Relax,' Heinrich said. 'I'm only messing with you. You guys're coming tonight, right?'

Helen's heart sank. 'Tonight?'

'You didn't tell her, bru?'

'Tell her what?' Jared asked.

'Texas hold 'em, high stakes – just the way you like it.'

Helen looked across at Jared, hoping he'd catch the appeal in her eyes.

'I was going to broach it, Heinrich. Give me a break, okay? I've just got back.'

'Too many ladyboys over there, hey, Jared? Not sure who should be wearing the pants?'

'Don't be a prick, Heinrich,' Susana said. 'Jared's probably tired.'

'Ja right. Like, when was the last time *that* happened?'

Helen looked at Jared, trying to gauge his reaction, but he simply stood up, opened his arms theatrically and bowed.

'Good to know you missed me, guys, but there's more than enough of me to go around. And for the record, Heinrich, there were a lot more ladies, than ladyboys in Thailand.'

'Thank God. You're acting like you're considering a gender reassignment.'

'Whatever.' Jared sat down, smiled at Helen, then stabbed a final bloody piece of meat with his fork, and dipped it into his mushroom sauce. After he'd swallowed it, he opened his wallet, tossing a generous wad of cash at Heinrich.

'Come on, gorgeous Helen.' He pushed his chair back. 'I want to go walk in my vines.'

♥

Their difficulties with Max seemed to have slipped Jared's mind completely, and in some ways, Helen was glad. She'd missed Bourgogne, and this would be her first time back in over a month.

As they pulled into the drive, she was struck once more by the beauty of the place. And Jared, normally garrulous, was surprisingly silent. He wound down the windows and sniffed loudly.

'It's so good to be home.'

They bumped into Prudence as they walked together towards the main house, her face alight with excitement.

'Mr Jared!' she cried, taking him in an effusive hug. 'Mr Max,' she called, 'your brother's back.'

'Hello Prudence,' Helen said, as the older woman studied her, then nodded at Helen in a not altogether unfriendly way. 'Helen, we haven't seen you for ages,' she said.

And then the front door swung open and there was Max.

'Big Brother Max,' Jared said, slapping him on the shoulder. 'Miss me?'

'Oh,' Max said, 'I cried myself to sleep every night.'

Max reached over and kissed Helen on the cheek, the touch of his lips as delicate as a butterfly's wing. She moved her face, and their noses bumped, making them both laugh.

'Hello Helen,' Max said. 'You're looking well.'

'Of course she is,' Jared said. 'I'm back, aren't I?' He grinned and put his arms around the two of them as Prudence fussed with his bags. 'After all those crowds, I need some space. Fancy a ride out to Elephant Rock?'

♥

They took two quad bikes, with Helen riding behind Jared like she had the first day she arrived at Bourgogne. It felt a little awkward, the three of them together, but Helen decided to give in to Jared's infectious enthusiasm, just as Max seemed to have done. Still, she turned once or twice at they rode, to see if Max was alright.

When they reached the viewpoint, Jared pulled the vehicle to a sudden halt, lurching them both forward, then flung himself off and sprinted between the rows of grapes.

'We're going to have a spectacular season!' he called. 'I can feel it in my bones!'

Max parked just behind them, watching his brother's antics with a tolerant expression.

'Does he always do this?' asked Helen.

'Often enough. Listen, Helen –'

Helen lifted up her hands. 'I care about you, Max. I really do. But I'm not a cheat ... however tempted I may have been.'

Max's face remained blank, then his eyes crinkled as he smiled. 'Well, at least you were tempted. Anyway, I've said what I needed to say. I don't want to hurt you. Or Jared. And I'll keep my feelings close to my chest. You don't have to worry – I won't mess things up for you.'

'Thank you.'

'And, Helen, another thing. The book proofs have come. I was going to phone you to see if you wanted to have a look.'

'*Of course* I would! I wouldn't miss that for anything.'

Jared popped his head around one of the poles. 'What's the delay? Are you coming for a walk or aren't you?'

And so they set off, the three of them. They walked up and down, and under and through, with Jared and Max examining leaves and fruit, palming handfuls of dirt that they filtered through their fingers as if they were panning for gold. They discussed nitrogen content and wheat growth and soil moisture, comparing mental notes on past seasons and previous harvests.

'The whites will be a bit later this year,' Jared commented. 'Mid-Feb, don't you think?'

Max nodded. 'I'll speak to Fanie about getting the labourers he rounded up last year. I'm not going with that machine again. Hand-picking's the answer; we can't risk losing any product. I think we'll need at least thirty extra people on site.'

Jared bent down to snap off a bunch of tiny grapes, tossing it under the vine. 'There are a lot of bunches that are going to have to come off,' he said.

'Why?' Helen asked, and Jared looked up at her from where he had crouched as though he'd forgotten she was there.

'Oh, we don't want the plant expending energy on the grapes we can't use. In the last month we only keep the best bunches.'

And Helen found herself wondering how one could tell which were the best.

♥

They arrived back at the house grubbier and thirstier than when they'd left. But Prudence, clearly anticipating this, had placed a jug of her lemonade, some glasses, and an ice bucket outside on a tray, all covered with a net to keep the flies away.

Max poured three glasses.

'At the harvest, can I help you pick?' Helen voiced a sudden desire to get her hands dirty.

'Sure,' said Jared, 'if you want to kill your knees. I, for one, am over that.'

'Yes,' Max agreed, 'Jared's much better at prancing up and down the rows shouting.'

'I do not prance. And I *definitely* do not shout,' Jared said to Max, glaring. 'Well, not unless it's absolutely necessary ... Though, now that I think about it, is most of the time.' The revelation made Jared laugh. 'See why we keep him, Helen? Max – our voice of reason.'

'Oh, he's more than that,' Helen replied.

'Good, good. So we're all friends now?' Jared unlaced his shoes and kicked them off under the table, then stripped off his shirt. 'I need to shower and change.' And within a minute he had disappeared inside, whistling cheerfully.

'If you want to pick grapes,' Max said, his eyes following Helen's admiring glance, 'then you really are welcome to. But you might prefer to sketch some of the action.'

'Maybe I can do a bit of both.'

'I don't see why not,' Max said. 'Maybe I'll join you. It's been a few years since Jared or I did the really hard labour. We might even be able to convince Jared. Burn off some of his excess energy.'

'You'd be lucky there,' said Helen. 'That man has more energy than a nuclear power plant.'

'Don't worry. He exhausts everybody,' Max replied. 'I don't think I've ever met *anybody* quite able to keep up with him.'

And Helen, who hadn't told Max how Jared exhausted her, wondered what she'd said by saying nothing at all.

CHAPTER NINETEEN

As they neared harvest time, Helen woke each morning with an increasing sense of anticipation. Jared's excited texts usually beeped at five or six am, and she never had the heart to tell him she was still asleep. When it came to Bourgogne, Jared was like a little boy in a toy shop, and in many ways Helen envied his ability to experience things as if for the first time. She wasn't going to put him off – Jared happy made her happy.

Since his return, she and Jared had settled into the relationship in a way that made her interactions with Max so much easier. Anybody could see she and Jared were besotted with each other. Inseparable. And though her friendship with Max could not be described as easy – it was too complicated for that – she knew they both took pleasure in each other's company. The memory of their night at the pool began to fade, and Helen didn't for a moment regret what hadn't happened. Though she knew how Max felt, she wasn't going to broach it any further. There wasn't any point.

On the first day of the harvest, Helen woke up early and was out of bed in moments, pulling on a pair of shorts, a T-shirt and a hat. She lathered herself with sun cream, knowing how hot it would be outside. Over the last few days, temperatures had soared to the mid-thirties, and she wasn't sure she'd last more than an hour in the vineyards. Yet if her life was going to be entangled with the winery, as she suspected it was, she wanted to experience the harvest first-hand.

At Bourgogne, Max and Jared stood outside one of the workshops, a crowd of labourers gathered around them. Helen recognised some of the faces from her walks and horse-rides through the vines, but most of the people were strangers. Dressed in blue overalls, some wearing scarves tied on their heads, and others wearing FIFA World Cup 2010 or African National Congress caps, the men and woman began to queue up. Simon was standing behind a table allocating each person some newly oiled picking shears and a red plastic stackable tray. Helen waved at the brothers, and joined the queue.

'Morning,' Jared said, his arms around her waist as he kissed her neck. 'You don't have to stand in line. I'm sure I can give you exactly what you need ...'

Max rolled his eyes. 'God, Jared, isn't it a bit early for that talk?'

Jared tucked his neck over Helen's shoulder. 'It's *never* too early ...' he retorted. 'But I was actually talking about the shears.'

'Of course you were.'

'Now, now, boys.' Helen pulled away from Jared. 'I'm happy to queue just like everybody else, just as long as I get a private demonstration of what on earth I'm supposed to be doing.'

'I'll leave you to it, then,' Max said, nodding towards Jared. 'But if he doesn't explain himself well enough, Helen, come and find me.'

'Where *are* you going?' Jared asked. 'I thought you promised Helen you'd join us.'

'I know your attention span,' Max said. 'I'll be back in an hour when Helen is dying for some scintillating and infinitely superior conversation.'

'Bite me,' said Jared.

'Thanks for the offer, but I'd rather bite Helen,' said Max with a shrug as he sauntered back up to the house.

♥

Helen realised soon enough what Jared had meant about the knees, and she knew she'd be hurting the next day. She watched as Jared cupped a bunch of grapes in his hand, pulling the cluster away from the vine. With the other hand, he clipped at the stem using the shears.

'So you pull gently,' Jared said, 'and make sure you keep some of the stem – it'll make them easier to handle. When we put them in the machines, the stems will be separated from the berries. Do you want to give it a go?'

Helen held the shears she'd been given. They were a little smaller than Jared's but she could see immediately as she held them to the vine that they were sharp.

'Careful, now,' Jared said. 'You don't want to drop them or cut yourself. Now place the bunch on the harvest tray. When the tray's full, you'll tip the grapes into the trough, and then they'll be fed into the machines.'

A little way away, the trough was set under a large oak tree out of the sun. As Helen wished she was. God, it was hot.

'Got it?' Jared said, misreading her expression.

'Well, it's not exactly rocket science,' she said. 'I think I can probably work it out.'

'It's not brains you need for this job, Helen – it's stamina.'

'And shade,' she grumbled.

Jared stood up and stretched. 'Maybe you should wear one of my shirts,' he suggested. 'Your arms are going to get fried out here as it gets hotter. And I'll get Prudie to pack us some drinks.'

Helen nodded, snipping her first bunch with the clippers. She eventually found a rhythm humming to herself; she aimed to fill a tray before Jared got back. And despite thinking that she might manage only an hour or so, Helen realised she found the picking rather therapeutic. It didn't involve all that much thought-processing, but the rhythm of her movements made her almost meditative. As the vineyards grew hotter, the sounds of insects grew louder. Bees. The odd fly. Cicadas. A few rows across, two pickers sang as they worked. She had no idea what they were singing about, but they sounded beautiful, catching melodies as they filled their trays. Helen realised she was content.

And Max had predicted correctly. At some point Jared returned with supplies, and a loose cotton shirt for her to cover herself with, but grew bored within forty-five minutes. He was faster than she was, and had filled and dumped a tray before he seemed to get restless.

'You don't have to stay with me, Jared. After all, you're the boss,' she teased him.

'I can't just abandon you. Some might accuse me of using slave labour.'

'Slave to love, what can I say?' Helen laughed. 'Anyway, I'll expect payment later in beer shandies and lunch.'

When she next looked up, Jared was already walking away.

'Well, you don't have to be a martyr; you can come back up to the house whenever you want,' he called back to her.

'Max will be down soon to entertain me,' Helen reminded him.

'Speak of the devil,' Jared said, as he noticed Max walking nonchalantly down the drive.

♥

Helen sat on the porch, waving a *Farmer's Weekly* like a fan.

'I don't know how they do it,' she said, looking towards the vineyards.

'No work, no pay,' Max said. 'This is peak season; they need to take advantage of the busy times, so they move from farm to farm.'

'Well, I'm in awe.'

'You're also very sweaty and dusty, and deserving of a nice cold drink,' Jared said, as he appeared around the corner with two shandies.

'Where've you been all morning?' Helen asked.

'I had some very important business to attend to. No, seriously Max,' Jared said, noticing the doubt crossing Max's face. 'One of the pumps on the tanks blew. I asked Heinrich to bring some parts over so I can fix it before we transfer the wine.' Jared gave Helen a shandy and a quick kiss, then gulped down his drink in a few seconds.

'What about me?' Max asked a little grumpily.

'Well, I'll kiss you if you like,' Jared said, plopping himself into a chair, 'but I didn't think you were into that sort of thing.'

'I guess I'll get myself a drink.' Max stood up.

'Well, seeing as you're up,' Jared said innocently. 'No harm in another. What about you, Helen? Still thirsty?'

♥

The tanks stood side by side like squat metallic wrestlers. In a way, Helen was a little disappointed. From the outside of the building, she was expecting something a little less like a factory, and more like a French *cave*. Something romantic and dominated by a central half-barrel, where she could take off her shoes, clean off her feet and jump up and down as the juice pushed luxuriously through her toes.

'Christ, Helen,' Jared said, 'We're not in the Middle Ages.'

'And it's not all it's cracked up to being,' Max said a little more kindly. 'Not nearly as hygienic either.'

Helen nodded, then moved forward. The high-ceilinged room smelt like fermentation, even though none had begun yet; she guessed the years of wine-making had embedded themselves into the stone walls. And at least it was cool. One of the troughs from the vineyard was already lined up next to an oval-shaped machine on wheels.

'It works on inflation and deflation,' Max explained. 'See that hatch?'

Helen looked at the opening on top of the machine, which reminded her of a submarine.

'We put the grapes in through there once the stems have been shaken off. We call that destemming. There's a contraption inside the crusher that basically blows up like a balloon, and then pushes against the berries, causing them to burst. It'll take a few hours, but eventually all the juice will be extracted. Skin and seeds float to the top, but the bottom three-quarters will be liquids.'

'With red wine, though,' Jared added, 'we keep the skins. And for rosé, we expose the juice to the skins for about an hour – for the colour.'

'For red wines,' Max continued, 'we do what we call "pump overs" about three times a day for a week. It's pretty much a circular flow-through of the liquids, and we remove the skins on the last press.'

'It all sounds so complicated,' Helen commented.

'Not really,' said Jared. 'It's fairly logical if we just follow the system. That's probably enough of a tour for now, don't you think?'

But Helen, who was not quite finished learning about the processing of the magical nectar, asked Jared, 'Where does the wine go next?'

'Into the tanks over there. We've got 5 100- to 15 000-litre tanks, depending on the cultivar and the harvest. We'll use cultured yeast, and the natural sugars will be converted into alcohol. For whites, it takes from a few weeks to a few months until all the yeast is used up. It's all temperature controlled.'

'It's really about getting the wines to the point where they're stable,' added Max. 'We check the acidity, and the wines only stay in the tank until they've settled. We have to wait for the fizz to die out.'

CHAPTER TWENTY

And then Jared's mood changed. It was as if at one specific moment, a switch had been turned off in his brain. Helen could scarcely understand it. While the harvesting of the white grapes had swept him into a frenzy, the red-grape harvest was heralded with a vague nod of recognition, and a slump back under the covers.

'He won't get up,' Helen told Max on the phone. 'He says you'll manage.'

'Of course he does,' replied Max, not bothering to hide the frustration in his voice. 'He drives me crazy sometimes, you know. One moment full of inspiration and plans that he starts to implement and never finish, and the next he's lost the will to live.'

'Well, I wouldn't say that exactly,' Helen replied, remembering his relentless drinking the night before at the Elephant and Barrel. Perhaps he was just hung over. She didn't, however, think this was worth mentioning to Max. It would only antagonise him further.

'I'd love to come over there and give him a piece of my mind,' Max growled, the anger in his voice was unmistakable.

'This is Jared you're talking about,' Helen said. 'Do you think that would even help?'

'Believe me if I did, I'd be there now.' Max sighed. 'I guess I'll have to cancel my meetings.'

'I'm sorry, Max. He just won't move.'

'I know. It's not like this is a first for us.'

She wasn't really sure what *that* meant, but it certainly didn't sound promising. 'Listen,' she said. 'I think I should go. I'll call you later with an update.'

When she'd put down the receiver, Helen went back to the bedside. 'Jared?' she said softly. 'Jared?'

He groaned, and rolled over. 'Leave me alone, for fuck's sake,' he said, pulling a pillow over his head. And then he slept.

He slept all day, leaving his tea to grow cold and his lunch, a tuna-mayo sandwich, to go grow dry and crusty at the side of bed. Helen checked on him every half hour, but he never moved. After a few times, she wondered if she should check his breathing. She leant in close, listening.

'Go away,' Jared muttered, not even bothering to open his eyes. 'Just go away, okay?'

Startled, she jumped away from him. For the first time since they'd met, Helen wished Jared apart from her. *What was wrong with him?* Helen tried to keep her temper in check. There must be a rational explanations for his behaviour. Jared clearly wasn't well. He was exhausted or maybe he was simply burnt out. But seeing as he wasn't going anywhere, she'd be the one to take a breather.

'I'm going out, Sally,' she said, picking up her handbag and car keys. 'I need to go to Paarl to buy some acrylic glaze. Call me if you need me.' She was too embarrassed to mention Jared's inert body upstairs, the sheets souring with his body heat. And now that she recalled, he hadn't even showered last night. If he surprised Sally downstairs, then so be it. She could handle it. 'Cheerio,' she said, with a brightness she did not feel.

♥

But in Paarl, Helen couldn't focus on art supplies.

Seeing a computer shop, she ducked in and, under the guise of testing out a laptop, typed a few keywords into Google: mood changes; sadness; insomnia; recklessness. The first result was a website on depression: *How to recognise depression and get effective help.*

A bit of Jared, but not him exactly. She flipped back to the previous screen, her eyes scanning the other options. And the same words starting repeating themselves, over and over again.

Bipolar disorder. Manic depression.

She opened each page, and realised she recognised her boyfriend in almost every one.

Her heart thumped. What had she got herself into? And why had nobody told her the truth?

'Excuse me, ma'am?' said a young salesman after she'd monopolised the laptop for close to half an hour.

'Yes?' she snapped.

'I just wanted to warn you. My manager's going to be back in five minutes and he doesn't really allow research on the machines.'

'He's really ill,' she said, her voice fading.

'My manager?' he said in confusion. 'Listen, I'm sorry, ma'am, it's just, um … Oh, I see. Can I get you a glass of water?'

'I've had to work it out myself because nobody told me.'

The youngster looked vaguely nauseous. He flicked his fringe in the direction of a woman behind the counter, who taking the cue, left her perch and fluttered towards them.

Helen stood up. 'Don't worry, I won't get you into trouble. I'm leaving.'

Driving towards Bourgogne, Helen realised that she was not just muddled. She was furious. She'd thought that of all people, Max would have been honest with her. Was perfect Big Brother Max really capable of subterfuge? And for what? It certainly hadn't worked out in his favour.

When she got out the car, she found him with the horses. He was sponging sweaty marks from Star's saddle, crooning to her softly.

'You've been out ,' Helen said.

'I needed to think,' Max said, dropping the sponge into a

bucket and beginning to rub Star's back with a towel. 'Things on my mind. And from the look on your face, you have too.'

'It's Jared. Why didn't you tell me?' she said.

'Tell you what? I've always said Jared gets sad sometimes. That's never been a secret.'

'But it's more than that, Max. It's much more, and you know it.'

Max glanced at Helen, then handed her a rubber curry. 'You could do Pinotage. She followed us into the fields; managed to get mud caked on her neck, how I've no idea.' Max stroked the body brush along Star's back and the patches he was working began to shine.

Helen took the brush, dropping her handbag and keys onto a patch of grass next to them.

'Hello, girl,' she said. 'I've missed you.' She began to brush along the horse's neck, clumps of mud falling to the ground. Her hands shook slightly and she wondered if it was from nerves or anger.

Max cut through the silence. 'Perhaps I need to tell you a bit about our upbringing,' Max said, not looking at her. 'My parents had this thing – a circle of trust, if you like – so that anything within the family was exactly that, *within the family.*'

Helen remained silent.

'When Jared started showing symptoms of bipolar disorder, my parents were concerned people would treat him differently. Badly. And hiding his illness became a way of life. A habit. When he acted out or became depressed, we protected him. Everyone in a family has a role – the nurturer, the bully, the prima donna, the martyr. I was always the protector, even more so when I lost my parents. I'm still Jared's protector, even if it means it has hurt you. Though that was never my intention.'

'But I don't understand. Why wouldn't you tell me when –'

'When it would have been better for me if you knew? Come on, Helen. What kind of person demeans someone else to get what he wants? You're a bright person and you've worked it out on your own. Besides, you wouldn't have respected me for telling you then – it would have seemed too convenient. I don't think you would have listened to me, even if I had.'

Helen sighed. 'Perhaps you're right.'

'I am.'

'But what happens next? Right now he's probably still comatose in bed. When I tried to talk to him, he just about bit my head off.'

Max half-smiled. 'Oh, yes, the sleeping lion. That's what my mother used to call him. He's probably gone off his meds again. He does that sometimes when he's manic – he feels so invincible he thinks he doesn't need them. We'll have to get him back on lithium or he'll get worse.'

Later Helen returned to the flat to find an unmade bed and Jared's clothes from the previous night dumped unceremoniously on her rocking chair in front of the window. No note. But no other sign of him either.

She began to strip off the bedclothes, trying to not to worry about where he'd gone and if he was in a state to drive. Picking up her phone, she dialled his number. *Answer, damn it. Answer. Answer.* Trying to be optimistic, she wondered if he was feeling a little better after a good day's rest. Maybe this was just a momentary lapse and they were already over it. When the phone went to voicemail she tossed it back into her handbag.

Where was he?

She walked to the kitchen to make herself a cup of tea. But the tannins did not sit well on her unsettled stomach. So much for English Breakfast in a crisis, she thought. She stood at the window, staring out towards the Groot Drakenstein Mountains.

Just after six, Helen's mobile rang loudly in the bedroom.

'Max!'

'Helen, he just got back.'

'Oh, thank God. Where's he been?'

'I don't know. He's not talking. I've called the doc. Are you okay?'

She was not. She was confused and anxious. But she said, 'I'm fine, Max, really. I'm just glad he's safe and sound. Maybe he can call me later if he's up to it.' The unsaid settled between them and Helen could hear Max exhaling. 'So...' she tried, 'I didn't even ask you earlier about the harvest? How did it go? It must have been running smoothly if you went for a ride?'

♥

In Jared's absence over the next few days, and then weeks, Helen took to dropping in at the Blignauts.

She kept her conversation neutral, emotionless, and focused instead on the portrait she was doing of Pieter. His face was what one might call 'lived in'; with every groove came an interplay of light and shade that fascinated her. Pieter seemed unconcerned by her study of him, picking up his tapestry and working on it as though she wasn't there. Sometimes he'd chat to her, but the conversation was largely one-sided. It didn't matter to her; it saved her the effort of being entertaining.

She reserved all her energy for her visits to Bourgogne, where she pretended she was full of beans. Max would open the door with a nod or a shake of his head, and with this, she would know. Today was a good day. Today was bad.

Though intellectually Helen could take in what was happening, on an emotional level she seemed unable to grasp how Jared could have changed so radically. In under a month, he'd lost more than four kilograms. Over nine pounds! He didn't want to eat, and much as she'd feared Prudence, Helen now admired her. With a tenacity Helen could scarcely credit, she watched Prudie cook up everything she knew Jared liked and then, with equal determination, sit next to him, trying to tempt it into his mouth. Most days Prudence came away disappointed.

'It'll pass,' Max said. 'It always does. The meds need to kick in.'

The 'De Villiers blues' now seemed rather an understatement.

'I'm sorry, Helen,' Jared said one late morning from the depths of his bed. 'I'm just all out of happiness right now.'

It wasn't as if Jared was completely unresponsive. He was

tired, incredibly so, but on some days she could see a glimmer of his old self. A drive on the quad bikes to Elephant Rock one afternoon brought a smile to his face, and Helen realised that Bourgogne was Jared's saving grace: the more time he spent outside walking the vineyards, the better his mood seemed to be.

'I love this place, Helen,' Jared told her. 'I may be a useless son of a bitch, but Bourgogne gives me purpose.'

'You're not useless,' Helen replied automatically, trying to push the thought away that they hadn't made love in a month. Perhaps that was the most difficult thing. Not the sex so much as the lack of contact. Jared used to be so tactile, but now he'd withdrawn like a hermit crab into a shell.

Yet it wasn't his fault he was ill. And Max said his doctors were already seeing an improvement.

'We'll hang in there, Helen,' he'd said. 'And wait for the sunshine to come back.'

♥

Despite everything, Max remained amazingly calm. How he was managing both Jared's workload and his own while still supporting his younger brother was beyond Helen. And he never complained. Not once. Well, not about the current situation.

One night when she arrived at Bourgogne after the gallery had closed, she found Max in his study, head in his hands. And he wasn't quick enough to mask the worry in his eyes when she opened the door.

'What is it?' Helen asked.

'Hm?'

'Come on, I'm not an idiot, Max. What's going on?'

Max sighed, pushing away the pile of post on his desk. 'Bills, bills and more bills,' he commented. 'Sometimes, I don't know if I can handle Jared better when he is high on life or when he is digging his way out of misery.'

Helen took the bank statement from Max, gasping at the totals.

'I had no idea,' she said. 'I always thought he was generous, but –'

'But this is just stupid,' Max finished for her. 'Funny how we haven't seen much of his crowd over the last month. They couldn't stay away in January.'

'To be fair, Max, it's not as if Jared's exactly been welcoming. I'm not sure if he even wants to see me.'

'Of course he wants to see you, Helen. He'd be crazy …' Max looked away, embarrassed.

Helen touched his arm. 'Listen, Max, if you think it would help for me to chat to Heinrich, I will. Maybe he could bring some of Jared's friends over for a meal or something. It might lift Jared's spirits.'

And the rallying of friends seemed to work, if only as a temporary cure.

Helen pulled out all the stops, hiring a spit roast to cook a Karoo lamb, which she'd heard would be terribly well received. She filled troughs with beer and ice, displayed bottles of wine and, with Prudie's help, made abundant salads to cater for the vegetarians. There was pap, roasted butternut and corn on the cob. However unreliable Jared's friends seemed to her or Max, they made Jared happy. And for that reason alone she was not going to let her poor planning discourage them from coming.

She watched him as he stood outside near the fire, where mealies wrapped in tin foil were cooking in the coals. He was nursing a beer, an intense look of concentration on his face as Heinrich explained something to him. Though he looked gaunt, Jared seemed engaged rather than his recent distant self. He sensed her glance, acknowledging her with a bright smile.

Later in the evening, as the sun began to set, Helen felt Jared's arms around her. 'I'm going to pull myself right again,' he promised her.

And though she nodded and kissed him, she wondered if it was as simple as he made it sound.

♥

Jared starting getting better, but remained unpredictable.

Helen had grown used to his moodiness – it had always come with the territory – but she was now aware of the extreme melancholy of which he was capable, and she felt as if she were walking across a suspension bridge, with a very long way to fall if she slipped. Would anything she could do or say trigger the depression again? Drinking coffee with Max at Calypso's, she wondered if she would be able to confide in him. But Max seemed to guess without her saying anything at all.

'You can't blame yourself,' he told her. 'Jared's responsible for his own emotional life. As long as you love him with everything you can muster, the rest is really up to him.'

Helen wondered how hard that was for Max to say. Yet as he sat back in his chair, she noticed he'd adopted a way of talking about her and Jared's relationship with an incredible objectivity.

'You really are too good to me, Max,' Helen said. 'I'm not sure how I would have managed all of this without you.'

'Of course you would have. You're a tough cookie.' Max cut a piece of omelette, scooping up the cheese that was glued on the side of the plate. 'How's Pieter's portrait coming along?'

'Almost done,' Helen said. 'I'm tempted to give it to him, but I don't think he'll let me. It hasn't been like some of my other paintings this year. For some reason, I can almost trace my own emotions in his face.'

'Transference,' Max said. 'You had to put your feelings somewhere. You're lucky to have an outlet like that. I've tried my hand at fiction once or twice, but I guess I'm just not imaginative enough.'

'Have you thought about what you'll do now the book is put to bed?' Helen asked.

Max smiled. 'Well, it's not as if I can write a sequel. I think I'll just contribute to the *Wine Magazine SA* and the *Franschhoek Tatler*. Try my hand at a wine blog or something.'

'When Jared is back on track you'll have more time for yourself again. Maybe go on holiday somewhere …?'

'Trying to get rid of me?' Max asked.

Helen blushed. 'That's not what I meant.'

'Are you going to eat that cucumber?' Max asked. 'It's been sitting there lonely on the side of your plate, and I don't think you're giving it the attention it deserves.'

Helen laughed, handing Max her plate. 'I hate cucumber,' she said.

'I know,' Max said, smiling at her. 'I've noticed.'

CHAPTER TWENTY-ONE

elen checked her watch for the umpteenth time.

Where was he? This was the fourth time this week that Jared had been late. She'd mentioned it last time, and the result had been an argument beginning something like: *Why do you have to be such a handbrake, Helen? I'm here aren't I?* And ending with: *I don't need this. Lots of other fish in the sea.* As Helen had learnt, reasoning with Jared when he was aggravated was almost pointless. At times like these he didn't listen to her anyway, and he could say such hurtful things that she felt physically ill. She knew that for her own good it would be better to accept his eccentricities and, in cases like this, wait with a book. But why, she wondered, did she always have to be the adaptable one?

It didn't make her feel much better, though, that she'd made such an effort getting ready. It was Susana's wedding – that friend of Jared's – to a local young winemaker, and Helen had put in the time and effort to buy a new dress and groom herself appropriately. Jared had made a big deal of taking her somewhere special en route.

When Jared finally pulled up outside the gallery, the top of the convertible was down. He hooted merrily.

Was she supposed to leap out and throw herself in gay

abandon into his car like a giddy teenager?

'Come on, places to go, people to see!' Jared called.

Helen pulled the front door closed behind her, waving at Sally, who looked at her with raised eyebrows. In the car, Jared leant over to kiss her.

'You look nice,' he said.

You're late – again, she wanted to say, but instead she said. 'Busy morning?'

'Not really. I kind of lost track of time. I was checking the tanks with Simon this morning. Then I thought I should get some extra wine barrels. You know they're like €1,000 a pop? That's a lot of dosh, Helen. Then some bloke phoned to debate pinotage wines for an article he was writing and you know how I feel about that.' (Helen didn't, but she wasn't actually all that interested to know either.) 'So by then I was still in the midst of ordering the barrels from France, and I suddenly recalled I had some French tapes in my room. New year and all that, thought I should brush up on my verbs. Conjugations. I used to have them down pat. *Je suis, tu es, il est ...*'

'Are you okay?' Helen asked. 'You're not making much sense.'

'What do you mean? Keep up, Helen! I'm talking about brushing up on my French.'

'Right,' said Helen. 'So did you order the barrels?'

'I thought I just told you I'm going to order them in the lingo. I need a couple of days. It'll impress the socks off the suppliers,' said Jared.

'You're going to master your French in a few days?' Helen said.

'Fuck, Helen, how difficult can it be? I did French till standard eight, and my teacher was an *actual* frog. Great accent. Sexiest pins you've ever seen.'

Helen hardly thought Jared's teacher's legs fifteen years ago were relevant. 'Great,' she said, not even bothering with false enthusiasm.

'Look at this day!' Jared carried on. 'Not a cloud in the sky.

We're going to have the *best* time! Did I tell you how sexy you look? And you smell like heaven. Makes me want to stop the car and ravish you on the spot.'

The familiarity of his comment made Helen loosen up enough to laugh. 'You really are far too charming for your own good,' she said to Jared.

'So that's a yes?'

'Keep driving, mister. You've promised me a morning out and I've been looking forward to it all week.'

'Okay, tiger, I won't let you down. Real croissants, first-rate coffee, the best apricot jam and conversation this side of the equator.'

♥

A few hours later, Helen and Jared were assembled with the other wedding guests on a terrace overlooking vineyards and a huge dam dotted with Egyptian geese and the odd mallard. Beyond, craggy blue mountains rose, framing the view.

'You never did tell me how you know Susana,' Helen commented as she accepted a glass of sparkling wine from a passing waiter.

'Ex-girlfriend,' Jared said. 'We dated in our early twenties. She studied oenology at Stellenbosch, came to do a stint at Bourgogne, vac work, you know. And, hey presto.'

'Love at first sight?' Helen immediately wished she hadn't asked.

'Is that actually possible? I always wondered. I mean, I can't speak for you, but when you saw me, I don't think you fell head over heels, did you? As for me, you were so hot I wanted to jump you there and then.'

'How romantic,' Helen said dryly.

'Oh don't tell me you didn't feel the same. I could see it in your eyes.'

'Then you *can* speak for me,' Helen said, wondering what was wrong with her.

Jared shrugged. 'I guess so,' he said brightly, knocking back his drink. 'Lucky me. Let's get another drink to oil ourselves for the service. Never been much of a fan of hatch, match and despatch.'

As the bride glided down the aisle – a narrow stretch of grass scattered with rose petals – Helen remembered her wedding to George. She'd been so sure of it all, and the fact that her bridesmaids had forgotten her bouquet did nothing to mask her joy. Helen had wanted to get married *that minute* and she hadn't been about to keep George Shaw waiting a moment longer. He'd stood there, handsome in top and tails, and when their eyes had met through the lacy veil, it had felt so *right*.

Next to her now, Jared had flicked off his lens cap and leant forward, blocking Helen's view, at the same time giving Susana an unsubtle wink. Susana glanced at him and beamed.

Click.

Jared checked his screen, frowned, and dug in his camera bag for a different lens.

As the minister ran through a happy-marriage checklist, Helen studied Jared, who seemed oblivious to any message that might be being transmitted. His knee bounced continuously as he scrolled through his photos deleting the ones he didn't want. Most of them had nothing much to do with the ceremony.

'Jared,' she remonstrated between her teeth, 'can you at least try to sit still?'

'Sorry,' he said. He put down the camera, pulling her hand into his. He shifted, once, again, then settled.

'Love is a magical four-letter word spelt G-I-V-E,' the minister said. 'It's also about honesty and truth. But don't be misguided on that one. Mutual honesty doesn't mean you're obliged to share every single thought, dream, fear, secret, or fantasy with your partner ...'

'Some things are better left unsaid,' Jared whispered in Helen's ear. 'Got it.'

Helen glanced over at Jared thinking that leaving things unsaid was one thing the De Villiers men had in common. She didn't like it all that much.

'The key to a happy marriage,' the minister continued, 'is what I like to call The Three C's: Commitment, Companionship and Communication.'

Jared check the hymn sheet. He turned it over, fanned himself, then looked towards the bride and groom. Helen could almost read his thoughts: *Vows, candle lighting, signing of the register. Fifteen minutes tops.* A few weeks or months ago, she might have found this amusing. Now she felt her temper rising, and forced herself to look away.

She'd always liked attending weddings when she was married. They'd seemed a chance to reaffirm how she and George felt about each other, and even if they didn't agree on everything, the wedding message gave them something to debate during the drive home. It didn't seem that Jared was taking much in. And it wasn't as if the subject of marriage had ever come up between them ...

Helen tried to tune Jared out, wishing she could focus on the couple whose lives together were just beginning, but she found she was now also distracted. Her eyes scanned the congregation and settled on Pieter and Magda, who held hands as they stood up to sing 'Morning has broken'. Magda looked up at Pieter and he smiled at her in a way that excluded everybody else. *Now that,* she thought, *was an inspiration.* As they sat back down again, Magda caught Helen's gaze, and mouthed something Helen didn't catch. But by the time Helen had had a chance to react, Magda had already turned away again so Helen was left in the dark.

♥

They walked to the reception through the vineyards.

'I need a drink,' Jared said, making a beeline for the bar. 'Coming?'

Helen nodded and followed him. As she accepted a gin and tonic from the barman, she turned to see Max coming along the vineyard path.

Standing close to him was a tall redhead whom Helen had never seen before. Helen realised she was staring. *Who was that?* Max hadn't seen Helen, but when he looked up, she waved cheerily. Max approached looking a little sheepish.

'Jared. Helen,' he said casually.

'Max,' said Helen, and realising that he was not going to be introducing his date, held out her hand. 'We haven't met,' she said. 'Helen Shaw and this is Max's brother, Jared.'

'Hello, Shona,' Jared said, making Helen feel silly.

'Oh,' Helen said, 'so it's just us who haven't met.'

'Shona Montgomery,' the woman said. Having shaken Helen's hand, she slipped it into Max's. 'Wasn't that a lovely ceremony?'

'Wonderful,' replied Helen. 'And what a setting!'

The brothers nodded, but contributed nothing.

The conversation was clearly doomed unless somebody found something to say. But Helen was at a loss. She'd had no idea Max was seeing somebody. She found that her cheeks were beginning to redden and she hoped no one had noticed.

'So, Shona,' Jared said after an uncomfortable minute. 'Any news on the venue for the gala dinner?' He turned to Helen. 'Shona is an events manager. She's organising this year's Bastille Day festivities.'

Shona smiled, and Helen noticed her perfect white teeth. She may not have been beautiful in the conventional sense of the word, but she was arresting. And that wasn't just because of her height or hair colour – she had stunning blue eyes framed by strikingly long lashes, and curves in all the right places.

'Well, I had the idea to transform a warehouse,' Shona said. 'It's a lot more effort than simply hiring out a restaurant, but I have a great team, and I think we can create just the right mood. Bonfire outside. Mushroom heaters. Candelabras. We'll choose wine from different estates for different courses. Max even suggested we do a Chinese auction to raise money for the Franschhoek Literacy Fund.'

'Sounds fabulous,' said Helen.

'Really?' said Shona, with a wide, disarming grin. 'Then I'll have to get you on my side to convince these boys to let us use Bourgogne. They seem a little reluctant ...'

'Where were you thinking?' Helen asked.

'The warehouse where the empty bottles are. We'll have to store them elsewhere for a few days, but I'm thinking of hiring a few shipping crates.'

Helen realised the dilemma immediately: to the De Villiers brothers, Bourgogne was sacred ground. There was no way either of them would want strangers treading over their private spaces, especially given Jared's recent upset. Pieter and Magda, however, might be more accommodating: they'd been talking just the other day about a warehouse near their vineyards that they barely used because it needed a little TLC. If the event was held there, Shona's team might be prepared to fix it up as part of the venue hire fee.

'You know,' Helen said. 'I think I have a better idea than Bourgogne. Have you met the Blignauts from Le Cadeau?'

Shona shook her head.

'They're here and at the wedding I'll introduce you when I see them. I think they might have just the right place for your dinner. The parking is better, and I know they're open to a few suggestions about what to do there.'

The sun was beginning to set and as the couples circulated between other wedding guests, Helen found herself alone with Max.

'Good save,' he said. 'About the warehouse, I mean. I tried to tell her, but I couldn't think of anywhere else to suggest.'

'No problem,' Helen said, looking towards the rose-and-lilac-tinted sky. 'Were you planning to keep her a secret indefinitely?'

'Shona?' Max asked.

'Yes, Shona.'

'The subject just never came up. It's only been a month. And what does it matter to you anyway?'

'*It* doesn't, but *you* do,' Helen said, realising she wasn't making all that much sense. 'I thought we were friends.'

'We are friends,' Max said, 'but that's all we are. Shona is a

Love and Wine

sweet girl. She's bright, ambitious, fun to be around.'

'And I'm not?'

'What is it with you, Helen? This isn't about you. Last time I looked, you chose Jared. I can't put my life on hold waiting for you to change your mind. And I've never met a woman who changes her mind about my brother, even after he's broken up with her.'

'Is that what's going to happen?'

'Did I say that? I don't think I did.' Max frowned.

'So, what about Jared and Shona?' It was an unnecessary stab at Max's pride, and Helen couldn't understand why she'd spoken. Or how she knew. Except that she just did.

He blanched. 'So you know about that? God only knows why Jared would tell you something like that, except to lay claim yet again to something that might just for a change be mine. It was one night, three years ago. It didn't mean anything to either of them.'

'Or so they say,' muttered Helen, as she looked at Jared and Shona. Though they weren't touching, their body language showed an intimacy that made her stomach twist. Jared said something, and Shona giggled.

'God Helen, if you trust Jared so little, why the hell are you with him? We're at a *party*. A *celebration*. Why don't you just *relax* and *celebrate*?' Helen felt tears beginning to well. *What was going on with her?* Max touched her shoulder, and looked into her eyes. 'Not every guy you meet is going to be George,' he said.

'This isn't about George,' she sniffed as she felt Max's hand. Familiar. Reassuring.

'Then what?'

'I don't know. I just don't know.' She sniffed, suddenly aware of the mascara she'd so carefully applied that morning. 'So are you happy, Max de Villiers?'

'I'd be happier if you were happy,' Max said, 'but on the whole, I am. With Shona in my life you're off the hook. No more worries about Max's hurt feelings, okay?'

189

CHAPTER TWENTY-TWO

nd perhaps it was easier.

Driving into Bourgogne, Helen didn't have to worry about whether Max would be hurt by her and Jared's walks into the vineyard. They didn't have to invite him to lunch unless they wanted his company, which they often did – because since she'd got to know Shona, Helen had found that she rather liked her. Shona was warm, straight-talking and bubbly. Shona looked at Max the way, Helen realised, he ought to be looked at. It was in some way a restoration of his power, and she noticed how his confidence began to build.

She wished sometimes that it was she who was responsible for that.

'That colour suits you,' Helen said, as Max opened the front door wearing a new T-shirt.

'Do you think so? Shona bought this for me.'

'Good taste,' smiled Helen. 'You really are looking wonderful, Max.'

'Isn't he just?' asked Shona, coming round the corner as she slipped her arm around Max's waist. 'Good you're here, Helen. I wanted to show you some of the designs; Max was positive you'd be able to tell me whether I'm on the right track or not.'

It wasn't long before Shona and Helen were seeing quite a lot of each other. Shortly after the wedding, Helen took Shona round to the Blignauts. Convincing them to host the gala dinner was a cinch: Shona's ideas were so innovative that Pieter and Magda accepted on the spot. By the time Shona was finished with the warehouse, they'd be able to hire it out again for other functions, so there was really very little for them to lose.

As Shona climbed back into Helen's car, she was excited.

'I didn't even know Le Cadeau existed until you suggested it!' she said. 'And it couldn't be more perfect.'

'I'm so glad it's worked out,' Helen said. 'Max introduced me to the Blignauts when I was working with him on the book. I've kind of developed my own friendship with them. There's not a lot not to like.'

'I know what you mean,' Shona replied, her eyes shining in a way that suggested she might be referring to someone else.

'You're seeing a lot of each other, you and Max' Helen commented as she drove back onto the main road. She was prying, she knew, but somehow she couldn't quite get used to the idea of Max with someone.

'Not as much as I'd like, actually,' Shona replied candidly. 'He's holding back a bit, but we've only been together a few weeks. That's only natural, isn't it?'

'Sure,' Helen said, wondering if that were true.

'It's all about playing games, isn't it, Helen?'

'What do you mean?'

'This part of a relationship: keeping the mystery alive, not sounding too desperate and never being instantly available. Sometimes I wish we could just dispense with all of that. To be able to say: "I like you a lot, do you feel the same way?" without all the rigmarole that goes with it.'

'But isn't that supposed to be the fun part? The guessing?' Helen asked. 'I'm sure Max will tell you in his own time. You just have to build up to it.'

'I can only hope. I wonder sometimes if he's upset about what happened between me and Jared. It doesn't bother *you*, does it?'

Helen looked across at Shona, wondering how she could be so guileless. Of course she wasn't happy about it. It wasn't that she was jealous, especially when she could see that Jared was the last person on Shona's mind. It's just that she didn't really want to reminded about *any* ex-lover of Jared's.

'I'd be a fool to think a man like Jared wouldn't have a past ... I just don't like to think about it too much.'

Shona grew silent. 'I probably made a mistake telling Max about us,' she said. 'It's just that I didn't want him finding out some other way.'

'From Jared, you mean?' Helen said.

'Well, you know how competitive those brothers are.'

Even Helen wasn't naïve enough to think that there wouldn't be a bit of one-upmanship between Jared and Max. But she didn't know Shona and Max's relationship well enough to say whether this was what was holding Max back either. The whole conversation was making Helen uncomfortable anyway, so she changed the subject.

'Jared says I should do an evening event at the gallery,' she said. 'A belated launch of sorts. What do you think?'

'Publicity is always good,' Shona mused. 'Especially if Cape Town's Who's Who are there.'

'I wouldn't know the Who's Who if I fell over them!' Helen grinned.

'That's because you're already in the right crowd. Anyone from around here would tell you that the De Villiers brothers are like Franschhoek royalty.'

'You aren't being serious?' Helen said. 'Thank God I didn't know that or I would have been completely intimidated.'

'How do you think I felt until I got to know Max better?' Shona said, 'I should be able to rustle up a few other celebs if you need me to. No harm in getting some of your work in the papers, especially if you're mostly relying on walk-ins at the moment.'

♥

A few weeks later, and with Shona's input, Helen had found the gallery's launch preparations had got completely out of hand. Was a marquee in the parking lot really necessary, and did they *have* to hire a string quartet when a lone guitarist would have done equally well? The more lavish the launch became, the more nervous she was. Who was going to pay for the oysters, the ice sculpture and the goodie bags? And what about the VIP transport and the mixologist?

'But why can't we just have wine?' Helen asked. 'We're in one of the most famous wine-growing regions in the Southern Hemisphere!'

'It's a party, Helen,' Shona said firmly. 'You want to draw the right crowd, don't you?'

Helen looked across at Jared, who surprised her by nodding. 'It's about appealing to every taste,' he said.

'Well, this isn't appealing to my bank balance,' Helen retorted.

But Jared chipped in: 'I'm happy to sponsor this one. My treat. Come on, Helen. It'll be fun!'

Helen remembered Max's head in his hands as he studied the bank statements.

'Maybe we should ask Max what he thinks,' she said, stalling, but Jared lifted her up and swung her around, kissing her firmly.

'I don't care what Max thinks. Nothing is too much for my girl,' he said. 'Relax and let me take care of this.'

'But –'

'But nothing. Let me spoil you,' said Jared, nuzzling against her. 'We're going to launch your gallery so that everyone will know who you are. I mean look at this stuff!' He threw open his arms to encompass the paintings. 'These are incredible! You just need a platform!'

'You think so?' she said, a little doubtfully.

'See, you don't even believe in *yourself* like you should. Well, I'll believe enough for both of us. How does that sound?'

And she had to admit, that did sound nice.

♥

Since Jared was feeling his old self, their social life had kicked into gear in a big way. It wasn't just the launch party, for which Jared was showing more enthusiasm than she was, there were invitations to the beach, to nearby vineyards, for picnics, birthdays, a few exhibitions and charity events.

'They always ask Jared,' Max grumbled.

'To attend?' Helen asked, an amused smiled crossing her face.

'No, for prizes. They know they can twist his rubber arm. Sometimes I'm surprised we have any wine left!'

'I've never thought that generosity could be a vice,' Helen said.

'It's only a vice when you don't necessarily have the resources to back it up. When Jared's like this, he'll give the skin off his own back. Thank God Heinrich hasn't got Jared hooked on poker – he'd probably wager Bourgogne on a bet.'

Max's serious face made Helen laugh.

'You think I'm joking?' he said.

Helen tried to curtail Jared's spending after that, but Max was totally right: Jared could not be held back. And nobody, not even Helen, could quite help but be swept up in his plans: *I think we should have a potjiekos cook-off on the beach at midnight;* or *Let's hire out the aquarium for a private dinner party.* One night he donned a Superman outfit and spent the evening pretending to save the world. He hurt his arm jumping from a tree but continued his mission regardless. Once he leant out the car window and handed a beggar at the stop street his entire wallet, forgetting about his credit and garage cards, which Helen then spent the rest of the afternoon trying to cancel.

He bestowed his largesse on everyone and anyone, and Heinrich took full advantage, with big nights out once or twice a week, plying Jared with shooters and down-downs that Helen thought they should have outgrown. She grew accustomed to being the unwilling designated driver. It was either that or wind her way home with Jared at the wheel, his right arm balanced over the open window, his foot flat on the accelerator and his left hand trying to catch a feel of her inner thigh.

And Jared didn't handle his hangovers well. By the next Helen morning, Jared's good mood would have dissipated as the alcohol evaporated from his pores.

Christ Helen, I thought I told you I don't eat this brand of cornflakes; it's like talking to a brick wall or *What's the point in getting up? Life's a big lie and then you die.*

On these days, the two Jareds were distinctive: aggressive, cold and insulting, or melancholic and clingy. She didn't really know how to handle either of them, and hated herself for wishing him back with Prudie and Max, who did.

'Nobody's perfect,' she tried to explain to Madeleine on the phone.

'Helen ...' Madeleine's voice expressed the caution she evidently felt.

'It isn't really him. Half the time he doesn't even remember what he's said.'

'That doesn't mean he hasn't said it. Or that *you'll* just forget.'

'I know.'

'And you must be on tenterhooks. How do you know what to expect from him?'

'I don't,' Helen said. 'But he needs me, and we care for each other. I'll just have to work it out. He is so much better when he takes his meds. I have to keep at him though. Anyway, he apologised this morning. With a bunch of roses ... he doesn't like it when he gets that way either.'

Sometimes Jared's moods lasted a few hours, sometimes a few days. Helen didn't think the drinking helped, and she said so.

'Please, Jared, just for tonight. Let's take it easy, okay?'

But the moment Jared and the group were in full swing, temporary resolutions were forgotten. It hurt her but there was nothing she could do about it.

CHAPTER TWENTY-THREE

A nother night at Heinrich's, and it wasn't one drink, or two, or three. Helen lost count, and by midnight everybody else in the room was rocking to Nickelback played at extreme volumes, despite several complaints from the neighbours.

Helen had tried to bend and buckle to Jared's enthusiastic dance moves, but she couldn't relax. Eventually Jared let her go, grabbed the hand of one of Heinrich's blonde bombshells and gyrated against her in a cringe-worthy display.

Without another word, Helen picked up her keys from the dining-room table, retrieved her handbag, and headed to her car. She drove along the quiet Franschhoek roads, knowing something had to change. *If you're more unhappy than you're happy ...*

Some people brought out the worst in Jared. People like Heinrich, with his broad rugby shoulders, rounded beer-belly, acerbic wit and chauvinism – Jared had some strange attachment to him that was beyond her comprehension.

Well, she thought, he could keep Heinrich, but she wasn't sure what she was going to do now. Break up with Jared? Read him the riot act? Give him another chance? Her inability to decide even that made one thing clear: she cared about Jared more than she'd thought she'd originally let herself. Helen looked towards one of the B&B's lit up with flickering lanterns outside. The little guesthouse looked so warm and inviting; not like her apartment with second-hand everything, and many recent unhappy memories.

Despite her hesitation, her car glided towards Bourgogne. She knew she should turn around; Max didn't need her sobbing on his shoulder at one in the morning. And what if Shona was there?

But she couldn't stop herself.

♥

The guard at the gate waved her through. By the time she pulled up outside the main house, a light was on in Max's room, and he was standing on the porch in a pair of sleep shorts and a T-shirt.

He didn't say much when she slammed her car door, just walked down the stairs to meet her, hugged her. His body was solid. Familiar. A protective wall around her.

And though she let herself cry, this was not the gut-wrenching release of pain that she'd thought she needed. Just being here with Max seemed to wipe that away.

'I'm here,' Max said. 'I'm always here.'

Helen leant in.

'Let's go get you some coffee,' he said.

'Shona?' Helen asked, looking towards Max's bedroom.

'She isn't here tonight,' Max told her. 'Come inside, and you can tell me all about it.'

They sat in the lounge. Helen felt her exhaustion like the pull of gravity, and curled her feet up next to her on the couch. Her head slid down to rest on a cushion, and Max leant over to stroke her hair.

'Is it normal to feel like this?' Helen said. 'I know he's sick, but in some way I felt as though once I knew, I'd be able to help him.'

'Jared doesn't want to be rescued,' Max said.

'Is that what I'm trying to do?'

'It's what everybody tries to do at some point, Helen, even

me. Especially with someone like Jared.'

'He's behaving like a jerk.'

'He *is* a jerk a lot of the time. Think of my life as an older brother, living in my younger brother's shadow. My parents tip-toeing around him. He has this charisma ... well, all I can say is that sometimes it's been hard. It *is* hard.'

Helen looked up at Max. 'But you always seem so at peace, so relaxed about it.'

'I'm not always ... I mean, when I see – ' Max was silent for a moment. 'People *choose* him.'

Helen opened her mouth to speak, but Max interrupted her.

'I don't blame them, necessarily. I don't. I've chosen him too, despite everything. I love him, *but*. That's how I've always thought about it: I love him, *but*.'

♥

She must have talked herself into a doze, because she woke up still on the couch, a dim morning light seeping in through the heavy curtains, her body stiff and cold.

She looked over to Max, who was awake but sitting quietly. He smiled at her.

'Okay?' he asked.

'I've kept you awake all night.'

'It doesn't matter. That's what friends are for, right? Come, let's have some breakfast.'

Minutes later, Helen was sitting at the kitchen table warming her fingers around a cup of coffee. Bacon sizzled noisily, and even with her anxious stomach she found it smelt delicious. Soon there were fried tomatoes, bananas, eggs. Some slices of wholewheat toast. She tried to think if Jared had *ever* cooked her anything ... but of course he hadn't.

Max piled up her plate, pushing some butter and jam towards her.

'Magda's apricot jam,' he said. 'You can't beat it.'

They ate silently, listening to the sounds of the waking

morning. They could hear Prudie singing, the geyser hammering as she turned on a hot tap. The wheels of Simon's wheelbarrow squeaking with each rotation as he walked towards the warehouse. A horse neighed softly.

'We should go riding again,' Max said. 'Like we used to. Star and Pinotage miss you.'

Helen looked down at the dress she'd put on for Jared the previous night: a red strapless number that was short enough to be risqué. Her expression was doubtful.

'Not today, obviously,' Max said. 'Shona's coming round, and she doesn't like horses. Actually, that's a bit of an understatement. She's terrified of them.'

Helen leant forward. She felt listless, heavy. When Prudie pushed the kitchen door open with her hip, her dark eyes took them both in.

Prudence nodded at her, then turned to Max. 'Good morning Mister Max. Should I make Mister Jared some coffee?'

Subtlety, Helen realised, was not Prudence's strong point.

'Thanks, Prudie, but no,' Max said.

Prudence frowned, then picked up a washing basket and walked down towards Max's bathroom to collect his dirty clothes. Her shoes dragged against the wooden floors, making dull scuffing noises.

'I'm just never going to make her good books, am I?' Helen asked.

Max grinned. 'Nobody's perfect.'

♥

By the time Helen got back to her apartment it was still early – just after seven.

She'd passed a few cars on the way back from Bourgogne, but Franschhoek was mostly still asleep. Her temples throbbed and she rubbed her neck. As she parked her car under the carport, she caught a glimpse of herself in her side mirror. She looked haggard, with grey smudges under her eyes, her hair frizzed into a weird halo. She locked the Opel, and walked to the gallery entrance.

Sitting on the front steps, his back and head resting against the front door, was Jared.

'Where the hell have you been?' he asked by way of greeting.

Helen looked at him, wondering how she could sidestep him to get inside. The last thing she needed right now was a confrontation.

'Out,' she said shortly.

'I've been here since five. I left my keys at Heinrich's place.'

Helen juggled her own keys in the lock, turning the handle. 'You shouldn't have been driving, Jared. And you could have phoned.'

'Left my phone there too.'

Helen shoved the door open. It swung quickly, bashing against the wall inside. She looked across at Jared, his pitiful look irritating more than enticing her.

'Maybe you two should move in together,' she suggested cattily. 'Now that half your belongings are there anyway ...'

Jared followed Helen in. 'So I messed up, Helen. Haven't you ever done that?'

Helen stopped momentarily. 'Where's your dancing partner, Jared? Did she dump you once you'd finished having sex on the dance floor?'

'Oh please. I wouldn't have banged Heinrich's bird. What do you take me for?'

Helen moved to the back of the room, opening the back blinds and turning on the aircon. She mulled what Jared had just said. *Heinrich's bird.* Once again it had nothing to do with his feelings for Helen. It was much more about his love affair with Heinrich Vermeulen.

'Actually, right now,' Helen said. 'I take you for a spineless prat. You're incapable of refusing a drink, and you're so self-obsessed that I think you've forgotten it takes two to make a relationship. And I don't mean you and Heinrich. I've done disappointment and esteem-shredding, Jared. And I'm not going down that road again.'

Jared looked at her with those emerald eyes. 'For Christ's sake, Helen. I said I was sorry.'

'Actually, I don't think you did.'

'Well, I *am* sorry. It all got out of hand last night, but I did leave and I've been waiting here for hours! But where were you, Helen? I could ask you that.' Jared moved closer to Helen, trying to take her hands into his.

'I was trying to clear my head, deciding what to do with my life,' Helen replied. 'That doesn't happen in a few short minutes.'

She pulled her hands away roughly, but he caught them a second time, locking her in.

'I can be better,' he said. 'You're the first person in my life who's made me feel that way. I love you, Helen and I'm sorry.'

Helen studied Jared, not saying anything.

'Look, I know Heinrich can be a bit of a tosser sometimes, but he's my mate. He's stuck by me when others haven't.'

'You mean like last month when you were too ill to get out of bed?'

'He doesn't know how to handle me when I'm like that.'

'And I do?'

'I don't have to see him as often, Helen. If that's what it takes …' Jared laced his fingers between hers.

Helen studied his face, trying to be objective. 'I'm not going to bar you from your friends, Jared. But you really upset me sometimes. And I'm not just talking about last night.'

'Do you want me to leave?' Jared asked pitifully.

'No,' she said suddenly. 'I don't actually want that. I want to fall asleep in your arms and see how we feel when we wake up.'

Jared smiled, and that familiar twisting sensation travelled through Helen's core.

'No funny business,' Helen said, trying to sound firm.

'Right,' Jared said, grinning naughtily. 'Nothing like that.'

♥

Things did get better. Several invitations to poker night were turned down, as were dinner with the group and a food-and-wine festival in Wellington in which Susana was involved,. Jared made an effort to spend time alone with Helen: they sat together on the couch in her apartment watching *American Idol* and old movies that they'd both already seen. *Shawshank Redemption. Fried Green Tomatoes. Dirty Dancing.* They played chess, though neither had the strategic stamina to see a game through. Sometimes Helen painted while Jared sprawled on her bed watching cricket, the commentary turned down low. They took walks in the vineyard, went on a bread-baking course (kitke, foccaccia, ciabatta, health loaf) and stopped in at art galleries in neighbouring towns where Jared would be instantly recognised and welcomed in.

Helen looked at the styles of more prominent or prolific local painters. Many came from Zimbabwe, the works inexpensive as the refugee artists tried to re-establish themselves. She liked the ochre and orange ethnic tones, but she didn't like the treatments; she enjoyed the stylised figures, but wasn't keen on the parity of detail. Landscapes depicting the Karoo, which Jared told her was a desert region of the Eastern Cape, sent shivers down her spine. The isolation. The space. She wondered what it felt like to paint under a sky that big.

'I'd like to go there sometime,' she voiced one afternoon.

'I'll take you,' Jared said. 'A little break before the launch. It'll be good to have a break, won't it, tiger?'

And so they went to stay on an ostrich farm near Cradock, and watched the enormous birds poke their heads through the fence. Once or twice Jared caught an extended beak with his hands. The ostrich would hold still in shock or surprise, retreating the moment he let go. Helen laughed when Jared caught the same bird a minute or two later, and it looked equally confused.

'Their brains are tiny – they can't remember what happened a moment ago.'

'Perhaps a short-term memory like that could be a good thing,' Helen commented. 'You wouldn't remember being sad.'

'But you're not sad are you, Helen?'

'No,' she said, taking his arm and smiling. 'I'm definitely not.'

Later, Jared proposed taking old tyre tubes to glide down the rapids of the Fish River. The farmer dropped them off in a large truck, helping them offload the wieldy rubber doughnuts on the riverbank.

'I'll meet you downstream,' he said.

'Are you sure about this?' Helen asked doubtfully as she eyed the gushing waters. 'There aren't any crocodiles in there?'

'Live on the edge, Helen,' Jared said. 'This will be a rush, I promise you.'

'But what happens if –'

'Walk on the wild side!' Jared exclaimed, as he pushed himself into the churning waters. Helen watched him lie back, his face a picture of ecstasy. 'Yee-haaaaaaaaaaaaaaaaaa! Get in before you get left behind!'

And with that, Helen pushed herself off the bank, kicking from the side with her soggy shoes. She felt a gentle, then a firmer tug underneath the tube as water swirled under her, and then she was barrelling forward, surrounded by froth and raging liquid. Up ahead, Jared had grabbed onto the branches of a dipping tree, waiting, and as she hurtled forward, he leant towards her with his free hand.

Linked together, the tubes floated in tandem down the river.

Helen looked at Jared's blissful expression, recognising what an unforgettable experience this was. There was nobody else about, the sun beat down, and she could hear the faint mooing of grazing cattle. At some point a small antelope peeped through the trees and approached the water's edge to drink. The pace of the river was both furious and leisurely: over the rapids, they had to focus on navigating between rocks and tufted islands, but where the water was deeper, they could drift on their backs, studying the building cloud formations above them. When they reached the weir, the farmer was waiting, chewing on a long piece of grass; Helen couldn't believe their journey was already over. Jared shoved Helen's tube towards the edge as the farmer moved in close to catch her. From the tube, Helen saw his knee-length socks were scabbed with burrs and soaked through.

'*Goed?*' the farmer said, and Helen beamed. She wanted to go straight back and do it again.

Jared manoeuvred himself to the riverbank and jumped off where he could stand.

'No one,' she said, 'will believe me if I told them how amazing that was!'

Jared grinned and kissed her. 'Stick with me, babe. I'll take you places you haven't even dreamt of.'

CHAPTER TWENTY-FOUR

n the morning of Helen's launch party, a sleeping Jared murmured softly, then rolled over onto his side, pulling the blankets around him in a tight cocoon. By ten o'clock he still hadn't moved, not even with the metallic clank of poles being hammered together as the marquee appeared on the parking lot. Nor did he wake with the sounds of the caterers setting up in the courtyard outside Helen's back door, nor as cars and vans negotiated the interruption to normal traffic flow with hooting and cursing. At eleven fifteen, the florist knocked over a vase, which shattered noisily.

Helen sauntered upstairs, apparently unconcerned, but she was beginning to wonder if Jared was actually still alive. Once she'd confirmed he was breathing, she collected a mop, bringing it down to the florist, who swabbed the laminate flooring, apologising over and over again.

Max arrived at midday, his Land Cruiser loaded with boxes of wine and crates of glasses from the tasting room.

'Where's that brother of mine?' Max huffed as he carried the first box out the vehicle. 'I've been calling him since eight.'

Helen rushed out to help him, unused to the tension in his voice. 'He's asleep,' she said.

'Now?' Max said, his morning's activities etched clearly in his armpits. Then the realisation hit. 'Oh shit. You've got to be kidding me.'

Helen shrugged. 'That's why I didn't wake him. I thought if he managed to roll out of bed on his own, he might be the better for it.'

'Please tell me it's just a hangover, Helen.'

Helen smiled, walking back with Max to the Land Cruiser. 'It's just a hangover, Max.'

'You don't lie at all well,' said Max grimly.

Jared still hadn't appeared by the time they were finished offloading the boxes.

'Do you want me to go and check on him?' Max asked.

'No,' Helen replied. 'It'll be fine.' But Helen's hands twisted together as she said goodbye to Max and she had to admit to feeling troubled. This was supposed to be her night, and she didn't want to worry about Jared right now. But she *did* worry about him; she couldn't help it. How had he managed to kick the meds *again*?

Helen walked into her apartment, wondering if she should bring him something to drink or eat. When she poked her head round the bedroom door, it was to find Jared sitting on the edge of her bed. He was naked and leaning heavily into his palms. When he lifted his head, his eyes were wet. He wiped them roughly, then attempted a smile.

'Big day, Helen Shaw. Hope I haven't missed anything,' he said.

'Not much,' Helen said. 'Just a bit of set-up. Shona's downstairs directing traffic. Are you okay?'

Jared stood up, his arrogant stride replaced by a cowed stance. 'Never better. I think I'll need to pop back to Bourgogne quickly though. Is Big Brother Max on the warpath?'

'He's been and gone.'

Jared's eyes betrayed his surprise. 'Well, well,' he said. 'Seems I got off lightly this time. I'll just go home for some clothes and stuff when I'm done. Anything we've forgotten?'

'I don't think so,' Helen replied.

Jared turned to look at her. 'Tonight is going to be great, just you wait,' he said, then closed the bathroom door behind him.

♥

Helen was dressed simply in a silver shift dress accessorised by the necklace Jared had given her for Christmas. She was wearing silver slingbacks with three-inch heels, and surprisingly for someone more comfortable in low pumps, she was relieved to be wearing them: they gave her height, and, she hoped, presence.

But despite her outward appearance as she glided around the gallery amongst the guests, Helen could barely stop herself from shaking. She missed Madeleine. Even June, who she hadn't seen in ages. In fact, she barely knew anybody in the room, though she could tell from the dripping diamonds and lavish outfits that her launch had become something of *the* place to be seen.

And that was mostly due to Shona, who just then stood at the entrance ushering people in, welcoming them with hugs and air kisses. Max was positioned slightly behind her. He looked at Helen, and offered a bemused smile; he looked as out of place as Helen felt. He pulled at his collar, clearly bothered by it. And still guests streamed in, milling between canapé-laden waiters. In the corner of the gallery a barman mixed a variety of cocktails, placing them in colour-coded rows in front of him.

The atmosphere was both sophisticated and celebratory, but Helen wondered if people would even notice her paintings. They certainly didn't seem to be getting much attention. Jared, however, was making headway in that department– she could see him talking closely to a vaguely familiar politician. Jared was pointing out the painting Helen had done of Christine Blignaut. The woman nodded appreciatively, and then indicated a Karoo landscape Helen had completed only days before. She seemed to like it. Thank God.

Jared took the woman's arm, heading in Helen's direction. Helen breathed slowly in and out, counted to ten.

'Helen Shaw,' Jared said, 'I'd like you to meet Nomvula Bala. She grew up in Somerset East, not too far from Cradock.'

'Oh,' said Helen. 'Then the Karoo landscape will be familiar to you.'

'You've really captured the Eastern Cape sky,' Nomvula replied, glancing back at Helen's painting.

Helen smiled. 'The sky was what drew me there in the first place. It's just not what I'm used to. Where I come from –'

'And where is that?'

They talked comfortably as Jared extricated himself, moving towards a man in a suit that fitted a little too snugly around the middle, and with whom he was soon involved in deep discussion about her kite-surfing frieze.

As the evening wore on, red 'sold' stickers started appearing under her paintings, and it seemed to Helen that her sense of foreboding had not been well founded. A few journalists had cornered her: *What inspired you with 'Orchard sketching'? Do you love animals? You seem to have a sympathy for portraying older faces – is there a reason for that? What brought you to South Africa? How long will you be staying? What sort of reaction have you had to your earlier work? Your response to the African landscape seems very intense ...* Helen tried to answer as best she could, often surprised by the media's perceptiveness: *The Scarborough paintings seem awfully melancholic; is there a reason for that?* Looking at those seascapes, she realised this particular reporter was completely right. Those paintings were sad, with grey skies hanging like heavy-bellied beasts over a turgid and churned-up ocean, the sand from the beach gusting and scattered.

Helen looked for Jared. His arm was around Magda, who was beaming as he led her away from Christine's portrait to the other side of the room. Helen had wondered about including that painting, but Max had convinced her. *It would be like leaving the chorus out of a song,* he'd said. *It just wouldn't be the same. Magda and Pieter will understand.*

Now, Pieter elbowed his way to Helen, his face set in a warm smile.

'You've outdone yourself, Helen,' he said.

'Yes, it's quite a party,' Helen replied.

'Oh, I was talking about the paintings. I've never been one for these sorts of occasions. I'm a farm boy, remember?'

'I still wish you'd let me give you that portrait,' Helen said softly.

'What for? I get to look at these wrinkles every day of my life,' he chuckled. 'And I'm not going to be here forever.'

'Don't say that.'

'Just look at that painting – you'd be blind not to see it. And because I'm an old man, I'm not very good at watching what I say ...'

'You're not going to ask about Jared, are you?' Helen said, her heart sinking.

'He's not well, Helen. I worry about you. And Max, he –'

'Max is dating Shona. You know, that tall redhead over there?' Helen tried to point without making it obvious.

'Then why, my dear, is he always looking at you?'

'Who's looking at you?' Jared swept in, putting his arm around Helen.

'You!' Helen smiled. 'I didn't realise you were an art expert.'

'Talk the talk, tiger,' Jared said. 'You're going to be sold out any minute. Oh, hang on, I'm just going to catch Alessandra before she leaves ...'

Jared quickly re-entered the crowd, the morning's sluggishness overcome, Helen believed, by sheer force of will. And then, as she lifted her eyes, she saw Max. He was sipping a glass of red wine, his gaze on her. He smiled, lifting his glass.

'Don't,' Helen said quietly to Pieter, whose expression had turned almost smug. 'It's just too complicated.'

And Pieter touched her arm. 'My dear, that's what makes life so exciting.'

'Jared's exciting,' Helen said softly.

'That,' Pieter said, 'I don't doubt for a second.'

♥

A week passed, two, with Jared being alternatively euphoric and morose. He stayed over, or he didn't. He called her all day, or he didn't get in touch at all. He arrived at the flat with flowers, or pitched up after ten looking jittery, then paced round the apartment as though high, poking through her drawers and cupboards, muttering to himself.

When she asked him about it, he looked at her as though *she* was crazy.

'Why are you always getting at me, Helen? What's really the problem?'

'I just don't understand what you're looking for,' Helen said.

'Why?' Jared replied. 'Do you have something you don't want me to see?'

One night he called up at her from the street to put on something sexy. 'We're going dancing,' he said matter-of-factly.

'It's eleven o'clock,' Helen tried to tell him, and all he did was laugh, his animation contagious.

'Then don't you think we'd better hurry?'

They returned at close to four, but rather than collapsing into bed, their bodies tingling for contact, Helen found herself alone.

'Duty calls,' Jared said as he left. 'I have to check the tanks.'

'For goodness sake, Jared, don't you need some rest?'

And Jared pulled her to him, kissing her one last delicious time, before picking up his keys. 'No time, Helen. I'll sleep when I'm dead.'

Helen tried not to focus too much on predicting Jared's behaviour; he wasn't like George. Before Rose, George's schedule had been so regular she could have set her watch by it. In retrospect she wondered how she hadn't noticed then that something, actually everything, had changed. Helen had been so obsessed by the baby-making that her husband had become a means to an end. She recognised that now, and perhaps that was progress.

She also recognised that there was an intensity to her relationship with Jared that was fired up by the sheer lack of domesticity. No routine. And that suited her, surely, she mused – because what was the point of building a home if you couldn't produce a family to put in it?

And did thinking that mean she had accepted her infertility?

She wasn't really sure. But she didn't feel the old bitterness in this new life she had made for herself. And maybe Max had been right that one day, when the time was right, there would be other options ... In the meantime, she had Jared who was kid enough for both of them.

♥

The first night that Jared didn't call or visit, she wasn't too concerned. In her bathrobe and slippers, she lay on the couch watching BBC Prime and sipping a glass of red. When she turned off the telly, she relished the silence of the empty room, settling into bed with a Douglas Kennedy she hadn't had time yet to read. After waking the next morning, she took a long soak with bubbles, then fixed herself a cheese-and-tomato omelette for breakfast. By lunch, she'd left Jared two messages, but he hadn't called back.

Night two and no Jared. This time she Skyped her Uncle Alec, who she hadn't spoken to in a while. And then Olivia. And then her mother. She kept the phone line free for Jared to call. He didn't. Helen tried to leave another message on his cell phone, but his voicemail was full. She slept that night, but she didn't sleep well. *Where was he?* And at seven the next morning, feeling distinctly unsettled, she climbed into her car and hurried to Bourgogne.

Hearing the Opel screech to a halt, Max stepped outside.

'Hey,' Helen said. 'Just thought I'd pop in.'

'Ah,' said Max, 'I was beginning to think you'd hijacked Jared permanently.'

Helen felt herself grow cold. 'What do you mean? I thought he was here. I haven't heard from him for a few days ...'

Concern flicked across Max's face. 'Have you called him?'

'A few times, Max. I've left messages, but I can't leave any more – it doesn't seem like he's picked them up for a day or so.'

Max turned towards the house. 'I think you'd better come in.'

In Jared's bedroom, his bed was made up and unruffled, the duvet's blue-and-white stripes exactly straight. His bedside table was clear except for a *Car* magazine still in its plastic wrapper and a well-thumbed copy of that South African wine book he liked. Jared's wardrobes were closed, the curtains and two windows ajar. The room smelt strongly of wood polish, but not really of Jared. Helen noticed something next to the bed. She bent down, extracting Jared's mobile phone. She picked it up. It was off. Deliberately so or the battery had run out.

'Well, that explains one thing,' she said.

Max opened the larger of Jared's wardrobes. It was really difficult to tell if anything was missing, the neat piles of clothing contradicting Jared's usual impetuousness. The other cupboard was a little less sterile. It was loaded with old tennis racquets, a cricket bat and a few suits lined up over them on a rail. On a shelf above, were several suitcases, one of which Helen recognised from fetching Jared from the airport. Yet to the left was a clear gap, as obvious as a missing tooth. Helen pointed at it.

'What's gone from there?' she asked.

Max frowned, trying to remember. 'God, I wish I knew. I don't come much in this room, but that's a good sign isn't it? That *something* isn't here.'

Helen moved to the first wardrobe, trying to run through some of Jared's clothes in her mind. She couldn't see his favourite pair of shorts, nor a blue T-shirt he often wore when it was really hot. Looking closely, she also couldn't find Jared's Hi-Tech walking boots and they certainly weren't in her apartment. They were so clunky, she tended to trip over them if they were around.

'His boots,' said Max, and Helen nodded. Max frowned, then turned swiftly. Helen followed him down the passage.

'Prudie!' he shouted. 'Prudence!'

After a moment, the old woman appeared dressed in her weekend best, a cerise hat pinned to her head at a jaunty angle.

'Did Jared tell you he was going anywhere on Thursday?' Max asked Prudence. 'The thing is, neither Helen nor I have seen him, and we're wondering –'

'He didn't say nothing to me,' Prudence said immediately.

Too fast, Helen thought. 'Did you see him leave, then?' Helen suggested.

Max sighed, looking at Prudence with a stern grimace. 'Prudie, if Jared is in trouble, we need to know,' he said.

'No trouble,' Prudence said. 'I saw him from the kitchen window. He was carrying a bag. Like a backpack. It was full. You could see how heavy it was. He waved at me.'

'Was he alone?' Helen asked Prudence.

Prudie bit her lip. 'I wasn't spying on him,' she said.

'Was he alone?' Max asked.

'I think so, but I couldn't see if there was someone else in his car,' Prudie said, then she shrugged. 'Anyway, he looked fine. He looked really happy.'

Which was more than Helen could say for herself. Right then, she wasn't happy at all.

♥

As soon as Prudence had departed, Helen had tried to go home too, but Max, seeing her face, had steadied her. He ushered her into the lounge, poured her a glass of Prudie's lemonade. It was sour and acidic at the same time, making her instantly nauseous.

'There'll be a simple explanation, Helen,' he said softly. 'Don't let your imagination get ahead of itself.'

He tried to keep her busy. Helen wasn't keen on the horse-riding trail he suggested, but she knew Max was right. There was nothing that she could do at the moment. She followed him reluctantly to the trail, her hands tight on the reins. Star whinnied, and Helen realised she was hurting her.

'Sorry girl,' Helen whispered against her ears.

Fully aware of Helen's tension, Max didn't wait for her. Pinotage was in full gallop, and Helen found herself trying to catch up, her muscles tense as she balanced herself, rising and falling into the saddle. And just as soon as she neared Max, he and Pinotage sprinted forward, drawing her and Star into a mad dash through the vineyards. When he finally stopped along a riverbank, Helen was breathing hard, sweat pouring down the length of her spine. She dismounted, letting Star lap thirstily from the water's edge.

'You didn't ride like that the first time you took me out,' Helen said, as she watched Max slip off his shoes and roll up his jeans to just under his knees, then wade into the water.

'I didn't know you could handle it.'

'And I can handle it now?'

Max tossed a stone in the river. It skipped once, then disappeared below, circles forming in the pebble's absence.

'Helen,' Max said. 'You can handle anything. You always have.'

'Has he done a disappearing act like this before?' Helen asked.

'Once or twice. He doesn't make a habit of it, if that's what you mean. But don't get yourself set on one conclusion. Jared's too complicated to be figured out *that* easily.'

'So what do you suggest?'

Max flicked an arc of droplets towards Helen. 'Take off your shoes, and come in with me. The water's glorious.'

♥

They arrived back at the stables at the same time as a car was drawing up outside the main house. Helen tensed, wondering if it was Jared. But even before the engine turned off, she knew it wasn't him. The arrival was too sedate, the car purring rather than roaring. Then she saw Shona striding towards them, her long legs even longer in her cut-off shorts.

Max separated himself from Helen, moving to kiss Shona.

'You been out already?' Shona said, as she put her arm around Max, then removed it just as quickly. 'You're all sweaty.'

'Riding,' Max said. 'Jared's missing, and Helen needed the distraction.'

'And now I need a shower,' Helen added. 'Will you call me, Max, if you hear from Jared?'

'Of course I will.'

She patted Max on the shoulder, keeping a respectful distance for Shona's benefit.

'You look after yourself, Helen,' Max said. 'And don't worry – he'll be back.'

CHAPTER TWENTY-FIVE

The three days that passed were as long as the ones Helen had endured during her IVF, when one embryo after the next died, and with them her hopes of having a child.

But this time she did not feel hopeless. She was angry. Worried. Troubled. Nervous. Tense. She framed conversations in her mind. Sometimes she was calm, discussing Jared's disappearance dispassionately. At other times, she imagined herself incensed, and her voice, no longer modulated and controlled, reaching fever pitch. At night she dreamt she had to go to the morgue to identify Jared's body. She'd never been to a morgue before, but in her dream he was stretched out on a gurney, a sheet over his inert form. When the mortician pulled it back, Jared looked afraid, his face a mesh of blood, his nose broken and unrecognisable.

Helen woke up sweating, unable to go back to sleep. Instead she switched on a light in the gallery and painted madly while still in her pyjamas – a sight for anyone passing in the street, but she was beyond caring what other people thought.

When the word got out about Jared, both Heinrich and Susana popped into the gallery to see her. Not on the same day or at the same time, but Helen could see they were concerned.

'Max said Jared's done this before,' Helen said.

'Jared's his own man,' Heinrich commented.

'I rather gathered from all the other *many many* times you mentioned it,' she snapped, then tried to smile as her eyes watered up. 'Oh God, I'm sorry. That was uncalled for. I'm just so worried.'

Heinrich patted her hand clumsily. 'I've checked the Cape Town flat, and I've been phoning around,' he said. 'Susana too. Nothing so far. But Jared's probably in the bundu somewhere, finding himself.'

'Right,' Helen said, nodding as if she had any idea of what he was talking about.

'Think about it. If Jared was anywhere in civilisation, someone would have picked up on it.'

♥

And then out of the blue, Jared reappeared.

It was near midnight when she heard the jangle of keys downstairs, and she started at the sound, clutching her ever-present mobile phone close to her.

'Helen?' Jared said. 'Helen, are you here?'

He was wearing a mud-splattered T-shirt, a pair of camo shorts, and his boots, which were caked in black sludge. Even from where she sat in the bed, she could see Jared's chin and neck was bristled like a wire brush. His hair was uncombed and he smelt of stale sweat and soggy clothes.

'Take those shoes off,' she said automatically.

Jared nodded, unlacing and kicking off his boots. 'You don't look pleased to see me,' he said absurdly.

'Absence makes the heart grow fonder?' Helen said.

'Something like that.'

Standing in her nightclothes, Helen felt extremely exposed. She walked to her bedroom door, pulling her gown off the hook. She wrapped it around her, as Jared stood there considering her.

'Where have you been?' she asked. 'You've been gone for five days and not one word.'

'I needed time out. Haven't you ever needed to get away, Helen?'

'Sure,' she said. 'That's why I came here to be mentally scarred by you.'

'That's a bit rough.'

'Right now, I'm feeling a bit rough. Go home, Jared. Clean yourself up and reassure your brother that you're okay. I'll see you in the morning.'

Of course, after he'd left, Helen couldn't sleep. She tossed and turned, running the conversation through in her mind. Had she been too harsh? What should she have said? How should she have reacted? She'd been as surprised as he had that her genuine concern of five days ago had turned into hostility. Disdain even. She hadn't even kissed him hello.

The truth was, now that he was back and the worry was over, she wasn't quite sure how she *should* feel about him. She thought about his eyes, his little-boy hurt ... Maybe she had been too hard on him. Then again, it wasn't okay to disappear for days without telling her. It really wasn't.

And now was it up to her to make the next move? Or was it up to him?

By morning, Helen was feeling bleary-eyed and emotionally wrought. More so, in fact, than she'd felt when he'd been missing. Feeling trapped by panic and worry, Helen realised she couldn't stay indoors any longer. She pulled her bike from under the stairs, mounting it as soon as the gallery door shut behind her. As she cycled into the street, she was stopped short by the familiar silhouette of Jared's yellow Audi parked nearby.

Jared was curled uncomfortably across the back seat, his height contorted to fit. He'd obviously been home to change – he was wearing a clean pair of jeans and a striped short-sleeved shirt.

'Jared!' She tapped lightly at the window.

He stirred, then lifted his head from his crossed arms which he had been using as a pillow. Seeing Helen, he sat up, then shifted over to unlock the door.

'Doesn't look like you slept well either,' Helen admitted.

Jared shook himself, then untangled his limbs to climb out the car.

'I was thoughtless,' he said, as she dug in her shorts for her keys. 'Arriving like that last night. Not keeping in touch. I picked up your messages earlier. I guess I'm not used to someone worrying about me like you do.'

'I wasn't the only one.'

'But you're the only one who matters,' Jared said.

CHAPTER TWENTY-SIX

ared had been back two days, and though Helen had spoken to Max, she hadn't seen him. Jared's return brought both equilibrium and chaos back into Helen's life. She had to admit that the time away had done him good. He seemed less frenzied, more attentive. Happier than she'd seen him in ages.

They'd reconciled as Helen led Jared into her apartment; their clothes had scattered across the lounge floor in what seemed like seconds. They hadn't even made it to the bed.

Helen didn't like confrontation, but making up had seemed a more-than-adequate substitute. And when their eyes met, their naked skin rubbing against each other, she couldn't really imagine the hurt she'd felt so recently. Downstairs, she could hear Sally unlocking, going through the morning rituals. As they'd bucked and rolled with and against each other, she'd bit on the edge of Jared's cupped palm, trying to stop herself from crying out.

Jared had rolled onto his side when their breath evened out. He'd shaved in the night, but traces of his stubble remained and Helen felt the tingle of his rough kisses along her spine. She'd pulled herself upright, studying his lean torso as he smiled at her.

'I think you may have missed me too. Maybe I should go away more often.'

But when Helen frowned, he'd run his hand though her hair. 'Just kidding.'

'You need to tell me at least,' Helen said, looking down.

'I know, I know. I'm a bad boy.'

♥

With the approach to Easter, the weather began to change. The nights were slightly cooler and rain began to threaten.

And then they heard that Heinrich was leaving. Not forever, but long enough to set Jared pacing and irritable.

'I don't get it,' he said. 'Why would Heinrich ever want to leave Franschhoek?'

'It's an opportunity,' Helen tried to say. 'He'll be back in two years.'

'An opportunity for what?' Jared grumbled. 'Missing the harvest. Twice. The planting. Bastille Day celebrations, festivals ...'

'Well, for one thing he's going to make a heapload of money in Dubai managing that engineering project.'

'Money's not that important.'

Helen smiled inwardly, thinking that something like that could only be said by someone who had too much money himself.

'I mean it, Helen. I wouldn't leave Bourgogne for all the money on this planet.'

'I believe you're right,' Helen said. 'You probably wouldn't, but when we go to that farewell, you're going to have to pretend you're happy. For Heinrich.'

'Why bother? We've known each other since primary school. He knows when I'm lying.'

'Well, he'll appreciate the effort,' Helen said.

'That bugger? He's never appreciated anything his whole life.'

♥

For some reason Heinrich chose a pub in Stellenbosch for his farewell. It wasn't a long drive, but they had to travel through the mountains past several roadworks.

The going was slow, and Helen chatted away to Jared, her voice bright as she tried to distract him. Still, his fingers tapped listlessly on the steering wheel. *Tap – tap. Tap – tap.* Then faster and faster until she couldn't keep her eyes off them. The noise began to grind on her nerves, and she found herself talking quicker and louder.

Jared looked across at her, a frown etched into his forehead.

'What's wrong with Franschhoek?' he interrupted her suddenly. 'Why not the Elephant and Barrel? Why frigging Stellenbosch, where we have to queue and wait for these idiots to wave a green flag in our faces? We're going to have to go back home the same way, you know.'

'They'll probably be done for the day by then,' Helen said, in her most soothing voice. 'Let's just relax, okay? Make the most of the evening.'

Jared looked across at her. 'You're probably glad to be rid of him. It's not like you ever saw eye to eye.'

'Jared,' Helen said. 'Heinrich is your friend, and I'm really sad for you.'

'Right,' Jared said. 'Sad. Thanks, babe.'

Helen watched Jared's knuckles whiten as he clenched. When Jared was like this, she never knew exactly what to say to him. She decided to say nothing. Especially when Jared rolled down his window and shouted at the road workers: 'Move it! We're not on a fucking Sunday drive here!'

The cursing seemed to calm him, and the moment they were moving again, he glanced at Helen, giving her a weak smile.

'How about some vibes, Helen?' he said. 'Let's get this party started.'

By the time they got to the pub, Heinrich was surrounded by his usual bevy of blondes hanging on his every word. Helen found she hardly knew anybody there, and though Jared had his arm around her, it was less reassuring than it was restrictive.

'I need to dash to the loo,' she said. Jared let her go, patting her as she left, and Heinrich immediately drew him into his circle. He handed Jared a beer, and held up his bottle in a mock salute.

As she retreated she admitted to herself that of course Jared was right. She couldn't be more delighted that Heinrich was leaving. Nevertheless, she also couldn't help wondering how this departure would unbalance Jared. And that was reason enough to wish him to stay.

Helen adjusted her handbag on her shoulder, and decided to order a rum and Coke for strength.

'A beautiful woman like you buying her own drinks?' she heard behind her as Max slipped next to her at the bar counter.

'I was just waiting for a De Villiers to pitch,' Helen said. 'You're just in time. Where's Shona?'

'Working,' Max replied. He nodded at the barman, 'Another of those, thanks.'

'Is this a good thing?' Helen asked tentatively.

'Heinrich leaving? I doubt it. He may have the backbone of a slug, but when it comes to Jared, well, Heinrich would do anything.'

'Jared has us,' Helen reminded Max.

Max stayed silent, long enough for Helen to notice. 'Sure,' he said. 'Let's mingle.'

They rejoined the group to the call of 'Speech! Speech!', and just as Jared was climbing onto a table. Throwing out his arms in a Shakepearean stance, he intoned with mock severity: 'We are gathered here today, to witness the departure of Heinrich Jonas Vermeulen from our midsts. In three days' time, this filthy bastard will be sunning himself in Dubai, and earning cash for the mere act of climbing out of bed. He will henceforth forget all of us, and spend his time shagging foreign women and organising fake marriage licences so he can have someone waiting on him hand and foot, and not get arrested for the privilege.'

'Hear, hear,' someone called.

'We are not here to celebrate Mr Vermeulen's loyalty or friendship,' Jared continued, 'because clearly if he cared anything

223

for any of us he would not be leaving, but then we all know what a selfish money-grabbing bastard he is.'

The crowd laughed. Helen did not.

'That said. Tonight is an historic event. And I say this with all seriousness. Because on this never-to-be-repeated occasion, the drinks are on Heinrich. So blow the bar bill, be merry and take this as Heinrich's final act of contrition for the women he has cheated on, men he has ripped off in poker and friends he has already forgotten. Raise your glasses, ladies and gentlemen, to the man of the moment – Heinrich Vermeulen.'

'To Heinrich,' everybody said.

As Jared climbed off the table, Heinrich replaced him.

'Of course if I had any friends worth remembering,' he said, 'Jared wouldn't be one of them. He appears so often in the papers, I couldn't forget him even I wanted to.' Jared shrugged at the tittering crowd. 'That said, his kind and heartfelt words are enough to warm any man's heart, so rather than getting choked up, I'm going to say goodbye. I'll be back soon. And just so you know, Dubai is only a plane-ride away. I also hear there are some nice tents in the desert where you can stay since of course I'll be far too important to put any of you up. Thanks for coming! Hasta la vista! Oh, and by the way, it's two-for-one till 10 p.m., which is, after all, why we're actually here.'

To the cheers of his guests – and no doubt a few stragglers – Heinrich downed his drink, balanced his glass on his head and climbed off the table in a magnificent display of equilibrium. Jared switched the empty glass with a beer from a passing tray, and Heinrich nodded with mock tearfulness, as if the emotion was too much for him.

Jared approached Helen and Max. 'Why the long faces, people?' he said. 'This is a party!'

And then the music was pumped up, and when Jared came over to take Helen's hand, her shoes peeled away from the beer-soaked floor. She felt, unflatteringly, like student again, shouting over the noise and trying to lip-read banter that would be forgotten by the morning.

They only left the pub at midnight.

♥

Jared was in a surprisingly cheerful mood as they got into the car. And buoyed by the evening's festivities, he wouldn't let Helen drive.

'I'm fine,' he reasoned, as she tried to extract the keys from him. 'I've danced off the booze.'

Too tired to fight a losing battle, Helen let the matter drop. She slid into the passenger seat, pulling off her shoes the moment she was inside. Her soles were killing her. She tucked her one leg under her, then adjusted the backrest.

After the throbbing noise inside the pub, the car was too quiet and Jared jiggled the dials on the radio as he navigated his way out the car park and onto the road.

'Good send-off,' she said. 'You did great.'

'You think? God, this music is *kak*,' Jared said. 'Why don't you dig in the cubbyhole for a CD – we've got to have something better than this.'

Helen couldn't see all that well, so she felt inside the space with her fingers. As she tried to pull out a few CDs to choose from, a smallish box fell into the foot well.

'Put the light on, will you, Jared?' She leant down to pick it up. 'I can't see anything.'

She wasn't intending to examine the box at all, but when she picked it up, the foil-wrapped contents scattered all over her lap. Helen looked down, not sure what she was seeing. Then the realisation hit her.

'Jared,' she said, holding up the condom selection, 'what's this?'

Jared adopted a wicked grin. 'A man has to be prepared, Helen. I'm never quite sure when I'm going to get the chance to bonk you.'

But there were the twirls and squiggles of Thai writing all over the box.

'You bought this in Bangkok,' Helen said. 'Why?'

'Oh, Helen. You're really making a big deal about nothing. I was in Thailand, for Christ's sake. Picking up a chick is about as mundane as ordering a Big Mac. Fast food. Forgotten the moment you've finished it.'

'Oh my God.' Helen paled.

'A man has needs; I was gone for three *weeks*. And Heinrich says men just aren't wired for fidelity.'

'I don't give a flying fuck what Heinrich says.'

'See, I told you. You *are* glad he's leaving.'

'Don't change the subject, Jared. This has nothing to do with Heinrich.'

'Then what are you on about? I was doing business, babe. None of it meant anything to me. I was missing you. I called you every day, didn't I?'

Helen's mouth dropped.

'And if I shagged Max while you were away,' she said, 'it wouldn't matter to you? I spoke to you every day, didn't I?'

The car lurched as Jared pushed on the brakes, pulling the car to the verge. The ticking of the hazard lights made Helen feel as though she was trapped in the bowels of a grandfather clock. Beyond time. Beyond anything.

'You screwed Max?' Jared's jaw clenched. 'Were you out of your fucking mind? I'll kill him! Messing on my turf.'

'Your *turf*?' Hysteria rose in Helen's voice. 'And of course I didn't screw Max – because I've been committed to *you*!'

'You don't own me, Helen. It's not like we're even married.'

'Thank God,' Helen replied. 'So how many whores were you with? Or don't you even remember?'

'They were *not* whores. You think a man like me has to *pay* for it? But what the fuck, Helen – it wasn't like it was love or anything.'

'Sure,' Helen said. 'And you know all about love, don't you, Jared?'

'What's that supposed to mean?'

'Oh, please. The only person you love is yourself. You don't even care about your own brother. Stealing his women. Slacking on the job.'

'Leave Max out of this.'

Helen looked at Jared, the Audi still humming gently on the side of the road. Just picturing him in Thailand made her feel ill. Dirty. *What had happened? How had this happened?* Suddenly she felt as though she were choking. She needed air. She heaved the door open and scrabbled out before beginning to retch, her sides hurting with the violence of her reaction. She was standing barefooted, the grass cool under her feet. Her stomach heaved again and she hung onto a small bush, trying to right herself.

'Christ, Helen,' Jared said, not bothering to get out the car. 'And *you* wanted to drive?'

'I am *not* drunk,' Helen said.

'Could have fooled me,' Jared said. 'Are you done, now? Can we get going?'

Helen began to tremble. Her whole being dissolved as she stood there, sobs rising in her throat.

'Get in the car, Helen,' Jared said.

He still had not moved. Not to help her back into the vehicle or comfort her. Or apologise. And as she looked across at Jared one thing became perfectly clear. She couldn't spend another moment with him. Pulling her handbag out the car, she slammed the passenger door.

'What the hell are you doing?' Jared asked, as he wound the window down. 'Get in the car. This isn't safe.'

'I'll take my chances.'

Even then, she was waiting for him to redeem himself. Get out the Audi, come round and hold her. Tell her he was so so sorry, that he never meant to hurt her. Drive her to her apartment, give her time to forgive him.

Tell her he loved her.

'Suit yourself.' Jared said, as he started to roll up the window. 'You want to be stupid, that's your prerogative. Last chance, Helen.'

And she watched dumbfounded as he drove off, leaving her

on the grass verge, her shoes still wedged under the passenger seat where she had kicked them.

Helen fell onto her knees, her body wracked with her crying. What was she supposed to do now – hitch? And from here of all places.

Then she remembered she still had her mobile. She searched for the familiar name, the familiar number.

'Max?' Helen said. 'Max? I'm in big trouble here. Can you help me. Please?'

CHAPTER TWENTY-SEVEN

Scarborough looked just the same, especially after she'd rehung Alec's painting. It had only taken a few hours to pack up her belongings in the Franschhoek apartment and shove them in the Opel. Madeleine had driven through in her husband's pickup, helping Helen bubblewrap the canvases that hadn't yet sold. Helen had paid Sally a month's notice, and their goodbyes had been fraught with tears and disappointment.

'I loved working here,' Sally had said. 'I was so proud of everything we'd achieved.'

Helen had nodded. 'Me too, Sal. Me too.'

She'd looked across the now-empty space. Her first gallery. 'I can't make this work without him, and Franschhoek isn't big enough for both of us. He was here first.'

And Helen felt the tears welling again.

'I've put Post-its on all the furniture Jared brought from Bourgogne. He can come and collect it when I'm gone. But he'll probably leave Max to do that, seeing as it was probably Max who supplied it anyway. Some of the kitchen stuff is mine, but I've left it. You can tell the landlady when she comes by. The rent is paid until the end of the month ... If Jared offers, not that he will, I've taken care of it. What else?'

'What if somebody wants to get in touch?'

Helen pulled her notebook from her handbag. She scribbled down the number at Scarborough, her mobile number and her email address. 'My flight to the UK's booked for four days' time. I'll disconnect the cell phone then.' Helen said. 'Madeleine and I are popping in at the Blignauts on the way out. They don't know yet I'm going. I'm going to set up a basic website for orders of the last paintings before I fly back to London. Mad will keep them in the coffee shop on the walls, and try to sell them there too.'

'And what about the book launch?'

'I won't go. Max will have to understand. It's his book anyway, more so than mine.' Besides, Helen didn't think she could face the memories.

Helen turned to the sound of footsteps coming down from the apartment.

'It seems pretty organised to me,' Madeleine said. 'You've left a few groceries in the fridge though.'

'Leave them,' Helen replied. 'I can't be bothered.'

And then she and Madeleine were off in their separate vehicles, and Helen was leaving Franschhoek as she had arrived: alone. Helen drove down her beloved Huguenot Street, taking in the coffee shops, the galleries, the buzz of tourists seeing Franschhoek for the first time. It was just so beautiful here, but not beautiful enough to keep her. Helen's heart clenched. She'd formed an attachment to this place. The history of it. The sense of it. As though it were grafted onto her soul – a vine to rootstock. But she was leaving it all.

And she was leaving Max. She could scarcely think about him without a sense of loss so strong that she felt herself collapsing inward.

She'd been too much of a coward to say goodbye; she wondered if he would ever forgive her.

When Helen pulled into Le Cadeau, she did so reluctantly, knowing that the brave face she was about to put on, was going to drain the last of her emotional reserves.

When she finally left Franschhoek, her nerves were raw and shattered.

♥

'Everything okay?' Madeleine asked as Helen checked Alec's house one final time.

'Just a moment,' Helen said. 'I'm going to dash down to June's and post the keys there. She's at the hospice on an emergency call.'

'Shall I drive you?'

'No need. I won't be a second – I'll take the shortcut down the path.'

Helen rushed down to June's, patting Desmond through the fence. 'Goodbye, beautiful boy. You look after June.'

Looking down towards the ocean from June's house, she remembered her first baptismal swim in the Atlantic. It was her first moment of hope in a long, long time, and for a brief second, she recalled how she'd felt coming out the water. Recovery was possible, she realised. Perhaps even a second time. She was just going to have to be patient.

Helen patted Desmond one last time, then bounded back up the hill to where Madeleine was waiting for her.

♥

'I can't believe I'm leaving,' Helen said as they crossed over the mountains.

'You can always come back,' Madeleine said. 'One day, when you're ready.'

'I'm not sure I'll be able to.'

'Time and distance are great healers, Helen. Despite what you're feeling now, just think how far you've come!'

'You're right of course.'

Madeleine laughed. 'Of course I am! Besides, you'll have to come back and visit me. You don't just make friends and then abandon them forever.'

She'd abandoned Max. Taken the easy way out and left him a note.'
I wouldn't do that,' Helen said. 'There's always Facebook.'
'God help us.'

Having driven along the coast, they began to hit a snag on the highway, with traffic much worse than usual. In fact, it didn't seem to be moving at all. They'd left with enough time to spare, but they hadn't anticipated *this*.

'Maybe I should check the radio, see if there's a traffic flash,' Madeleine said as she jumped from one channel to the next. And from the fuzz and the white noise, they both heard the beginning of an announcement on the news:

It's been confirmed that the car wreckage found on Helshoogte Pass between Stellenbosch and Franschhoek in the early hours of yesterday morning belonged to wine personality and bon vivant Jared de Villiers. Brother of the deceased, Maximillian de Villiers, has expressed his extreme devastation at the tragic news, but declined to comment. Friends of the family have confirmed Jared's recent breakup from British artist Helen Shaw, who has been unavailable for comment ...

Helen gasped, as adrenaline surged through her. 'Oh God, oh God. Why didn't Max call me?'

♥

Helen stabbed out the numbers she knew by heart on Madeleine's phone.

Hello, this is Max de Villiers, I'm not available to take your call at this moment, but please leave your name and a message. BEEP. This mailbox is full. Please try again later.

She tried Bourgogne.

Thank you for your calls and support. Unfortunately we cannot answer at this time. Do, however, leave a message.

Helen listened to Max's voice on the newly recorded message, and her heart contorted. He sounded absolutely wrecked. Wooden. His voice cracking under the strain. As she sat there, the phone held to her ear, she felt tears streaming down her face.

Poor, poor Max.

'We'll go straight to Bourgogne,' said Madeleine.

And Helen nodded, unable to get any words out.

♥

By the time they arrived it was almost dark. Helen's fingers knotted around each other as the familiar territory came into view. To think that if they hadn't turned on the radio she may have known too late. Boarded a plane, and left Max, and what was left of Jared, behind.

Across the sky, pink clouds reflected the light from a dipping, bloody sun. Helen rolled down the window, trying to calm herself by breathing giant gulps of dusk air. When they turned into the main entrance, the security guard approached the car.

'Sorry, Madam,' he said to Madeleine. 'I'm not allowed to let anybody in.'

Helen opened her window so that the guard could see her better.

'It's me, Joseph,' she said. 'I just heard.'

Joseph inclined his head, a look of sympathy in his dark eyes. 'Mr Max has been looking for you, *sisi*,' he said. 'Please drive up, and park in front of the house.'

'I'll wait here for the moment,' Madeleine said diplomatically when they reached the top of the drive. 'Call me when you're ready. And take your time.'

Helen squeezed Madeleine's hand, wishing Max would fling open the front door like he'd done so many times before. Stand there and analyse her moods, like he always did, so that he knew what to say, what to do. This time, she was going to have to know how to act, and already she was at a loss.

'Go on, then,' Madeleine urged. said. 'Go now.'

♥

Helen slid out the car. She took each step, one by one, shocked by the porch draped in shadows. Not even the front light was turned on. The flowers in the pot plants next to the front door withered. Helen moved closer. She lifted the knocker and banged twice, the banging making her feel ill. At first there was no response, but then softly down the passage, the sound of approaching footsteps.

'Helen,' Max said, his hooded eyes red and swollen, his hair unkempt. And as he fell against her, drawing her into the house, his sobs shredded her soul. She didn't know where she found the strength to walk him inside, settle him in a couch in the living room, and hold him until he stilled.

She didn't know where she found the strength, but she knew that being here was all she could do to make things bearable for both of them.

CHAPTER TWENTY-EIGHT

adeleine had left Helen at Bourgogne without disturbing her and Max. By the time Helen had managed to move Max to his bedroom, it was past midnight, and she realised she'd completely forgotten her friend. Rushing outside to tell Mad what had happened, she found Madeleine gone, Helen's suitcases stacked next to the front door with a note balanced on the top: *Call me when you need me,* followed by her number, which Madeleine must have remembered was programmed into her old SIM card.

The days passed miserably. Too miserably even for her to paint or draw.

On the morning of Jared's funeral, Helen could hear Prudence bumping around the kitchen. A glass shattered, then a dish, followed by Max's even tones. *It doesn't matter, Prudie. It's just stuff.*

Helen stood up immediately and dressed. She slipped on her shoes, then walked towards the kitchen to see how she could help. As she went down the passage, she remembered her late mornings when she'd first stayed at Bourgogne

But everything was different now.

Everything.

Jared was gone.

Shona, her hair tucked in a pixie style behind her ears, was folding serviettes at the kitchen table. The women greeted each other in muted tones. Max looked a little better today. Less pale. More robust. Planning a funeral like Jared's had kept them all busy. Focused. Helen wondered how they would manage in the evening once the milestone was passed. What would they talk about? What would they do?

Max poured Helen a cup of coffee, then refilled Shona's cup. 'Do you want me to start carrying stuff to the tasting room?' Helen asked. 'I can ask Simon to help me.'

Prudence nodded, then blew her nose into a pale pink handkerchief. 'He's waiting outside the kitchen,' she said. 'He's been here since six.' Prudence waved at the stacks of plates, the coffee cups and the glasses. 'There's a lot. You might need more people.'

As Helen positioned the plates on the tasting-room counter, she remembered being alone in this place with Jared. It seemed that everything about Bourgogne reminded her of their time together, stabbing at her temples in sharp jabs. She put the cups and saucers down carefully, then holding her sides, burst out into the sunlight to breathe. She narrowly missed Heinrich on the way out.

'Heinrich!' she said in surprise. 'I thought you'd already left for Dubai.'

'I did,' he said sombrely. 'I came back.' Heinrich rubbed his rounded belly. His movements were anxious, jerky. He looked at Helen, with a temporary uncharacteristic lack of something to say.

'I'm so very sorry about Jared,' Helen remarked.

'Yes, guilt's a terrible thing, isn't it?' Heinrich replied.

Helen's mouth dropped open in surprise. She felt as though he'd punched her.

'You abandon him the moment I go overseas. And you of all people knew how he was. What the hell were you thinking, woman?'

'Couples break up, Heinrich. I'm sorry but I had my reasons.'

'Sure. That's why I'm loading chairs in the vineyards, just like

Jared and I always talked about. Except as far as I remember, we'd planned that for a wedding not a fucking funeral.'

Even with these few sentences, Heinrich's face had turned puce, a sheen of sweat pumped up over his forehead.

'You're upset, Heinrich,' Helen said as she stepped back. 'I can see that. I'm upset too.'

'*You're* upset? And you think knowing someone for less than a year entitles you? You think you and Jared were special? Think again. There's nothing special about you Helen. Nothing.'

Helen tried to focus on controlling the tremors that were building inside her. She wasn't going to give Heinrich his petty victory.

'You'll miss him, I know that,' Helen said.

'Twenty-four years of friendship, that's what you've fucked up.' Heinrich replied. 'Do you understand me?'

'I'm not taking the blame for this one, Heinrich. Jared was a fast driver. Reckless. And it was an accident. A terrible, tragic accident.'

'Oh please. He knew that road so well he could have driven it blindfolded. With one hand.'

Helen straightened. 'I don't have to listen to this.'

'You mean you don't want to.'

She turned away, marching back inside the tasting room. Helen managed to close the door before she collapsed, sliding down the wall to slump in a corner. She pulled up her knees, wrapping her arms around them then rested her head. Her entire body trembled than shook as she cried. Softly at first, then louder, the sort of grief-sodden weeping that couldn't be stopped voluntarily. Helen heard Simon come in the room. He approached her tentatively, then left the building, the front door slamming behind him.

When he returned, Max was with him, and Helen tried to quieten herself. Heinrich was right. She didn't deserve to feel like this. But the guilt that lurking below the surface suddenly seemed inescapable.

'Is this my fault?' she asked Max, as he slid down the wall

next to her. 'Did I do this to him? Heinrich says this is my fault.'

'Heinrich needs someone to be angry with,' Max said.

'That doesn't answer my question.'

'Darling Helen,' Max said. 'You know as well as I do Jared always did exactly what he liked. Whatever happened, you weren't there. Whatever choices he made that night were *his* choices.'

'What are we going to do?' Helen asked.

'I honestly don't know. Missing Jared is like missing my arms. I'm cut off. I'm taking it a minute, then an hour, then a day at a time. I think that's all we can expect to do.'

♥

The sun beat down over the rows and rows of plastic chairs laid out between the vineyards. In front of them all was the coffin, a fynbos wreath draped over the top and a photograph of Jared placed reverently in front of it.

What a perfect-looking man. What a waste.

Helen stood to one side, feeling at a loss. She wasn't family, but she wasn't exactly part of Jared's circle either – Heinrich's bitter comments to her that morning had made *that* perfectly clear. So it was with relief that she felt a papery grip at her elbow.

'Sit with us, my dear,' said Pieter Blignaut. 'If you wouldn't mind?'

And Helen allowed herself to be led to a chair, her body heavy as lead. Most of the tributes passed in a blur. Until Max stood up.

'There's a song I've always liked by Tim McGraw,' he said. 'It's called "Live like you were dying" and what always used to occur to me when I heard it was that it described my brother completely. Jared de Villiers took life by the horns, as though every single moment was going to be his last. Jared never walked anywhere; he ran. For Jared, coming second wasn't an option. He loved speed. He loved action. And as an older brother, I often worried about him because he was absolutely fearless. But Jared wasn't invincible. He was as fallible as the rest of us are. Though he could walk in a room and make you feel like you were the only person there, it didn't mean that he was immune to praise or sympathy or insecurities. Jared needed reassurance, guidance, love. And he got that from the people sitting here today, and also from those that can't be with us. I know there are lots of rumours about Jared's death, and perhaps we will never know what really happened that night. Ultimately I wonder if it matters. Because Jared is gone, and assigning blame won't bring him back.

'Today as I stand here, I can't even express my sense of desolation. I am the last remaining member of my family. Bourgogne will be the poorer for it, because Jared loved this land. He had an affinity for the vines I've never witnessed in anyone else. For him, each planting was a rebirth; each harvest, a triumph. This year, I will be planting new vines on my own, and I don't think I am big enough for the task. Because Jared was larger than life, and eclipsed me in more ways than I can count. I'm standing here today as someone Jared used to call Big Brother Max, and all I want is to be that person again. But it can never be.

'What I can do, however, is to keep on living, and tending this land that he loved, keeping his voice in my head when I lose faith in myself. Because one thing I know for sure: Jared would not have let me give up. It just wasn't his way. Jared was a fighter, touched sometimes by sadness that most of us couldn't really understand. He was exuberant, charming and yes, sometimes a little self-involved. He had the world at his feet, and now that world, my world, has changed forever.

'Wherever you are now, Jared, I am going to miss you with every ounce, every inch of my being. But I am not going to let you down. I'm going to live this life and the life you left behind. Take care, my boy, I will always treasure the times I spent with you and I am so glad you can be laid to rest here on Bourgogne, amongst the vines that you loved so very much. Goodbye, Jared. My brother. Farewell.'

As Max moved towards his seat near the coffin, Helen felt the emotion rushing through her. She dug into her handbag, extracting tissue after tissue, as the tears rolled down her face. And just as she looked up, her eyes met Max's, their connection so instantaneous and honest that she felt a physical jolt. For seconds that seemed like hours, they were locked together, and it was then that Helen realised what was really happening: Jared was gone, but Max was here.

He always had been.

Max in Langebaan, lifting her out of the ocean suds as she mourned the loss of her marriage, her unborn children. Max in the fairy-lit garden, his eyes on her naked body, his undeniable attraction for her, the love written all over his face. Max on Pinotage, racing Helen and Star through the Franschhoek foothills. And Max, dear Max, collecting her from that grassy verge in the middle of the night, asking no questions when he knew she would have told him everything he wanted to know.

Helen's heart beat furiously, as though trying to knock itself from her sternum. Her breathing echoed in her ears. And when Max finally looked away she was overcome by such dizziness that she had to sit down.

'Are you alright?' Pieter asked her.

And Helen nodded.

But she wasn't, not really. Not when the truth of her feelings had surfaced at this moment of all moments.. Not when they were about to walk the coffin to the De Villiers graveyard, lower Jared's body into the earth next to his parents, and say goodbye forever.

And certainly not when she saw Shona, her hand at Max's elbow, as she coaxed him forward to take his place next to the pallbearers, waiting to walk Jared to his final big sleep.

CHAPTER TWENTY-NINE

elen stood on the wooden walkway at Scarborough, a misty grey haze descending over her.

'You're mad,' June said. 'I'm not sure even Desmond is mad enough to go with you.'

But the Labrador seemed impervious to the rain, pulling on his lead so that Helen couldn't change her mind. Helen looked towards the ocean. Clumps of khaki kelp rolled and tossed in the water. Some of it collected between the rocks, chafing back and forth as the sea rose and subsided. Desmond barked loudly, yanking Helen down between the rocks onto the sand.

Helen took off her sandals, leaving them together with a towel on a slippery rock behind her. She undid Desmond's lead, letting him bound forward to grab a submerged piece of driftwood between his teeth. The sand crunched between her toes, massaging the soles of her feet. She shivered, and then pulled off her shorts and her shirt, dipping a tentative toe in the icy water.

Desmond returned to her side looking at her in a way that somehow reminded her of Jared. And for some reason, this made her laugh.

'Oh go on then,' she said, taking the wood and tossing it down the beach for him to fetch.

Then she waded in deeper, to her waist, then to her

shoulders, feeling the pull of the ocean as it ebbed and flowed. Desmond, not to be outdone, paddled out to her, his treasure gripped firmly in his mouth.

'Back to the beach, boy.' Helen lobbed it onto the sand as far as she could.

This time, Desmond didn't swim back to her, staying firmly on solid ground but deep enough in the shallows to wet his paws. Satisfied that he wasn't going to follow her, Helen swam out further, ducking and diving under the waves.

It had only been five days since the funeral, and on all of these days Helen had pushed herself to exhaustion. When she was physically tired, it gave her less energy to think and that, she believed, was a good thing. She knew that she was copping out, avoiding rebooking her ticket to London, but she didn't feel strong enough to make decisions like that. What she did feel was that she was waiting for something. In limbo and unable to propel herself forward.

Driving back from the funeral with Madeleine, Helen hadn't been able to get the image of the lowering coffin out of her mind. That, and a vision of Max, who instead of dropping a flower onto Jared's coffin had taken a hefty clump of Bourgogne soil in his right hand, and scattered that instead. How well he knew his brother, who so loved the earth and his vines. He never really was a man for flowers.

Later, as people had gathered in the tasting room around cheesecake and scones, and little sausage rolls and mini quiches, Helen had walked back to the graveyard, where the gravediggers were finishing off. She'd watched the careful levelling off the ground, listening to the scrape of metal on sand. When no trace of the gaping wound had remained, they'd draped a rectangle of thick green material onto the newly cleared space, lining it up neatly like a picnic blanket.

Helen hadn't spoken much more to Max. She'd cleared away plates with Prudence, fetched glasses. Found teaspoons. As the morning had worn on, midday Merlots had surfaced with lunchtime Chardonnays. And rightly so, because who was Jared without wine? Helen had looked across at Heinrich as he helped open bottles, and had found some peace in his silent acknowledgement. She wanted to believe this was an apology of sorts. But under the circumstances, it was the best they could do.

Still, Helen couldn't get Max out of her mind. She'd seen the way he'd separated himself from Shona near the end of the day – he'd stood up, filled his glass and wandered off into the vines. She'd noticed the slumped collapse of Shona's shoulders, the way her eyes, welling up, had traced his retreat. And shamefully, rather than feeling sympathy, Helen had been filled with relief.

Now Helen bobbed in the water. She liked the isolation of this beach, the muted swirls of the water matching her mood. Pushing up and down in the foam, she realised she was going out too far. She waited in the waves for a rush of tide to pull her to the shore. It didn't help to fight the water, and she had no fight left.

By the time she reached the shallows, Helen could hear Desmond whining nearby. Darting back and forth, he'd abandoned his driftwood for an old fish carcass, the bones and flesh hanging together like a half-knitted jumper. Helen wondered if it would make him ill and moved as if to take it from him. He growled at her, low and deep. *I found it. I found it first.*

And as Helen stepped away the realisation hitting her: *I found him. I found him first.*

♥

Helen pulled up the zip on the dress Madeleine had lent her from her 'younger, thinner days'. When Madeleine had opened the door and recognised Helen's look of urgency, she'd gone into full combat mode. Outfit. Shoes. Helen's hair brushed out straight and sleek. And mascara, which Helen hardly ever wore.

'Now do a twirl.'

Helen turned, tucking her hair behind her ears.

'Helen, stop being so self-conscious – you look amazing!'

Helen hugged Madeleine. 'You're a wonderful friend, you know that?'

'I try. Now get going. You're already more than fashionably late.'

The evening was already in full swing. A crowd at a book launch was not guaranteed, but this was no average book launch. How could it be after all the coverage from Jared's so-recent death? Their publisher had vetoed any suggestions of cancelling it. Though no one would be so callous as to say it, you couldn't engineer *this sort of* publicity. The De Villiers family history was flying off the shelves, with a second print run already being talked about.

Helen slipped the strap of her handbag over her shoulder, her fingers trembling. She stood to one side, watching people mill about. Now that she was here, she wasn't quite sure what to do. A waiter passed with a glass of Bourgogne Chenin Blanc, which she took gratefully. In front of her, to the left, a book-signing queue had formed. Helen saw the piles of books stacked all about the shop.

Despite all the work she and Max had put into it, she hadn't yet seen the finished product. She picked up a copy, and as she paged, her head was filled with memories. Helen bit her lip, trying not to cry.

Decided now and her copy purchased, Helen took her place in the line snaking its way from Max's table. Though he was too far away to see *her*, Helen was able to study Max from a distance. She watched how he smiled, his head angled in attentiveness as he listened to the woman shoving her book towards him. His hair was a little longer now than when she first met him, his face showing some of signs of the recent stress – his skin paler, frown lines more pronounced. But this only made her more anxious to get close to him. Her heart crashed in her chest. How much longer could she wait? She wanted to push her way to the front, steamroll all these human obstacles out of her way so she could get to him. Every minute, every second that passed, stretched like elastic. Though the queue was moving, it definitely didn't feel like it.

Then Max looked up.

And this time he saw her.

Helen smiled, holding up their book. She couldn't recall exactly how it happened, but she was somehow propelled forward, the crowd opening up as she walked to the table.

'My partner in crime, ladies and gentlemen,' Max said. 'The talented artist and illustrator, Helen Shaw.'

She heard clapping, a few cheers, but she was only vaguely aware of it. She was only focused on Max, who was pulling her to his side of the table. And it was as if the crowd wasn't even there.

'You're here,' Max said. 'I can't believe it.'

'Max,' Helen said truthfully, 'I don't think I could be anywhere else.'

With his solid arms around her, her body tucked against his, she recognised how well they matched. Max bent his head, kissing her softly on her hair, but it wasn't enough: she lifted her face to his, offering her lips, herself.

Helen touched his face, seeing a smile ignite his eyes.

'I'm sorry. I've made so many mistakes, wasted so much time. I wanted to tell you –'

'You *did* tell me,' Max said, 'just not in words.'

'I love you, and I need to be with you. I don't know why it took me so long to realise it.'

Max smiled back. 'You're a slow learner, Helen Shaw. I loved you and everything about you from the first moment I met you.'

Helen kissed Max again. 'So why didn't you fight for me? Why didn't you fight? You knew what your brother was like and –'

Max cupped her chin in his palm. 'You know as well as I do it would never have been a fair fight with Jared. It was just too complicated. And Helen, I wanted you to decide for yourself.'

Helen studied Max's beautiful hazel eyes, the emotion almost overwhelming. 'I *have* decided,' she said. 'I have. I did. I just wish I could turn back the clock, take away the pain and sadness I've caused you.'

Max smiled. 'Everyone gets hurt at one point or another,' he said, weaving his fingers between hers. 'That's how life is. But there *is* something you can do for me now.'

'Just name it,' Helen said.

Max's lips met hers. 'Come home with me, Helen,' he said. 'Come home with me to Bourgogne.'

ଓଃEND୨୦